T. S. Arthur

What came afterwards.

A novel being a sequel to Nothing but money by T.S. Arthur

T. S. Arthur

What came afterwards.
A novel being a sequel to Nothing but money by T.S. Arthur

ISBN/EAN: 9783743303416

Manufactured in Europe, USA, Canada, Australia, Japa

Cover: Foto ©Andreas Hilbeck / pixelio.de

Manufactured and distributed by brebook publishing software
(www.brebook.com)

T. S. Arthur

What came afterwards.

.

WHAT CAME AFTERWARDS.

A Novel.

BEING A SEQUEL TO "NOTHING BUT MONEY."

BY

T. S. ARTHUR,

AUTHOR OF "OUT IN THE WORLD," "LIGHT ON SHADOWED PATHS," "NOTHING
BUT MONEY," ETC. ETC.

CARLETON, PUBLISHER, 413 BROADWAY.
1865.

WHAT CAME AFTERWARDS.

CHAPTER I.

T was an evening in winter. A man, just above the medium height, with a pale, delicately cut, intellectual face, sat by an office table, above which depended a shaded gas-light. He was leaning over a book, now examining a page intently, and now turning the leaves with rapid fingers — not so much reading, as searching for some fact, formula, or illustration. His face, we said, was pale; but the paleness was not of ill health, nor in consequence of prolonged physical exhaustion; for the skin had a clear, healthy look, and the strong brown eyes, that glanced up, now and then, in pauses of reflection, were full of fire. The face, as we said, was delicately cut; the forehead high and broad; the eyebrows thin, but darkly defined; the lashes well fringed and with a graceful curve upwards; the nose long, rather prominent, but straight, with wide, almost transparent nostrils; full lips, and slightly receding chin.

There was not a hard or harsh line in his face. The artist-soul, which had been at work upon it for many years — the snow-flecked hair said many years — drew, it was plain, her inspiration and ideals of beauty, from heavenly spheres. Truth, purity, self-discipline, high thoughts and noble purposes, with love of the neighbor, had all guided the artist-soul, as it wrought upon the material investure, and cut it into a representation of its own interior life. So the soul is ever at work upon the face, giving to it the form of its quality. If you have skilled eyes, you may read the men you meet by the lines of their countenances.

He sat at an office table, the strong gas-light flooding his face, and giving it an almost supernatural beauty. There were many cases standing against the walls of the office, which was spacious, and carpeted ; — cases of books ; of chemical and philosophical apparatus ; of drugs and curious specimens in bottles ; and of anatomical preparations. Orderly arrangement, and an air of taste and comfort, were in everything. The man and his surroundings were in harmony.

"Is the Doctor in ? "

The door opened so quietly, that he was not aware of the presence of any one, until a child's voice asked the question. Glancing up, he saw a little girl, not over eight years of age, standing just inside of the office door, which she still held ajar. She was poorly dressed, but clean. Her face, which could not be called a plain one, had little of that healthy glow and round-ness which we see in children who have plenty of food, air and exercise. It was the face of a child to whom life had not been all sunshine; for over it shadows of real things had passed so often, and dwelt so long, that cheerfulness had faded out. She had a look of endur-ance, if not suffering. Her skin was fair, and she had blue eyes, that should have been dancing in light; but they were dreamy and sad, and full of questionings. To her, life had come on the darker side, and its mystery and sorrow weighed sluggishly on her heart. The Doc-tor, who possessed the rare faculty of reading counte-nances as some men read books, saw all this at a glance.

"I am the Doctor," he replied, leaning back from the table, and looking intently at the child.

"Mother says, wont you come and see little Theo." The child came forward a few steps. Her eyes rested full on the Doctor's face — not boldly, but with that confidence seen in artless children.

"Who is your mother?" asked the Doctor.

"Her name is Mrs. Ewbank."

"Where does she live?"

"In Green street, four doors from Franklin."

"Which side?"

" On t'other side."

" What's the matter with Theo ? "

" He's sick."

" In what way ? "

" I don't know ; but he cries 'most all the time, and
ne's fallen to skin and bone, as mother says. He's
cried all day — and he's so hot ; and wont eat anything."

" In Green street, four doors from Franklin ? "

The Doctor took a slate and commenced writing on
it with a pencil.

" Yes, sir."

" What is the name ?   Mrs. Ewbank ? "

" Yes, sir."

" Does your mother want me to come around this
evening ? "

" Oh, yes.   She's crying ; and is afraid Theo wont
live."

It was on the Doctor's tongue to ask the child about
her father ; but it crossed his mind that such a question might give pain, and so it was withheld.

" I'll be around this evening, tell your mother," he
answered, kindly.

The child threw him a grateful look, and then went
out.   As she did so, the Doctor bent over his volume
again, and commenced running from page to page in a

rapid, searching manner. He did not observe that another door had opened, nor that almost noiseless feet were crossing the room. A hand was laid gently on his shoulder. Without starting, or a motion of surprise, he leaned back from the table, and turning, looked up into the pleasant face of a woman. In actual record her years were forty-five; in appearance, she was younger by half a score. The flowers of summer had been tempered for her by the shadows of great rocks, or the cool recesses of arbors wrought of vines that loving hands had planted. The wild blasts of winter had rarely been able to penetrate the sheltered home in which she dwelt; and even when their chilly breath came in through a suddenly opening door, or neglected cranny, it was soon subdued by the tempering warmth within. Life had, thus far on her journey, given her more of peace than sadness — more of interior satisfaction than disquietude. And yet, a second glance at her almost youthful face, revealed the fact, that she had not passed thus far in the ways of life, without a share of discipline — of sorrow — of sickness and pain ; but they had wrought their true intent, softening, elevating and refining — bearing back, and to the circumference of her being, the inherited natural with its evils, and ministering to the birth of that spiritual life, the full development of which gives the stature of an angel.

1*

"Lena." As the Doctor uttered her name, gently, a smile crept around his lips, and the intenser light of his eyes, which professional thought had kindled, softened to a look of tenderness.

"Studying a case, I supppose," she said, question and affirmative uniting in her voice.

"Yes, and a difficult one," replied the Doctor, as he still leaned back, and looked at his wife. She moved around, and stood more nearly in front, the light falling strongly on his face from the shaded lamp, while hers remained partly in shadow.

"I should think, by this time," was remarked, "that you were so familiar with all forms of disease, and their treatment, that no case would be found difficult."

"As evil is Protean, so is disease. When the moralist has discovered all forms of evil, and noted their remedies, the physician may hope to attain for disease a like consummation," said the Doctor.

"In that view, the healer can never be perfect in his art."

"Never. Symptoms — effects — the ultimate signs of causes he does not see — are all that meet his observation. Sin is the mother of disease — therefore, all diseases have a spiritual origin. Physical evil is only the result of moral evil, descended to a lower plane of life. As the cause is, so will the effect be ; and the effect must give an actual sign of the cause, and vary as to its quality and force. You can see, then, how, with an almost infinite variety, diseases will manifest themselves, and while holding a type, or classification, set at naught, in many instances, all the physician's previously acquired skill and demand of him a new application of remedies."

Something like a sigh parted the air, as the Doctor's wife answered —

" And so, his work will never grow lighter."

" Why should it, if he have strength ? " asked the Doctor. His countenance was as serene as his voice.

" True. Why should it, if he have strength ? But, dear " — her voice fell to a lower tone — " your strength is failing, while your work demands increasing vigor."

" I am not conscious of the failure." The Doctor smiled into the face of his wife.

" You bear the signs," she answered, tenderly. " Here," she laid the tips of her fingers softly on his hair, " they are gathering fast. Every day I can see some spot on which a snow-flake has alighted. And, as your head whitens, the summer flushes grow paler on your cheeks. Are deepening orbits and shrinking flesh, the signs of strength ? No — no, my husband ! "

" You are too quick at reading signs, Lena. The plump and the ruddy are not always the most enduring.

The clear eye, the healthy skin, the compact muscle —
these show the right condition, and give warrant of endurance. And, above all, the calm temperament, and
Heaven-aspiring soul."

"But a dwarf may not be equal to a giant's work."

"No; and he would be a very foolish dwarf to attempt so impossible a thing. But, a dwarf, working
bravely up to his strength, may do a great deal more
than a self-indulgent giant, and be none the weaker."

"You generally beat me in argument," said the
Doctor's wife, smiling. "But, convinced against my
will, I hold the same opinion still. I feel that you are
taxing yourself too severely — and I see it, also; and
unless your reasoning harmonizes with my perception, I
cannot fully accept your judgment. In most cases,
your thought and my intuition reach to the same conclusion, and then I *know* we are right. I doubt now;
and think you will be wise to take the benefit of my
doubts, and spare yourself a little."

The Doctor reached his hand towards the table, and
shut the book over which he had been poring when his
wife came in.

"That's right. Now come up stairs," she said, drawing upon his arm.

"Is tea ready?" The Doctor took out his watch.

"It will be, in ten minutes."

"Half past six." The Doctor laid his hand on the book he had just closed. "In ten minutes, you say? That will give time to finish my —— "

"Indeed it will not," said the wife, interrupting him, and speaking with the firmness of one who intended to have her own way. Seizing the volume resolutely, she returned it to one of the book-cases.

"Now, sir, my will must, for once, be law," she added, with mock seriousness.

The Doctor leaned back in his chair, and fixed his eyes on his wife, meeting her animated countenance, as she turned from the book-case, with so sober a gaze, that she was, for a moment, half in doubt whether he were not offended.

"Do you know who is up stairs?" she asked.

"Who?"

"Lena and little Ned."

"No!" The Doctor was on his feet in a moment.

"Yes; they've been here all the afternoon."

"Have they? Well, that's pleasant." And he was already on his way to the door of his office. In the door, he turned, and saw his wife standing near the table. She had not moved.

"Come," he said.

"Oh, it's of no consequence about me," was answered, in a voice simulating so well a hurt spirit, that the

Doctor was for the moment deceived. Going back, he drew an arm around his wife.

"She is yours as well as mine, dear."

"All very well to say that. But, I understand. You couldn't give *me* ten minutes. Oh, no! But at Lena's name, you start away like an impatient lover."

"Jealous of your own child! What a riddle is woman!" said the Doctor, standing full before his wife, and looking away down into her large, black eyes, that were always so full of light that few could gaze into them steadily. A kiss reconciled all. A husband's kiss — the heart of a loving wife never gets too old for that sign, but leaps to it, always responsive, and with a thrill of pleasure. With his arm still around her waist, the Doctor and his wife went from the office to one of the drawing-rooms above.

"Lena!" How tenderly the name was spoken! How warmly the small, fair hand was clasped! How lovingly manhood's lips rested on lips that were given to their pressure with the pure abandonment of a daughter's heart. Then little three-year-old Ned was in grandpa's arms, and clinging around his neck.

"How is Edward?" The tone in which this question was asked, made very plain the fact that Edward, Lena's husband, stood in high regard with the Doctor.

"Very well." The daughter's love and the wife's

love, blended sweetly in the rich young face, dark as her mother's, and as full of affluent life.

" He will come to tea ? "

" No."

" Why not? "

" For the same reason that we cannot, once in an age, get you to tea."

" Crowded with professional duties? "

" Yes ; that's the only reason. He has a consultation at six. I've said a hundred times, when I saw how you were robbed of social hours, that I'd never marry a doctor. But, it was my fate. You would have office students ! "

" Not a very hard fate, I imagine," said her father, smiling.

" I will be as brave and enduring as possible, knowing that it might be worse," answered the daughter, with feigned seriousness.

As they talked, the tea-bell rang. Assembled at the table, five persons made up the circle. Doctor Hofland and his wife ; Lena, their oldest daughter, with her boy in a high-chair, next to his grandfather, and Annie, the youngest daughter, just blossoming into the full spring-time of luxuriant eighteen. Their only son, Frank, holding the rank of a lieutenant in the navy, was on board of a national vessel, in the Indian seas.

" If Frank were only here ! " The mother's thought, as she gazed around the table, went off to the absent one. " Then," she added, our circle would be complete."

" There would still be a vacant place," said Lena.

" Whose ? "

" Edward's."

" True." And yet the mother's heart did not come rounding into fulness in her tones."

" He loves you just as dearly as if he were your own son, mother."

" And I love him very much. He could scarcely be dearer, if he were my own flesh and blood. Yes, it would take him, also, to make our circle complete."

" He seems to be making his way very rapidly into the confidence of some of our best people," said the Doctor.

" Yes. Almost every week, he is called to a new family," said Lena, with pride and pleasure in her voice. " If it goes on as it has begun, he will speedily acquire a large practice."

" I hear him well spoken of in influential circles," remarked Doctor Hofland. " As it now stands, he is on the right road to a high place in his profession."

" He was called in to Mr. Larobe's last week," said Lena.

"Ah! Mr. Larobe's! Who's sick there?"

"Mrs. Larobe's oldest son."

"Leon Guy?"

"Yes."

"What ails him?"

"Some nervous disease. He's lost the use of both legs. Edward says that he's a most pitiable object — emaciated, and with a countenance so exhausted by suffering, that the sight of him leaves an impression of sadness. His mother has taken him to the sea shore, to medicinal springs, and once to France, for consultation with physicians in Paris. But, all to no good purpose."

"How long has he been suffering in this way?" asked the Doctor.

"For a number of years. Up to his tenth year, he was a healthy boy. Then, from cold, or some shock, I don't remember which, the balance of health was destroyed, and he has been growing worse ever since."

"He must be a young man, now?"

"Past sixteen, I think."

The Doctor's eyes fell from his daughter's face, and his countenance grew serious.

"We cannot pity the mother," he said, thoughtfully, "however we may feel for the child. If there is such a thing as retribution, it must fall upon her head."

"It is falling, I think," remarked Mrs. Hofland, "and with crushing weight — hurting her in the most vulnerable places. Some one told me recently, that her daughter, Blanche Guy, was simple. This, in all probability, accounts for the fact that she is never seen on the street, and but seldom in the carriage, with her mother."

"Simple?" the Doctor mused. "I shouldn't wonder," he added, "if that were really so. I saw them riding out not long since, and remarked in passing, an unsatisfactory something in the girl's face. Feeble-minded — poor child!"

"Better feeble-minded, I should say," returned Mrs. Hofland, "than evil-minded, like her mother."

"Safer by far," answered the Doctor. "With such a father and such a mother, what hope of a moral equilibrium in the child? The chances are heavily on the adverse side. In a foreclosure of the rational, so that responsibility may cease, lies, it would seem, in occasional instances, the only barrier to floods of evil in which the soul would inevitably be lost."

"But, what bitterness for a woman of Mrs. Larobe's quality of mind. How the perpetual presence of an imbecile child must drain the wine of life from her soul, and leave only bitter dregs," said Mrs. Hofland.

"And these are not all her troubles," remarked the Doctor. "To the hopelessly invalid son, and worse diseased daughter, another calamity has been added.

"What?"

" In her hands, if all that is said be true, Adam Guy was bent at will. Her subtle power, against which he had no armor of defence, o'ermastered, and, I fear, destroyed him. For one, I have never been clear as to a state of insanity warranting his removal to a madhouse ; and the fact, that he was taken to a distant private institution, under circumstances of haste and concealment, never fully explained, has always left with me a suspicion of foul play. Poor man ! His dreadful death, while attempting escape, closed the door on a mystery which no one cared to investigate. Though rich, Guy had no true friends ; and when he was in mortal peril, there was none interested enough to spring to his rescue. But, I did not mean to speak particularly of him. If there has been foul play, Justin Larobe was the wife's accomplice. Executor under the will of Mr. Guy, in little more than a year from the day of his death, he became the widow's husband. From that time, I venture to say, the subtle, cold, self-poised, and selfish woman found herself matched against one of superior subtlety and strength. Adam Guy was triple armed and defended only on one side, and vulnerable at almost every other point ; but, Justin Larobe is of another class. Guy sought wealth through the avenues of trade — honest trade in the main ; but, Larobe has more of the spirit of a freebooter. Under legal covers, and statutory licence, he plunders right and left,

as opportunity offers. Of course, such a man is ever
on the alert — Argus-eyed, for prey as well as for pro-
tection. He observes the motions of all who approach
him ; and reads those who try to read him, from Introduction to Finis, before they have spelled through the
first chapter of his record. Such is my estimate of Justin Larobe, and such, I doubt not, the widow of Adam
Guy has found him. But, as I was going to say, she
has met with another calamity. There has been, I understand, a separation between herself and husband."

"Not legal?" said Mrs. Hofland.

"No ; only formal."

"On what ground?"

"That is mainly conjectural. Rumor says, they
have not lived happily for a long time ; and rumor
also says, that Larobe has acted with but little disguise
since their marriage, on the subject of her property,
which the law has placed almost entirely in his hands.
Certain settlements were sipulated for ; but the cunning
lawyer, who had, as executor under Mr. Guy's will,
everything in his own hands, while formally making
these settlements, contrived to fail in giving them a
legal value."

"And is going to absorb everything," said Mrs.
Hofland.

"That is an inference, which goes beyond the range
of probabilities. My belief is that he will not drive her

to desperation by any such an excess of wrong. He
knows her quality, and just how far to test its strength.
There is enough between them in my opinion, to ruin
both, should either take the witness stand against the
other. So while contending one with the other, in a
bitter antagonism, the last things must be at stake before Mrs. Justin will fling off all disguises, and risk
a final struggle with him before the world. Confreres
in evil, are chary of an open fight. They know too
much about each other, and therefore will not risk too
much."

"I pity all who are in suffering, be they evil or
good," said Mrs. Hofland. "And, somehow, I pity
this woman. The good have much to sustain them
when night falls, and pain oppresses. But, to one like
Mrs. Justin, there is no balm in Gilead. If there is an
open rupture with, and separation from her husband,
the dark days of her life have come. I never believed
however, after the way in which her step-children were
treated, that any good was in store for her. It was not
wise to alienate Adam. A bond of interest would have
held him; and he might have been, at this time, a
powerful friend. He is said to be growing rich."

"Like his father," replied the Doctor, "he knows,
by a kind of instinct, where the veins of metal lie, and
rarely fails, in digging down, to reach them on the first
trial."

"He did not follow in his father's steps, however; did not become a merchant."

"No; but tried the lottery and exchange business. His love of money led him to prefer a closer contact with the precious thing, and a quicker result. Stocks, that enrich so many and ruin so many, he never tries, I am told. But his property investments are large, and most of them in improving neighborhoods. In the simple item of advance in real estate, I have heard his gains estimated at almost fabulous sums."

"Is he getting rich so very fast?"

"We must take all these reports with grains of allowance. But, you know, that he wedded an heiress."

"Miss T——. Yes; and she is said to have brought him fifty thousand dollars."

"At least that."

"If I were a man," spoke up Annie, the youngest daughter, who had until now, made no remarks, "I would not have taken her for a wife, had her fortune been twice fifty thousand. Homely and, disagreeable! Faugh!"

"She is no beauty," remarked the Doctor.

"She's coarse and vulgar!" said Annie, with some warmth.

"She could hardly be otherwise," said Mrs. Hofland, "for both father and mother were coarse and vulgar. I remember, very well, when they kept a shop in West

Market street for the purchase of old iron and rags. He was miserly, and his wife a woman, I should think, after his own heart. In the course of time, a part of the lower floor of their house was fitted up for a dram shop, and here, at almost any hour in the twenty-four, from six in the morning until ten or eleven at night, you could have seen Mrs. T——, waiting on her customers, black and white. A few years more and the old iron, rag, and dram shop were closed, and Mr. T—— presented himself to the public behind the counters of a well-stocked retail grocery. From this period, Mrs. T—— was no more seen in public life. But, she began to show herself in vulgar finery on the street, and to seek to intrude herself among people of refinement and education. In this last essay, she attained only a limited success. The sphere of her true quality was too dense, and thus too easily perceived. True refinement could not breathe freely in her presence. The daughter grew up undisciplined, poorly educated, and coarse within and without. At her father's death, she became the possessor of fifty thousand dollars, and, by virtue of this golden attraction, won the admiration of Adam Guy, and bought herself a husband."

"Bought! You may well say bought." Annie spoke with ill-concealed disgust. "But think, how low the idea of marriage in the mind of Mr. Guy. To take such a woman into so intimate a life-relationship, just for money! Isn't it shocking — disgusting — painful. He is not wedded to a wife, but to gold.

"All base cupidities," said the Doctor, "have a transmuting power, working inversely to that of the fabled stone sought for by old alchemists, and wholly changing the relation of values. In Adam's case, the earthly dross was rendered invaluable, while the divinely endowed soul sunk to a poor insignificance; and he seized the one with avidity, while almost spurning, with contempt, the other. He could not understand nor appreciate a heart; but in yellow gold he saw beauty and perfection."

"It is sad; very sad;" remarked Mrs. Hofland. "These things always pain me. But, now that we are speaking of Adam, the thought of poor Lydia comes into my mind. I wonder what has become of her?"

The Doctor shook his head in a sober way.

"Her father not only disowned, but disinherited her."

"So I have understood. Poor child! I'm afraid she has found her way in life along rough and thorny paths. But, these oftener lead to final peace, than more flowery ones."

"I fear that she did not, in marrying, act wisely."

"Few act wisely who wed as she wedded. I never saw her husband, but, from the little I gathered from Lydia, he was weak and inferior, and love was not the power that moved him to the conquest of her heart."

" What is his name ? "

" Brady, I think."

" John is dead."

" Yes," replied the Doctor. " Intemperance and debauchery made quick work with him."

" There was another son."

" Yes. I saw him to-day."

" What of him ? "

The Doctor shook his head. " No credit to himself, or to any one else, I'm afraid. He received ten or twelve thousand dollars on becoming of age, and lived fast for two or three years, when he found himself penniless, and of course, friendless. The habits acquired during this spending term, were, in no way, favorable. But, necessity is a stern disciplinarian. He had to work, or starve ; and so sought employment among our merchants. The small salary at command of an indifferent clerk, was not sufficient for the habits of one like Edwin Guy. He lost his place in a few months. Rumor gave the reason, and it was not honorable to the young man. Again he found a place, and kept it longer ; but, not over a year. He was far from being well enough disciplined for the position of a clerk. Then he fell into the hands of a clique of politicians, who have used him ever since. Being neither honest nor scrupulous ; yet having a specious exterior, and some smartness, he is just the kind of implement for them to work with. Of course, the workman must live, and he has a place in the Custom House, which he holds in virtue of his willingness and ability to serve the party in power."

" I would rather my son were dead," said Mrs. Hofland, with feeling. " Poor Lydia! To think that her child should come to this ! "

There was silence for some moments, when Mrs. Hofland went on.

" There was one more child — the youngest — a daughter. What has become of her? She must now be at least twenty-four years of age."

" She is not with her step-mother. At least, I have not seen them together for a long time."

" She was sent away to school, and alienated from home as much as possible ; treated, as I have understood, more like a stranger, than a child."

" Her father's will gave her a few thousands of dollars," said Doctor Hofland. " Some fortune-hunter, in a small way — or one whose imagination increased her ten thousand to fifty or sixty — has, in all probability, drawn her from lonely and desolate ways, and blessed or cursed her life in marriage."

" I have little confidence in the blessing," sighed Mrs. Hofland. " Little — very little. My poor friend Lydia ! — so true hearted, so pure, so good ; to think, that it is of your children that we are now speaking. Alas !

Alas! It has been well said, that marriage is a blessing or a curse — a good or an evil — the road to happiness or misery. With a husband of another quality, what a different life would have opened for my friend. To-day she might be sitting among us, crowned with blessing."

Doctor Hofland now pushed his chair back from the table, and resting his hands on the arms, was about rising.

"Why, father!" said his daughter, Lena, "you are not going away from us yet?"

"Yes. I have several patients who must have an early call this evening."

"Oh, that is too bad. Can't they give you one half-hour?" asked Lena.

"Sickness will not wait, my child. We must not prolong our enjoyments at the expense of others' sufferings. But, I will be home again in an hour."

And the Doctor bent over his grandson, who sat next him in a high chair, and left a warm kiss upon each ruddy cheek.

A few minutes afterwards, and he was out in the clear, cold air of a January night, on his way to Green street, near Franklin, to see the sick child of a stranger, who had sent to ask his aid.

CHAPTER II

THE house was small and poor. A dim light shone through one of the second story windows, and the Doctor could see, as he looked up, a shadow on the ceiling, as of some person walking in the room above. His knock at the door was almost immediately answered by a child, who held a candle elevated above her head.

"Does Mrs. Ewbank live here?"

"Oh, it's you, Doctor! Walk in, please."

Doctor Hofland recognized his visitor of the evening. The child stepped back, and he entered, closing the door. He was in a room instead of a hall, the door opening directly on the street.

"I'll call mother," said the child, as she set the candlestick on a table. "Please to take a chair, sir."

The few minutes that intervened before Mrs. Ewbank came down, gave Doctor Hofland an opportunity to make, by the feeble light of a single tallow candle, a running inventory of what was in the room. The floor had no carpet. Five old cane-seat chairs were against the walls, and a small mahogany table, dark and dim with age, stood under the window, which had neither shade nor blind. A papered fireboard concealed the hearth. Two small frames hung just over the mantel-piece, but the light was so feeble that the Doctor could not make out from where he sat, whether they contained miniature portraits or fancy pictures. An impulse of curiosity led him to cross the room for the purpose of examining them closely. They were evidently miniatures, one of a man, and the other of a woman, in the ripeness of early prime. The first impression was that of familiar faces; but not being able to make out the features distinctly, he was turning for the candle, when a woman entered the apartment. She had descended the stairs so noiselessly, that her coming was not observed.

Though scant and poor, the room was clean and orderly; a fact which the Doctor had not failed to observe. He was not surprised, therefore, to see in Mrs. Ewbank a neat, though plainly attired person. She wore a dark wrapper, carefully buttoned, and her hair was evenly parted, and brushed smoothly away over her temples. Though apparently some years past thirty, and showing signs of wasting sickness, or of trouble that exhausts more than sickness, her eyes were large and bright, with something of youthful fire in them, that a mother's present anxieties could not extinguish. What most impressed the Doctor, was the refined aspect of her countenance, and the manner, which showed cultivation.

"Doctor Hofland," she said, in a low voice, yet fixing her eyes intently upon his face, and in a questioning manner. The tone struck him as familiar, and stirred for a moment old feelings, in a vague, uncertain way. But he failed to recognize in her features those of an acquaintance or friend.

"Mrs. Ewbank?" he responded.

"Yes sir."

"You have a sick child?"

"Yes, sir. Will you walk up and see him?"

She led the way, and Doctor Hofland ascended to one of the chambers above. He found the furniture almost as meagre as in the room below; but the same order and cleanliness prevailed. On the bed lay an emaciated child, a year old, in whose pinched features he saw at the first glance a sign of approaching death.

"How long has he been sick?" asked the Doctor, as he sat down, and laid his fingers on the wasted little hand, limp as a wilted leaf.

"He's never been a well child since he was born, Doctor."

There was something so familiar in the answering voice that Doctor Hofland looked up curiously into the woman's face. She turned partly away, as if to avoid the scrutiny.

" What seems particularly to ail him ? How is he affected ? "

" I can hardly tell you, Doctor. He cries a great deal, and don't eat. There's something the matter inwardly."

A slight spasm went shuddering through the little frame, and a low cry cut the air. A moment, and it was gone, and the pinched features settled into quiet again. The Doctor bent down, and examined the face carefully. While doing so, a man in the next room coughed two or three times, at which he raised himself and listened, noting, with a professional ear, the sound.

" My husband," said the woman.

He turned to the sick child again, watching its face, and observing the respiration. He then wrote a prescription.

" Send for this, and give him one of the powders every hour through the night when not sleeping. If he sleeps, don't disturb him."

" Do you think him very ill ? " asked the mother, in an anxious voice.

" He's a sick child." What less could the Doctor say, when he saw death written all over the ashen face ?

" But you can help him, Doctor ? " said Mrs. Ewbank, in a pleading voice.

" It would have been better if I had seen him earlier,"
remarked the Doctor. He wished to prepare her for
what seemed inevitable.

"I know it was wrong in me not to send," the poor
mother answered, in a distressed way. " But———"
She checked herself, and left the words that were on
her tongue unspoken.

" Why didn't you send before ? "   The Doctor's interest was still further awakened.

But Mrs. Ewbank did not reply immediately, and in
the pause that followed, the sound of coughing was
again heard in the next room.

" How long has your husband been coughing in that
way ? " asked Doctor Hofland.

" Only about a week, so badly.   But, he's coughed
for a long time."

" Has he taken medicine, or seen a physician, within
a week ? "

" We got some cough mixture from a druggist's ; but
that only relieved him for a little while.   It kind of
stupefies him."

" And leaves the cough harder afterwards ? "

" Yes, sir.   He's worse when the effect passes off."

The doctor shook his head.   There was a pause, and
then he asked,

" Shall I not see your husband ? "

" Oh, Doctor !   If you will ! "   Hope and gratitude

were in her face — and tears in her eyes. "Wait just a moment," she added; and then passed into the chamber where her husband lay, to prepare him for the Doctor's visit. She came back quickly, saying — "Now Doctor," and the physician entered. Though everything, as perceived by the feeble rays of a single poor candle, was clean as in the other rooms, and in order, yet the articles were scant; and the whole air of the apartment dreary. The remains of a wood fire smouldered on the hearth, but there was little pervading warmth in the atmosphere.

At a glance, Doctor Hofland saw that Mr. Ewbank was not a coarse or common man. His mouth and nose were cleanly cut; his eyes full of intelligence; and his purely white forehead of ample breadth. His hair was very dark and fine, and curled back from the transparent skin of his temples, through which was perceived the azure net work of veins.

"My husband, Mr. Ewbank : Doctor Hofland." There was an air of refinement about Mrs. Ewbank, now more particularly observed. Not much change took place in the countenance of her husband ; though, as the Doctor sat down, and laid his fingers on his pulse, he kept his large bright eyes fixed steadily on him.

"You have a fever," remarked the Doctor.

"Yes, I've been feverish for some days." A fit of coughing followed this reply.

2*

" What excites this cough ? " asked the Doctor.

" A creeping and tickling here in the throat pit. And he touched the spot.

" Does the coughing produce pain ? "

" Now it does. The jarring seems to have hurt my chest."

" The pain is not lancinating or acute ? "

" No — it is a sore pain, as if the lungs were bruised."

Still holding the patient's wrist, the Doctor bent his head thoughtfully for some moments. Then he asked—

" May I see the cough mixture you have been taking ? "

Mrs. Ewbank went to a closet and brought out a large vial. After smelling and tasting the contents, the Doctor shook his head.

" Do you think it has done him any harm ? " the wife asked, with much apparent anxiety.

" It has done him no good, at least. Don't give him any more of it."

" It contains opium," remarked the patient.

" Yes, and gave you a temporary relief. But, when the effect wore off, your cough was dryer and harder than before."

" That was just the effect."

" And you have grown more feverish ? "

" Yes."

" I will give you something better." The Doctor

spoke with cheerful confidence, and drawing a memorandum book from his pocket, in which were some loose bits of paper, wrote a prescription.

" Take, according to directions accompanying the medicine, and I think, when I call to-morrow morning, that I shall find a decided improvement."

The Doctor noticed a gleam of hopeful light break over Mrs. Ewbank's face. He then retired, and, in passing through the next room, stopped to look at the sick child again.

" He is sleeping," said the mother, in a whisper, as she stooped over the bed.

The Doctor did not reply. After standing there a few moments, he turned and left the chamber; Mrs. Ewbank following him down stairs.

" You will come in the morning?" she said.

" O, yes. I'll be round early." There was something unspoken in her thought, and he paused that she might give it utterance. But she stood silent, and evidently in debate with herself. He was moving towards the door again, when she said —

" Doctor," apparently speaking under self-compulsion. He turned and looked at her with kind encouragement in his face.

" Is there a Dispensary in the neighborhood ? " Her voice shook, and a flush came to her pale cheeks. Doctor Hofland understood too well the meaning of this question. Moving back from the door, he regarded her, earnestly, for a moment or two, and read that in her wasted countenance, of which he had not guessed in the beginning — read of hunger, and the exhaustion of life through lack of food. Under the sharp inquiry of his eyes, she shrunk back, and held the candle so that her face would be more in shadow.

"Send your little girl with me," said the Doctor.

Mrs Ewbank moved to the stairway and called — "Esther!"

"Yes, ma'am," was the child's response, and in a moment quick feet were heard in the chamber above.

"Bring your hood, the Doctor wants you to go with him."

"It is cold out, my dear," said Doctor Hofland, looking narrowly at the child, as she came down stairs. "Haven't you a cloak, or a coat? That shawl is too thin."

"Oh, I'll be warm enough," was answered, in a brave, cheerful way. And so they went out together. The nearest drug store was at a distance of three squares. On the way, Doctor Hofland asked a few leading questions, in order to gain, without drawing his companion into undue communicativeness, some idea of the condition of things at home.

"Have you always lived in Baltimore?" was one of his questions.

" Oh no, sir. We haven't lived here very long."

" How long ? "

" Maybe about a year."

" Where did you live before you came to Baltimore ? "

" In Albany."

" State of New York ? "

" Yes, sir."

" Did your father keep a store in Albany ? "

" Oh no, sir. He kept a school."

" Ah ! A school ? "

" Yes, sir. But he got sick, and lost it. And then we came here."

" Has your father taught since he has been in this city ? "

" Yes, sir, for a little while ; but not in his own school."

" He gave lessons in somebody else's school ? "

" Yes, sir."

" What did he teach ? "

" Latin and Greek, sir. But he can teach anything."

" He doesn't give lessons now ? "

" No, sir. They got another man in his place ; and he's been too sick to teach for a good while."

" How long is it since they got another man in his place ? "

The child thought for some moments, and then replied,

" Ever since August. I know it from my birth-day."

" That was in August ? "

" Yes, sir."

" How old were you then ? "

" I was eight years old, sir."

" Eight years.   And your name is Esther ? "

" That is my name."

" Called after your mother ? "

" No, sir, after my grandmother.   But she's dead."

They were now at the druggist's shop, and entering, Doctor Hofland ordered the two prescriptions.   While they were being prepared, he scanned the child's face closely.   Some would have called it handsome ; but he saw in its regular oval so many signs of endurance and suffering, that, as he gazed upon it, his heart was touched.

" Give me two packages of oat meal," he said, to the druggist, as he received the compounded medicines. " Now, Esther," turning to the child, " tell your mother to make a large bowl of gruel, and let your father drink as much of it as he can."

" Before he takes his medicine ? " asked the child, lifting her earnest eyes to the Doctor's face.

" Yes.   First the gruel, remember ; and if his cough doesn't trouble him, he needn't take the medicine for an hour afterwards.   Good night, dear.   Run home as fast as you can ; and tell your mother by no means to omit the gruel."

CHAPTER III

HEN Doctor Hofland came back to his office, he found a man awaiting his return — a young man, with a hard, sensual face, and something of a dissolute air.

"Doctor Hofland," said the visitor, rising, with a respectful manner, as the Doctor came in. The Doctor bowed, in assent.

"Can I have a few words with you confidentially?"

"I presume so," replied the Doctor. "Be seated again."

The young man sat down. His manner was disturbed, and a little mysterious.

"I believe," he said, trying, though with only with partial success, to assume a cool demeanor, "that you were acquainted with my father, the late Adam Guy."

"Yes, sir, I knew him."

"You attended him, in his last dreadful illness."

"I was not his physician," replied the Doctor.

" But you visited him, I know ; for I saw you at our house."

" I was called in, as consulting physician, and saw him for a few times."

" Exactly. That is sufficient. Now, Doctor, you may not know it — but there was foul play with my father; and I'm bound to rip up the whole business. I'm going to sift matters to the bottom."

" Foul play in what respect ? " asked the Doctor.

" In all respects. That she-devil, his wife — excuse me ! but I always lose myself when I think of her — managed to rob us children of nearly the whole of our father's property, by means of a will that, I am satisfied, could be broken in law. And I'm going to break it. Now, Doctor, you can help me. You attended my father, and know whether he was in condition to make a will. If it can be proved that he was *non compos* at the date of the will, then it is thrown overboard, and we come in, as heirs at law, for an equitable division of the estate. You see how it is, Doctor. What do you think ? What is your opinion ? Was the old gentleman sound or not ? Fit to make a will or not ? "

Disgust struggled with pity in Doctor Hofland's mind, and kept him silent. Edwin Guy scanned him sharply, trying to read his thoughts.

" What is your opinion, Doctor ? " The young man

was impatient for a response. "Of course, you have an opinion. You were with him. You saw exactly how it was. You know whether he was sane enough to make a will."

Doctor Hofland thought as rapidly as possible, before committing himself in a reply.

"You are Mr. Guy's youngest son?" he said, avoiding the answer that was expected.

"Yes sir, I am. Edwin Guy is my name."

"Your brother John is dead?"

"He is."

"What of Adam, your oldest brother? Is he going to move with you in this matter?"

There was a change in the young man's face — anger and contempt swept over it.

"No, sir! The will was adroitly made, giving him the full sum to which he would have been entitled in a legal division of my father's estate. That settled him. Pocketing his share, he turned his back upon the younger children, and left them a prey to robbers. Thus bribed to abandon us to our fate, I hold him as an accomplice with my step-mother and that precious scoundrel, her husband. But right is right, Doctor, and I'm going to see this matter through. If I can establish the fact that my father was not in a sane condition when the will was made, there will be a new distribution of property, to the advantage of myself and sisters."

"What of your sisters, Mr. Guy? Where are they?"

This question dashed the young man. He reddened, and then stammered an admission that he was not particularly advised in regard to them.

"What about Lydia? Is she in Baltimore?"

"Indeed, Doctor, I am unable to speak with any certainty in regard to her. She threw herself away, as you perhaps know, in a disgraceful marriage, and became separated from the family. Nothing has been heard of her, so far as I am advised, since our father's death. My step-mother may know something of her whereabouts; but as we have been strangers for years, no information that she possesses would be likely to reach me."

"She may be dead," said the Doctor.

"Possible." There was not even a pretence of feeling in the young man's voice.

"You have a younger sister?"

"Yes, sir, Frances."

"Is she living with your step-mother?"

"I think not."

"When did you see her?"

The young man lifted his eyes to the ceiling, and mused for some time.

"It's over two years since I saw Frances," he said, at length, with as much indifference as though not a drop of kindred blood were in their veins.

" Is she married ? "

" I've never heard of such an event."

So thoroughly disgusted was Doctor Hofland with the unfeeling, almost brutal spirit shown by Edwin Guy, that he felt no inclination to aid him in any effort to break the will of his father.

" If called to give evidence," said the visitor, going back to the leading purpose in his thought, " how clearly could you state the case? In other words, if asked whether my father were sane or insane, what would be your answer? "

" There are degrees of insanity," replied the Doctor, " and it would be for the court to decide, on the particulars of evidence, its estimate of the degree in your father's case. There was certainly a temporary derangement of the faculties."

" Temporary! Anything but that, Doctor? It proved to be inveterate. You are aware that the family was compelled to send him to an asylum, where, in the violence of his insanity, he threw himself from a window and was killed."

" Did it never cross your mind," asked the Doctor, dropping his voice to a more serious tone, " that in the precipitate removal of your father from our Maryland Hospital to a private mad house in another state, some wrong may have been involved? "

" Wrong? Wrong, sir? I am not sure that I take

your meaning." There was a sudden knitting of the young man's brows.

" I never assented to his being taken from home in the first place."

" Ah ? "

" No, sir. In my view, the case did not threaten the disaster that followed. Doctor L——, who is now dead, was your family physician, and I was called, I think, at your father's desire. But without advising with me, and certainly against my judgment, he was taken to the Hospital while under the influence of an opiate. In a few days, he was so much better, that the resident physician consented to his being removed by Doctor L—— and your step-mother. I learned this on personal inquiry at the Hospital. You may judge of my surprise when, not long afterwards, the fact came out that instead of being taken home, he was borne off to the private asylum where he died."

" Is that so ? " exclaimed Edwin Guy, starting to his feet, with lowering brows, and eyes that had in them a strange glitter.

" That is so," replied the Doctor.

" Who took him to the Hospital ? "

Without reflecting as to the prudence of his answer, Doctor Hofland replied —

" Mr. Larobe and your step-mother.

" Ha ! Larobe ! Good ! I begin to see light !

Something wrong? Of course there was something wrong!"

And the young man stalked backwards and forwards across the office in a wild, excited manner. But suddenly composing himself, he sat down close to the Doctor, and bending towards him, said, while he rubbed his hands in suppressed excitement and expectation —

"What else? Mr. Larobe was with my step-mother — her accomplice in the matter. And they took him from the Hospital, and removed him to a distant asylum?"

"No; Doctor L—— accompanied your mother when your father was taken from the Hospital."

"Doctor L——, oh!" There was a tone of disappointment. "But no matter. The thing is plain as daylight. I'm much obliged to you for the hint. Something wrong! I believe you! I always said that woman was capable of anything; and I always said that her day would come. Murder will out, you know, Doctor; and it's coming out now."

"Don't take too much for granted," replied Doctor Hofland; "I have only given you a fact or two, and must warn you against quoting or involving me in a single item beyond what I have said. My evidence will only serve in a limited degree; and if, through any eagerness to make out a case, you rely on me to prove a tittle more than my present language declares, you will damage instead of promoting the cause of justice. You have all that I know or think it advisable to suggest. In my view, your father's case was a simple one, and should not have led at so early a stage of aberration, to his removal from home. If the will dates prior to this removal, the question of his ability to devise property is an open one, and may be decided by the courts either way. Unless you have a cloud of witnesses to prove insanity as existing when the will was made, an attempt to break it may only involve you in years of costly and fruitless litigation."

" I'm obliged to you for the advice, Doctor," said the young man, resuming a cool exterior. " You've set me to thinking in a new direction." And with half-closed eyes, and shut, protruding mouth, he sat musing, with an occasional satisfactory nod as he followed the train of thought which had been awakened in his mind. Then rising and drawing his cloak about his shoulders, he bade the Doctor good evening, and retired.

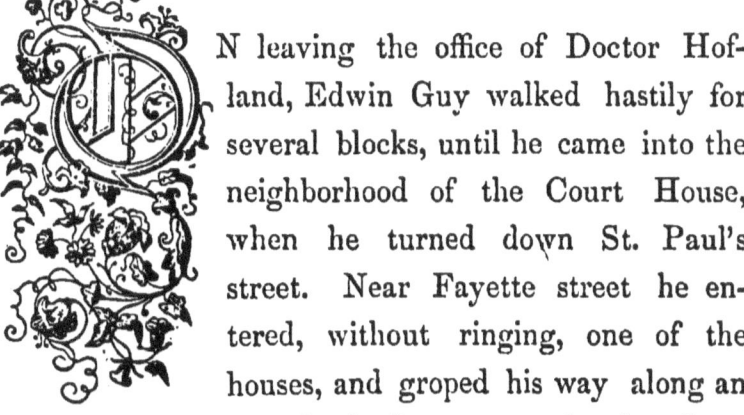

CHAPTER IV

N leaving the office of Doctor Hofland, Edwin Guy walked hastily for several blocks, until he came into the neighborhood of the Court House, when he turned down St. Paul's street. Near Fayette street he entered, without ringing, one of the houses, and groped his way along an unlighted passage, to the back room on the first floor. In this room, furnished as a lawyer's office, a man sat by a table, writing. He looked up as the door opened, showing a large face and head, and a pair of calm, cold, steady eyes. His age was about forty.

Guy, after shutting the door, took a chair at the table opposite to this man, and then they looked at each other for a few moments in silence.

"Did you see him?" The lawyer, for that was the man's profession, spoke first. His voice was firm and penetrating, yet not burdened with any special in-

terest. A close observer, and one skilled in human nature, would however have detected beneath his unmoved
exterior a wily, alert spirit.

"I saw him," replied the young man.

"To any good purpose?"

"You will think so, when you hear what I have
learned."

"The Doctor's evidence will serve you in the case?"

"I'm not sure of that. He doesn't think my father
was so very insane when taken to the hospital."

"What?" The lawyer betrayed a momentary impulse; for instantly his thought compassed the true
significance of this answer.

"There has been foul play beyond anything I had
imagined, Mr. Glastonberry. It makes my hair stand
on end to think of it."

"Foul play in what respect?"

"In respect to my father."

"Doctor Hofland is not satisfied that he was insane?"

"No, sir. He was consulting physician at the time,
and they removed my father to the Hospital while stu-
pefied with opium, without a word of conference with
him."

"Is that so?"

"It is, on the word of Doctor Hofland; and I reck-
on he wont lie."

"If Doctor Hofland says so, you may believe it."

" Of course I believe it.   And who, think you, were the accomplices in this thing ?   Who, think you, conveyed him to the Hospital ? "

" I cannot guess."

" My step-mother, and —— Justin Larobe ! "

" No ! "

" Yes, sir ; on the word of Doctor Hofland, as declared to me this night.   His informotion was obtained from the resident physician at the Hospital, of whom he made inquiry at the time.   And I learn farther, that in the few days my father remained in the Hospital, he improved so rapidly, that the physician made no objection to his being taken home again at the request of my step-mother, who, in company with the late Doctor L———, then our family physician, called in a carriage, and removed him."

" Taking him home ? "

" No, sir.   He never saw home again ! "

" What ? "

" He never saw home again.   A short time afterwards, Dr. Hofland learned to his amazement, that my father had been taken from our excellent institution, and placed in a private mad-house on Long Island, where the catastrophe occurred that ended his life."

" Grave matters are involved here, my young friend,'' said the lawyer.   The case assumes an entirely new aspect."

8

"It does, Mr. Glastonberry. I saw that in a moment. I question now whether an attempt to set aside the will, under an allegation of insanity, would be successful. The testimony of Dr. Hofland, on which I mainly relied, would damage instead of helping the case. He does not think the mental disturbance of my father was at all serious in the beginning."

"The move, if now attempted, must be in some new direction," said Mr. Glastonberry, dropping his head, and partly closing his eyes.

"One thing is clear," remarked Guy —"Larobe and my step-mother plotted to get father out of the way, and plotted successfully. Their act was little less than murder. It can be proved that they drugged him while sick, and then carried him to the Hospital ; and further proved that he was taken from thence in an improved condition, and sent to a distant asylum, kept by an irresponsible foreigner, where he met with a violent death. An ugly look all that would have, bruited to the world in a court of justice."

"Very ugly." Mr. Glastonberry spoke as if to himself.

"If successful in breaking this will," resumed Edwin Guy, "there will be so many to share in the estate, that my proportion cannot be large."

"How many children are there ? "

"Six or seven — six, if my sister Lydia is dead ; and

I guess, seeing that nothing has been heard from her in eight or ten years, that she is safely out of this troublesome world."

" She may have left children."

Guy shrugged his shoulders, and frowned, saying —

" I didn't think of that."

" Say seven children; and the law will give your step-mother one-third of the estate."

" And her three cursed imps nearly half of what remains, after that great slice is taken out," growled the young man.

Just so. The whole estate possessed by your father at the time of his decease, you estimate in round numbers at two hundred and fifty thousand dollars."

" Yes."

" Deduct your step-mother's one-third, and we have left about one hundred and sixty-seven thousand dollars, to divide between seven persons, or something over twenty-three thousand to each. It will be safe to call this twenty thousand. Now you have already received ten thousand dollars under the will. As a fee for recovering the balance, you offer me one-half. The case may be on trial for half-a-dozen years. Larobe is a hard man to fight at law. Does this view look enticing ? "

" No, sir, it does not ;" was the strongly spoken answer.   o

"Our fox may prove too swift for us in the open
field ; we must hunt him under cover."

"Just my own conclusion. The fact is, Mr. Glastonberry, to speak outright and downright, I'm for getting my own in the surest and safest way. Larobe
and his she-devil of a wife must disgorge ; and from
what I have learned this evening, there is a process by
which that desirable result may be effected. A crime
lies between them ; I know it, and can ruin them with
a word!"

Guy had been seated since he entered the lawyer's
office ; but in closing this sentence, he started up in an
excited manner, and gesticulated with some violence.

"I can ruin them at a word," he repeated —"and
what is more, I'll do it, unless ——"

He did not complete the sentence, but Glastonberry
understood him.

"One thing must not be forgotten," said the lawyer,
in his cold, deliberate way. "You have a cunning fox
to deal with in Larobe."

"A swift-footed hound, keen of scent, is usually a
match for the cunningest fox. I'll put you against Larobe, any day ; and I'm not slow myself, when the
game's on foot.

Glastonberry's upper lip was raised in a peculiar way
— drawn back, as we sometimes see it in a dog — showing two or three of the teeth on one side. The move-

ment seemed nervous, and passed in a moment. It did not appear, from all the signs in his face, whether he relished his client's compliment or not.

" What do you propose ? " he asked.

" If the Doctor's story is true, there's been foul play towards my father."

" Unquestionably," replied Mr. Glastonberry.

" And Larobe is a party to the foul play."

" I take that for granted."

" Very well. A man with a crime on his conscience is always a coward. You can frighten him into any-thing, if he is fully assured that you know his secret."

" In some cases that is so."

" Will it not be so with Larobe ? "

" His character, as a man of honorable dealing, does not stand very high, you are aware. Two or three estates of orphans have been queerly managed under his administration ; and he has coolly braved the odium of legal inquiry into his conduct, suffering damage to his good name in consequence."

" I can shake the penitentiary, nay, the gallows, in his face," said Guy, fiercely.

" He will understand the value of all that to the tenth part of a scruple."

" Of course, he will," answered the young man, losing a portion of his excitement under the chilling composure of the lawyer. " And its value is not to be determined with feathers in the opposing scale."

"In this line of attack, Edwin," said Mr. Glaston-berry, "great caution is needed. If Larobe were a merchant, of ordinary calibre; or, in any other profession except law, he might be advanced upon with the prospect of a certain victory. But he is wily, crafty, and well entrenched in any position he may have taken. He knows every inch of the ground he stands on; its weak and its impregnable side. If you approach him as an enemy, he will comprehend your strength and resources, as compared with his own, and by feints and covert movements, seek to betray you to destruction — and he will do it, if you are not wholly on your guard."

"How can he damage me?" asked Guy.

"Conspiracies to extort money are regarded as serious crimes; and, moreover, in our courts, a lawyer, as party to a suit, has two chances to one in his favor."

"What do you mean by that?"

"Simply, that, from a certain *esprit de corps*, the Bench and the Bar generally sustain each other. It is a difficult thing to get one lawyer of standing to conduct a case against a brother in the profession, who holds a good position. If Larobe can trap you in any way, and then dispose of you under legal process, depend upon it, he will do so, and you may find yourself across the Falls, and under lock and key, before even conscious of danger. Instead of hurting him, you may ruin yourself."

" Then you advise an open and above-board suit to break the will."

" No ; I do not advise that."

" What then ? "

" Simply, that you govern yourself in all things, as I direct. There is a safe way, and also an unsafe way, in this business."

" I am in your hands, Mr. Glastonberry."

" Hold yourself strictly to my suggestions," answered the lawyer, " and I think we may gain more by private arrangment with Larobe, than in a perplexing suit. I must, of course, be unknown in the affair. It will not do for you to come here for consultation in the day time ; nor must we ever be seen talking together on the street. In fact, we should avoid recognizing each other on meeting. It will suggest itself to Larobe, that you are acting under advice ; and he will be Argus-eyed in his efforts to learn by whom your well considered advances upon him are instigated. If I am known, my power will, in a great measure, be gone. You understand ? "

" O yes. I see the bearing of all that. You can trust in my discretion. I know what is at stake."

" Very well. Now we understand each other clearly. See me again to-morrow evening. In the mean time, it may be well for you to call on Doctor Hofland, and get from him a repetition of what he said to-night, and anything further he may feel inclined to communicate.

But, I must particularly caution you against the utterance of threats towards Mr. Larobe, or the use of any expressions that may give the Doctor a hint of what you intend doing. Note his language exactly, in all he says about your father, so as to remember his very words. I think—" he added, encouragingly—"that we have a rich case, and one that will pay, if we manage our cards aright. We must not be precipitate ; but move with stealthy circumspection. Larobe must not be startled, too suddenly, by a threat. He must be toyed with, and entreated, as it were. Your first visit should be one of solicitation, rather than demand. An approach to get his ear, and open the way for other advances. But I will think out the programme minutely, and to-morrow evening speak by the card."

Mr. Glastonberry then arose, and going to a closet, brought forth a small waiter, on which were glasses and a bottle of wine.

" It is sharp out to-night," he said, " and you must warm yourself before going, with Amontillado."

And he poured two full glasses of the pale, sunny liquor.

" You perceive the flavor," said Glastonberry, as Guy, after sipping at his glass, noted the taste on his palate.

" True Amontillado," was replied, and then the glass was emptied and set down, but held between the fingers, dumb in invitation to be refilled — an invitation that did not wait.

"You're a judge of wine, Mr. Glastonberry," remarked Guy, approvingly, as he smacked his lips, after emptying his second glass.

"I know a good article," answered the lawyer. "Try another glass. It is light," and he filled for his companion again.

When, half an hour afterwards, they parted, the bottle stood empty on the lawyer's table.

CHAPTER V.

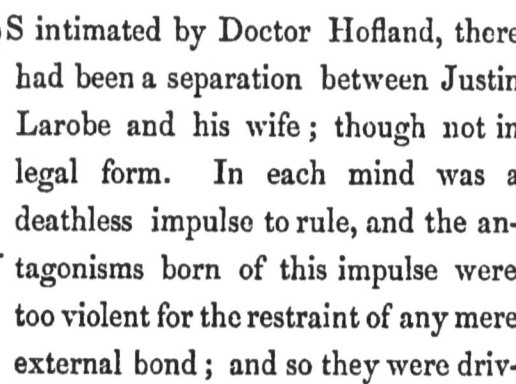

S intimated by Doctor Hofland, there had been a separation between Justin Larobe and his wife; though not in legal form. In each mind was a deathless impulse to rule, and the antagonisms born of this impulse were too violent for the restraint of any mere external bond; and so they were driven asunder. The parting had been in such hot blood, that no recognition of mutual rights had taken place. As enemies they drew apart, each hating, yet fearing the other; for, they held between them a deadly secret. The household was not broken up. That remained with Mrs. Larobe; and as issue had failed in the marriage, no irritating questions in regard to the disposition of children were involved. Mr. Larobe, in separating from his wife, had taken a suite of rooms at the City Hotel, where he was living at the period of which we are now writing.

On the night after the interview between Edwin Guy and Mr. Glastonberry, as described in the last chapter, Larobe sat alone in his chamber. He was a man rather below, than up to the medium stature, but stoutly and squarely built. The lower part of his face was narrow, but the upper portion broad and high. A pair of small, tawny gray eyes, looked at you, warily, from beneath heavy and projecting brows; and a peculiarity in them was, that their color came so near to that of the deep orbital cavity, that you did not, at first, detect their sinister expression. His head was thickly covered with short, coarse hair, that was beginning to turn grey. Mr. Larobe was reading, and sat very still, apparently absorbed in his book. The time wore on until nearly ten o'clock, when two knocks came upon the door; not by a servant's hand — his ear told him that. Rising, he crossed the room, and opened the door.

"Edwin Guy!" Larobe uttered the name in no simulated surprise; his heavy brows falling, as he spoke.

"Mr. Larobe," said the young man, stepping into the apartment. The lawyer moved back, and Guy advanced, shutting the door behind him. In the middle of the room, half way to the glowing grate, he faced around, and planted himself squarely before his visitor, who, naturally, stood still, confronting him. Both frowned — both looked defiant. Each recognized an enemy, who would inflict harm if possible.

" To what am I indebted for this visit ? " asked Larobe, coldly.

" I have several things to say," replied Edwin, speaking with as much coolness as possible, and at the same
time taking, though uninvited, a chair. It was plain,
by the lawyer's manner, that something in his visitor
puzzled him. He did not consent to this freedom of
conduct in his own apartment, by taking a chair also,
but stood even more erect and solid, with his arms
thrown behind him.

" Say on." Larobe, in tone, at least, feigned indifference well.

" As you are aware, sir, I have never been satisfied
with my father's will." Guy looked at him, keenly, as
he said this. It was a simple feeler. The only change
noted, was a warier expression in the deep set, brownish
gray eyes, that were fixed on him, snakily.

" And you are aware, sir, that I have no power to
change it," was answered, evenly and coldly.

· I think its conditions will have to be changed,"
said Guy.

There was a meaning in his voice, more than in his
words, that caused Larobe to move from his solid balance, with just the slightest sign of uneasiness.

" All parties are bound by the terms of a legal instrument," said the lawyer, slowly, distinctly, and without
apparent feeling. " A will, to an executor, is a letter

of instructions, from which he cannot depart. In regard to your father's will, every provision has been carried out to the letter. If you question this, demand an investigation. You will be patiently heard in the Orphan's Court. But if, as I infer from your remark, it is against the will itself that your complaint lies, then you must go past the executor, and test its binding force in law."

" An insane man cannot make a will," remarked Edwin Guy, in dead level tones, while he kept his eyes watchfully on Larobe's countenance.

" True; but your father's will bears date anterior to the loss of reason."

" I am not sure of that."

" You surprise me, Edwin!   How long have you entertained this view ? "

" For a long time."

" It can at least be said," remarked the lawyer, with manifest irony, " that you have been exceedingly patient under this impression of fraud and wrong. Had the case been mine, I would have seen to the bottom of it years ago."

" Some men act hastily, while others bide their time. I was only a boy when my father died, and ignorant of the dark things passing around me. The thought of crime and violence never entered my young brain, and when, long ago, the suggestions were made, I turned

away from them as too horrible for belief. But, one
fact after another came to light, until the accumulated
evidence forced an almost unwilling conviction. I did
not act hastily; but went on searching, inquiring, pondering, willing to bide my time; *and it has come,
Mr. Larobe!*"

Guy threw a quick, strong emphasis into his voice, in
closing this sentence, which gave the lawyer's nerves,
self-poised as he was, a sudden start. Turning himself,
by an almost imperceptible movement, he withdrew his
face from under the direct scrutiny of a pair of eyes
that seemed looking right down into his heart. Before
answering, he took a chair, placing it in a line parallel
to the one in which Guy was sitting, so that he might
look towards, or away from his companion, as suited
him best. He did not speak immediately. Guy waited for him, struggling to repress the mounting excitement, which made every pulsation of his heart audible
in his ears.

"If you know of anything wrong, Edwin," he said,
at length, in the manner of one who offers disinterested
advice, in the hope of serving another —" bring it to
the light. I was simply executor under your father's
will, the purpose of which I have carried out faithfully.
You received, at my hands, on the day you were twenty-
one years of age, all that it gave you. I could do no
more. If there was anything wrong in the execution

of this will; if, as you seem to think, dark and criminal things are involved; in Heaven's name, drag them forth to view! Count on me for giving you all aid that may lie in my power."

This, though understood by Edwin, was unexpected, and he pondered it, before answering. When he spoke, his words were —

"I have learned that my father was drugged before his removal to the Hospital."

"Drugged!" exclaimed Larobe, in feigned astonishment.

"Yes, sir, drugged!"

"By whom?"

"Ah, there's the pinch! The fact is ascertained beyond question. He was heavily under the influence of opium when received at the Hospital."

"That may be satisfactorily accounted for, I think," said Larobe. "Your father's derangement was preceded by days and nights of sleeplessness, and morphia was administered, under the advice of his physician, as the only means of tranquilizing his nerves; and he may have been more or less under its influence when taken to the Hospital. To my mind this view is reasonable."

"If that fact stood solitary, your inference would be reasonable enough. Unhappily, it does not," replied the young man.

" What other facts have you learned ? " asked Larobe.

" He was removed from home without the knowledge or consent, and against the judgment, of at least
one of his attendant physicians, and in the absence of
both."

" Is that so? " The lawyer did not turn his face
towards his companion, but sat, with his chin drawn
down, and his eyes looking inwards.

" Without question, that is so. And it farther appears, that my step-mother, with a male accomplice —
of whose identity I am not yet clearly advised — accompanied him to the Hospital, delivering him in person,
to the officials of the Institution."

" That may all be satisfactorily explained," answered
Mr. Larobe. " It is the same with actions as with
natural objects; a different point of view, gives a different appearance. I don't see a case in this."

" And it still farther appears," resumed Guy, " that
my father showed immediate signs of improvement; and
these were so marked, that the Resident Physician consented, after a few days, to his being taken home again,
and with that view permitted him to leave the Institution, in company with his wife and another person.
Now, sir, in tracing the case thus far, judge of my surprise and horror, when I learned, that, instead of being taken home, a sane man as he was, his wife and
ner accomplice spirited him off to a private mad-house

on Long Island, where he met, not long after, with a
violent death. Sir! there is a murder at the bottom of
this dark transaction! Yes, sir! A murder! And
by all the solemn obligations of a son to his father, I
will drag the foul transgressors into open day, and have
them punished!"

Starting to his feet, in excitement, the young man
took a position in front of Larobe, and gazed upon him,
with stern accusation in his eyes. The lawyer, cool
and wary as he was, found himself, unexpectedly, in so
perilous a strait, that entire self-composure was almost
impossible. To betray weakness or fear, would be to
give his enemy a power over him that might be used
with terrible effect. So he waited, before answering,
to collect himself. He then remarked, with a thoughtful air, as if pondering what Guy had said —

"That has a dark look, certainly."

"A dark and devilish look! ejaculated the young
man, fiercely.

"From whom did you gain this information, Edwin?"

"I am not yet at liberty to give names; but, witnesses ready to prove all, and more than all, I have said,
will be forthcoming. Among these is a man who held
the place of keeper in the mad-house where my father
was taken. He has already given me some shocking
particulars in regard to his treatment there."

" What ? " The lawyer was off his guard, and gave a sign of alarm that Edwin Guy did not fail to note.

" ' He was no more insane than you are now, when he came to our place ; ' these are the man's very words, Mr. Larobe. Just think of it ! Do you wonder that I am excited and in earnest? That I have sworn to uncover this great iniquity ? "

" What did he say about your father's death ? " asked Larobe. Guy perceived, by the lawyer's tone and manner — by the holding of his breath for an an- swer — that, in his reply to this question, he felt a deep and personal interest. And so, he withheld the answer until he could think for a little while.

" There was some mystery about that," he remarked, at length, as if unwilling to communicate what was in his thoughts.

" Mystery ? "

" Yes. The man evidently knows more than he cares, just now, to communicate. But I understand the kind of influence needed, and shall bring it to bear."

" In attempting to escape from a window, your fa- ther fell to the ground, and was killed. I never heard, or suspected, anything more," said Larobe.

" That was the story, I know. Beyond this simple casualty, as it was called, nothing reached the public. All the actors in this infernal business were cunning and secretive ; but it happened, as it usually does in all

hellish schemes, that Satan left one or two points unguarded, through means of which he might betray to
ruin the easy fools who trusted him. The devil, Mr.
Larobe, is a false friend; and all who swear by him are
equally false, and as ready to betray each other. Doctor Du Pontz, if I remember aright, is the name by
which the keeper of the asylum on Long Island is
known ? "

" Something like that," replied the lawyer.

" A Frenchman ? "

" Probably."

" You have seen him ? "

" No, I believe not." Larobe seemed trying to recall
the man's identity.

" Then I have been misinformed. I understood that
you were, several times, on Long Island, during the
time of my father's imprisonment.

Larobe shook his head, slowly, as he answered —

" I was never on Long Island in my life."

" A simple question of evidence," said Guy, in an
undertone, as if to himself.

" What do you mean by that ? " demanded Larobe,
forgetting himself.

" By what ? " coolly asked Guy.

" By your remark, that it was a simple question of
evidence."

" Whether you were ever at Du Pontz's mad-house on Long Island, or not ? "

Larobe was losing ground in this passage at arms with the young man, and he felt it bitterly. How should he regain the failing advantage? Not, surely, through any betrayal of passion ; though he felt the intimations of Guy as a biting insult. Fear, however, was stronger than anger, and admitted as the safer counsellor.

" I think, Edwin," said he, after a hurried repression of feeling, facing round, and looking steadily at Guy — his voice had now a velvety softness, and a friendship of tone not exhibited before —" that we had best clearly understand each other. You have come here with a certain purpose in your mind; and I am of opinion, that through a frank statement of that purpose, you will more readily attain to it, than by any covert movements. I cannot understand your drift in this seeming effort to involve me, in transactions of a dozen years back to which I was in no way participant. You contemplate some legal action, I infer ? "

" I do," was promptly answered.

" Before commencing, let me suggest a careful consideration of the question, whether, in this action, you will have me as a friend or an enemy."

" Thank you, for the suggestion," said Guy, in a conciliatory manner. " Enemies are never to be desired.

Of course, I desire to have you as a friend ; but it may happen, that interest will come in the way of friendship. If, as appears from all I can learn, you were an active abettor in my father's ruin of mind, and subsequent death, I don't see how, in any legal or personal sense, you can stand to me in any other relation than that of an enemy. Understand me, Mr. Larobe. I am in possession of evidence in regard to my father's treatment that will astound the community when it comes to light, and I shall prosecute to conviction all parties who were in the conspiracy against him."

" To what end ? " calmly inquired the lawyer.

" That wrong may be punished, and justice established," said Guy, in a firm voice.

" Justice ? " queried Larobe. " To whom ? Your father is dead, and no legal decision can affect him."

" It can affect his children, wrongfully despoiled of their interest in his estate."

" What was your interest ? '

Edwin dropped his eyes and seemed to be thinking.

" Not above twenty thousand dollars, in equitable division under the law, if your father had died intestate. Are you aware of that ? "

Edwin did not reply, and the lawyer added,

" Ten thousand were devised and paid. If you succeed to the utmost, you cannot get beyond an additional ten thousand, subject to fees and legal claims, which, under the law's delays and requirements, will amount to half that sum. I am speaking as your friend, and showing you the best that lies beyond."

" You forget interest," said Edwin. " Interest on ten thousand dollars from the date of my father's will. Six or seven thousand dollars must cover the most liberal estimate of expenses ; and I can find half-a-dozen prominent lawyers in an hour, any one of whom will engage to conduct the suit for that fee in prospect."

He was watching Larobe closely, to see the effect of this last sentence. It went home. Some minutes passed in silence ; a silence that Larobe felt to be telling against him more and more, the longer it was continued, for it showed his perplexity and indecision. Guy could afford to wait his companion's response ; and he did wait.

" You are aware," said the lawyer, in a deliberate way, breaking the pause, " that your step-mother and I are not on friendly terms."

" I have heard as much," answered the young man.

" I cannot, therefore, speak for her. Perhaps —"

But he left the sentence unfinished.

" There has been no divorce ? " said Guy.

" No — no ; nothing of that kind."

Larobe understood the remark. As husband, under the State laws, he had control of his wife's property, nearly the whole of which was personal, and not freehold. And so he was still in perplexity of mind.

"Edwin," he said, after another period of silence, "this is too grave a matter to admit of hasty decision. Everything depends on your knowing where you stand. A false step may be ruinous. As intimated a little while ago, I can be your friend, and serve you — or, if you elect, I can be your enemy. It is for you to say in which attitude I am to stand."

As if deliberating on the lawyer's suggestion, Guy walked the floor for some time, his hands behind him and his head bent down. Pausing at length, and lifting his eyes, he remarked —

"I think you understand the case, Mr. Larobe?"

"Perhaps I do," was answered.

"And you wish to be my friend?"

"I have said so."

"Turn the subject over in your mind. Look at it upon all sides, and determine for me, if you can, what course will be the wisest. I will see you again to-morrow evening."

"Whatever is done, Edwin, should be well considered in advance," said the lawyer, with cautious reserve.

"No one understands that better than I do, Mr. Larobe, and therefore I suggest twenty-four hours' deliberation. To-morrow evening I will be here again. Good-night."

And he went out abruptly. There was a covert threat in his good night tone which the lawyer's wary ear did not fail to notice. For nearly an hour after Guy's departure, he sat so motionless before the fire, that an observer would have thought him sleeping. But sleep was a stranger to his pillow through all the watches of that troubled night.

CHAPTER VI.

ROM the City Hotel, Edwin Guy waited leisurely down Monument Square to Lexington street, where he stopped and waited several minutes on the corner, narrowly scrutinizing every one who approached from the direction of the Hotel. Satisfied, at length, that Larobe was not following him, he started up Lexington street at a quick pace, and passing the Court House, dropped down St. Paul street to the · neighborhood of Glastonberry's office, into which he disappeared. The cold, still face of the lawyer looked ' at him inquiringly, as he took a chair opposite to where he sat at the office table. It was one of those unreadable faces that we sometimes see in men, which, like a turbid stream, hides everything beneath — smooth, sluggish, mysterious.

" You have seen him ? "

" Yes."

4

"Give me the interview as accurately as possible; word for word if you can — and the effect produced on Larobe."

Guy related, with minute particularity, all that had passed between him and his father's executor.

"He's frightened — so much is clear," said Glastonberry, in his imperturbable way.

"Frightened out of his boots," returned Guy.

"No, not so badly as that. He's an old fox, my friend, and will double on his track and throw you off the scent."

"He'll never throw me off; make yourself easy on that head," answered Guy, confidently. "He betrayed enough to-night, to show that he believes me in possession of facts which may be used to his harm. He intends to avoid all legal issues if possible."

"No doubt of that. But none knows better than he, the questionable policy of secret compromise with an enemy. If he can hold himself clear from that perilous necessity, he will do so."

"Do you think he can, Mr. Glastonberry?"

"There is a way —"

"How? — Where?"

"It would take too much time to explain to-night. Besides, I am not fully posted; I only know that there is a way — difficult to be sure; but one along which he may choose to venture as a means of escaping the trap you have laid for his feet. Let me, once more, enjoin upon you the greatest prudence. Keep your own counsel. Above all, remain strictly silent, even to your nearest friend, touching the matter now in progress, so that no one may have it in his power to report a sentence from your lips. Suspect all who approach you with a word about family affairs ; and on no account suffer a remark on the subject of Mr. Larobe's relation to your father's estate to drop from your lips. You will be watched with unsleeping vigilance from this hour. Larobe will surround you with men under pay and instructions, whose business it will be to lure you into imprudences of speech, that may be tortured into evidence to prove an attempt on your part to extort money. Forewarned, forearmed, my young friend. You are embarking on a dangerous venture."

" But with a good pilot at the helm," replied Edwin, in compliment to the lawyer.

" If my ship obeys the helm, the passage will be safe. If not, the peril is imminent."

" She will obey the helm, Mr. Glastonberry. Trust my word for that."

The only response to this, was in that peculiar lifting of the upper lip, before mentioned, as if a portion of it were drawn back by a cord, showing the canine teeth.

" I shall see him, as per appointment, again on tomorrow night," said Guy. " What programme is to be followed ? "

" Be, for one thing, more reserved and more mysterious," replied Glastonberry, " as if you were conscious of having said too much during the first interview. Seem more inclined to legal measures than any other. If he intimates any confidential adjustment — any further division of your father's estate in your favor — show little favor towards the proposition. If he argues the case, listen with owl-like gravity, and put on the appearance of a man who carefully weighs two nearly equal advantages. You must play him as an angler plays his trout, and give line so long as he drags firmly on the bait. He will thus weary, weaken, and entangle himself, while you remain alert for the moment of advantage."

" Suppose he makes an out and out offer of the full sum due me from my father's estate, throwing the will aside ? "

" Draw back from the offer. Don't seem in the least moved by it. Speak of the wrong to other heirs as well as the wrong to yourself. But, it is not at all likely that any such offer will come. If it should come, however, it will show him to be more frightened than now appears, and, of course, deeply involved in crime against your father and his children."

" He will never permit an investigation, Mr. Glastonberry, if in his power to prevent it. You may set your mind at rest on that. I saw enough, last night, to remove all doubts on this head."

For half an hour the conference went on. Then came the bottle of wine, over which the subject was continued until it stood empty on the table between them, when they parted.

On the next evening Guy went to the City Hotel and called at Larobe's rooms. To his knock at the door no answer came. He stood awhile, and then knocked again. But all was silent within.

"Mr. Larobe is not in the city," said one of the waiters who happend to pass at the moment.

"Are you sure?"

"Yes, sir."

"When did he leave?"

"This morning."

"Where has he gone?"

"I do not know, sir. Perhaps they can tell you at the office."

To the office Guy went, but the clerk answered his questions with an indifference of manner that was irritating. He did not appear to know or care anything about Larobe.

"You are certain that he's not in the city," said Guy.

"I haven't seen anything of him, to-day. Probably he's gone out of town."

Nothing more definite than this was obtained, and Guy left the Hotel in some perplexity of mind.

" What does it mean ? " he asked of Glastonberry, to whose office he went, hastily, on leaving the hotel, speaking with evident concern.

" Something, or nothing, so far as we are concerned," answered the lawyer. " Business, wholly unconnected with this affair, may have taken him from the city."

" I'm afraid," said Guy, " that I went a little too far."

" In what respect ? "

" That story about information received through a former attendant in the insane Asylum, may have led him to visit Du Pontz, in order to ascertain just how much it is worth."

" Not at all improbable. I'd give something to know if that were the meaning of his absence from the city."

" Would you regard such visit as a good omen ? "

" Yes. It would prove, what we suspect, that he is seriously involved, and in alarm. To-morrow we must set inquiry afoot in a dozen directions, in order to ascertain the precise facts. If he has really gone to Long Island, our game is safe. I'd give five hundred dollars to be well assured of the fact."

" Do you know the exact location of this Asylum ? " asked Guy.

" I never heard of its existence until the present time."

" It is somewhere on Long Island."

" So you have informed me."

" And the proprietor's name is Du Pontz."

" So you say."

" Suppose I make an effort to find the place, and if successful, see what I can get out of this Frenchman ? "

Glastonberry shook his head, saying, " Not yet my young friend. We must make haste slowly in this business. That may be one of our moves in order to get the vantage ground ; but there's time enough."

The result of this conference was limited to the one purpose of finding out the meaning of Larobe's absence from the city, and tracing its connection, if any existed, to the business on hand.

And now let us return to Doctor Hofland's new patients in Green street — to Mrs. Ewbank, and her sick child and husband. The Doctor's suspicions were not at fault. There was neither food nor money in the house, and the two packages of oat meal which he had sent with the medicine, served the purpose intended — quieting the " hunger-pain" in more than one stomach that night. Tearful sorrow came with the morning. One lonely watcher sat through the waning hours, from midnight until cock crow, sleepless, while all slept ; and as the day dawned faintly along the dark horizon, laid her wet face down in helpless, almost despairing sorrow, against the chilled face of her unconscious child, thanking God, even in the bitterness of her bereavement, for death.

It was all over with little Theo — all over in this
world; and he had passed into the company of angels.
How cold it was! Mrs. Ewbank had not observed it
before. Shuddering, she drew about her the shawl
which had lain loosely over her shoulders. There was
no fire in the room. Long ago it had gone out, for
lack of fuel. But the cold shudder was not felt until it
ran along her nerves from contact with that strange ici-
ness, which is the sign of death.

Covering the face of her departed, after a long, long
yearning look, Mrs. Ewbank went silently into the next
room, where her husband, Esther, and another child,
five years old, were sleeping. Moving a chair to the
bed, on which her husband lay, she leaned forward,
burying her face in a pillow. There had not been in
all her life, so dark, so hopeless an hour as this. Literally, they were without money, food, or fuel. Death
had come in, as if to snap the last fiber of endurance;
and for the time, Mrs. Ewbank gave up in despair, and
asked that she might die. Even as the prayer went up
her husband awoke, and, partly rising in bed, saw her
position.

"Lydia." He spoke to her in a voice of tenderest
concern.

She did not move, nor answer.

"Lydia." He called her again, reaching forth an
arm from beneath the bed-covering, and touching her.

As he did so, the cool air of the room penetrated his thin night-garment, chilling the blood, and producing an almost instantaneous fit of coughing.

" Oh, Henry ! " exclaimed Mrs. Ewbank, starting up in a hurried manner, and pressing her husband back upon the bed, while she drew the covering around his shoulders and neck. " The room is wintry cold. Such imprudence may cost you your life."

As warmth returned, the coughing subsided.

" How is Theo ? "

Mrs. Ewbank did not answer in words. She only laid her face, all wet with tears, close against her husband's, and sobbed uncontrollably. He understood the meaning of this, and lay very still, with shut lids.

" The Lord gave, and the Lord taketh away." Mr. Ewbank tried to speak firmly, but his tones were weak and tremulous, and he could not finish the sentence. His wife understood what was in his heart — knew how far the pain had reached — how bitter the loss ; for that child had been as the apple of his eye.

" Safe in Heaven," he whispered, a little while afterwards. But his wife did not make any response. " The night will not always last." He tried to lift her out of the depth into which she had fallen. " This may be that darkest of all dark hours, Lydia, which gathers its thickest gloom just before the coming of day light. It

4*

can't be darker than it is now, darling ; and God still
lives and is merciful."

How tenderly — how hopefully, in tone, as if to in-
spire hope — was this said. But there came no response.

Coldly, drearily, the winter light stole in, as the
morning advanced; dusky gray yielding to the purer
crystaline, until white and yellow beams poured through
the windows. And still the heart-stricken, despairing
wife and mother, sat motionless by the bed-side, her
face hidden.

" Mother ! " It was Esther's voice. The sunbeams
had awakened her with their morning kiss, given as
tenderly as to the happiest child in all the land.

" Mother ! " she called again, for Mrs. Ewbank neither moved nor answered. " How is Theo ? "

The child was now sitting up in bed, and bending
forward, her serious face turned towards her father and
mother. The truth seemed, all at once, to flash upon
her mind, for she slipped quickly out of bed, and with-,
out stopping to dress herself, pushed open the door that
led into the next chamber. She remained there only
for a moment; then came back sobbing bitterly, and
crept into bed again, where she lay weeping and
grieving.

" Esther ! " At the call of her father, the child
started up.

" Wont you dress yourself, dear ? "

" Yes, father." She was out of bed in a moment.

Slowly Mrs. Ewbank raised herself, as by strong internal compulsion. The light fell over a face so ashen
pale, so exhausted, so hopeless, that Esther, child as
she was, lost all sense of individual suffering, in pity
and alarm for her mother.

" God has taken Theo," said Mr. Ewbank, to Esther, as she came near the bed. He spoke calmly.
The bitterness with him had already passed; for his
thought had gone up from the child on earth, to the
child in Heaven. " God has taken little Theo, and
given him to the angels. He will never be sick any
more, nor have pain."

Esther covered her face with her hands, and leaning
over on to the bed, sobbed aloud. Waiting until he
could command his voice again, Mr. Ewbank said —

" It is best, my dear, that he should go. We couldn't
cure his sickness, nor ease his distress, and so God took
him to the heavenly land where there is neither sickness nor suffering."

As Mr. Ewbank said this, his wife passed to the next
room where her dead child lay, closing the door behind
her. Uncovering the white face, already restored to
calmness and beauty, for a moment it seemed to her
that he was only in tranquil sleep; but the chill strik-
ing down to her heart, as she laid her lips on his icy
forehead, swept this illusion aside.

" God has taken little Theo," she repeated, in thought, her husband's words, trying to find comfort in them.

Not long she remained standing by her dead, but, drawing the sheet over his face again, went down stairs, continuing into the cellar, where she groped about try-ing to find pieces of wood and chips with which to make a fire. The effort was only partially successful. A washing tub stood in one corner. She took hold of it, and turned it over; seemed to be in debate — then, as if acting from a hurried resolution, caught up an ax, and at a single stroke laid the vessel a wreck at her feet. Gathering a portion of the short, dry staves in her arms, and taking up a basket partly filled with chips and splinters, she returned to the chamber where she had left her husband and children, and kindled a fire on the hearth. While engaged in doing this, a knock was heard on the street door.

" I will go down," said Esther, starting away.

" Mother ! Mother ! " she called, at the bottom of the stairway, in a few moments. " Come here, wont you."

Mrs. Ewbank hurried down. A black man stood at the door, with a large basket in his hand.

" Are you Mrs. Ewbank ? " he asked.

" Yes. I am Mrs. Ewbank," she replied.

" Then this basket is for you."

" For me ? Who sent it ? " she asked.

"I was told to leave it, ma'am," answered the negro, showing his white teeth. "And here is a letter."

Breaking the seal, she found a fivedollar bill enclosed, and these lines, pencilled —

"Use this as you have need; and if you are in want of fuel, say so to the bearer."

The black man lingered, while Mrs. Ewbank read the note. She was so bewildered that she did not, at first comprehend the truth as a reality.

"Shall I bring a load of wood, ma'am?" he asked.

"Yes."

The man bowed, saying — "It shall be here right away," and went out.

In the basket were loaves of bread, tea, ground coffee, sugar, butter, a bottle of milk and a bottle of wine; some eggs, fresh meat, and dried beef nicely chipped. As Mrs. Ewbank laid these articles out, one after another on the kitchen table, a few rays of light came in through the dark clouds that encompassed her mind, and her heart, which had been lying, for hours, almost like a stone in her bosom, moved with a few living pulsations. Not for herself, but for those who were dearer to her than life, went up an emotion of gratitude. Brief thanks formed themselves on her lips. A thought of her dead child, lying in one of the rooms above, stayed her feet, as she was going to the cellar for the remainder of the shattered tub, with which to kindle a fire in the kitchen stove — a thought of the living gave them motion again.

"Go up and dress Jasper, and see that the fire burns while I get some breakfast. As soon as the room begins to feel warm, let in just a little air through the back window. Open it about an inch at the top and bottom, and see that it doesn't blow on your father, and set him to coughing."

"Shall I tell him?" asked Esther, light playing in the large, sad eyes, that were lifted to her mother's face.

"Yes, you may tell him." The mother caught her breath to repress a sob, and Esther went up stairs. It was nearly half an hour before Mrs. Ewbank followed with a cup of tea, a soft boiled egg, and some toast, on a waiter, for her husband.

"Take Jasper down. You'll find some breakfast there," she said to Esther. The two children went out, and Mrs. Ewbank, after placing the waiter on a stand, shut the back window, which had remained open a small space at the top and bottom, as directed, to air the room. Then getting a shawl to throw over the arms and shoulders of her husband, she brought the stand to the bed-side, saying, in an encouraging voice —

"Now, Henry, you must eat every mouthful of this."

"Have you eaten anything?" he asked, looking with tender concern into her wan face.

"Never mind me. I'll do well enough. Come! Eat some of this nice toast, while I break and prepare an egg."

Mr. Ewbank, with a forced effort, raised the cup of tea and swallowed a few mouthfuls. As he was removing it from his lips, he saw tears falling, in large drops, silently, over the cheeks of his wife. Her hands, busy with the egg, moved in an uncertain way — the tears were blinding her. Sinking down into the bed, Mr. Ewbank drew the covering over his face to hide a sudden rush of feeling which he had, for the moment, no power to subdue. How could he eat with his dead darling in the next room; dead, and he in such extremity, that even for the commonest burial rites he must be indebted to charity. A thought of the Potter's Field for that precious clay, wrung an involuntary groan from his heart.

"Oh, Henry! Don't give way now," sobbed Mrs. Ewbank, turning to the bed, and stooping down over her husband. "It seems as if light and help were coming. You said the darkness would not always last; and I leaned, in my feebleness, on your confidence in God, and did not utterly fall. If you had given way — if your trust had failed, Henry, I should have died. Bear up a little longer, my husband. Our Father in Heaven has not forgotten us. You said that we were in His remembrance, and that, when suffering had done its work, the light of His countenance would shine upon us. Is it not beginning to shine, Henry? Is it not a little lighter than it was? Who sent us food in this last extremity? Oh, Henry! take courage."

Mr. Ewbank drew the covering from his face, and looked at his wife in wonder. It was the first time he had heard from her lips a sentence that expressed confidence in God. Her mind had always been very dark in this direction; the windows looking skyward, shut. Now she talked of hope — of faith in God's providence — of the dawning day; and tried, in this his moment of weakness, to impart strength.

"You have spoken truth, dear wife!" he answered. Self-possession restored. "In all the circumstances of our lives, even to the minutest particulars, God is present. I confidently believe this. He is present to us now in loving kindness — not in anger. I see it — I feel it."

"Take, then, what He has sent." And Mrs. Ewbank turned from the bed to the stand on which she had placed the food prepared for her husband. "It is for the preservation of your life."

She took the plate of toast and held it for him to eat.

"Will you not eat, also? It is for you as well as for me. Both of us have work to do, and we must take food in order to gain strength. Let us walk side by side, Lydia; step for step; in the way that opens for our feet — leaning upon each other, in our weakness, for mutual support. I think, with you, that the darkest hour is past — that light is in the east. Let us prepare, thankfully and hopefully, for the coming day. It will show us our work, and we must have strength to per• form it."

It was hard for either the husband or wife to keep back the tears that were almost flooding their eyes, as they compelled themselves to share the food which had come, heaven-sent, in their extremity. It refreshed, revived and strengthened them both. But, higher strength had Mrs. Ewbank gained — strength of soul — in that moment of despair, when she saw her husband's heart fail, and sprang to his aid, pointing him to the Strong for strength — to the God in whom he had trusted. Then were opened the long shut windows of her darkened mind, and light from heaven streamed in. She felt new confidence in the future ; and a calmness of spirit that gave a serener aspect to her countenance than it had worn for months.

In this state, she shut herself up with her dead child, and alone, performed the last tender, tearful services its pure body would ever receive at her hands. Then, in its white robes, she bore it in her arms to the chamber of her sick husband, and held it for him to look upon. As he laid his lips to the snowy forehead, he murmured, tremulously —

"Of such is the Kingdom of Heaven."

There were many tears on the baby's face when the mother carried it back. She was on her knees, by the bed-side, as Doctor Hofland entered the chamber ; not having heard him in the room below nor on the stairs.

CHAPTER VII

IT was a sight to move the coldest neart. Doctor Hofland stood still, looking upon the dead child and the kneeling mother ; stood still for nearly a minute, an unwilling intruder where his presence seemed like a desecration. The mother was, to all appearance, as motionless and unconscious as the child. Silently retiring, the Doctor entered the next room. The air felt softer and warmer here, for there was a fire on the hearth. As he came in, Mr. Ewbank, who was alone, and lying with his face to the wall, turned in the bed. He did not speak. The Doctor sat down, and taking one of his hands, held his fingers on the wrist.

" How was your cough through the night ? "

" Easier."

" Has it troubled you this morning ? "

" Very little."

"Pulse softer and slower. No fever. A very decided improvement. In a few days we shall have you
up, Mr. Ewbank."

There was a look of gratitude in the sick man's glis-
tening eyes, for Doctor Hofland spoke with kindness
and sympathy.

"Death has been here since I saw you last night."
The Doctor's voice dropped to a lower key.

"Yes ; and he came in mercy." The tones were
not steady.

"All the ways of God are merciful."

"I believe so." The sick man shut his eyes. It
was the outward, involuntary expression of his inward
state. He was walking, in the dark, by faith, not by
sight.

"I am glad to hear you say this, my friend. Such
confidence in God is an anchor to the soul; a light
from heaven when the sun is obscured."

A silence followed.

"When did little Theo die?" asked the Doctor.

"About day dawn."

"So the two mornings met; for him the spiritual
morning — for us the natural."

Mr. Ewbank did not reply, but fixed his eyes intently, and with a look of inquiry, upon the Doctor's face.

"Death to us; but resurrection to him."

"I know, Doctor," said Mr. Ewbank, speaking

calmly, "that the angels have taken him. I know that it is well with our child. If a word of mine could restore him, that word would not find utterance. But we are natural and human; and he was very dear. For myself, I can bear this sorrow; but, my poor wife!" His voice shook as he closed the sentence.

"As our day is, so shall our strength be," answered the Doctor. "God will comfort her heart as well as yours."

While he thus spoke the door leading from the next room opened, and Mrs. Ewbank came in. Her face was calm.

"How is my husband, this morning?" she asked, as she took the Doctor's offered hand. Her eyes were fixed on him, and full of earnest appeal.

"Better — much better," was the assuring reply.

"You think so, Doctor?"

"Yes. He is better in every way. With good nursing and right medicine, he will be about again very soon. I think I understand his case, ma'am. You see how much he is improved already. So, take heart. We shall make a sound man of him."

That was promising too much; and yet, while Mrs. Ewbank knew it was more than could ever be accomplished, she took heart in the assurance.

"I will send another package of medicine, to be taken according to directions," added the Doctor, as he made a movement to go.

" Wónt you look at him, Doctor? " Mrs. Ewbank
laid her hand on the door through which she had just
come. They went in together, and she shut the door
behind her. Then turning down the sheet that covered her dead baby's face, she said, while her voice
trembled through the calm surface she was striving to
throw over it —

" It is best so, Doctor. I see it now. But it was
very hard to give him up — very hard to see him die.
I thought it would kill me."

She drew the white sheet over the dead again. Then
turning to Doctor Hofland, she regarded him steadily
for some moments.

" You do not know me," she said, at length.

" Know you! " a flash of surprise swept over the
Doctor's face.

" Lydia Guy, that was."

" Impossible ! " returned the Doctor.

" I do not wonder that you say impossible," mournfully answered Mrs. Ewbank. " And yet, I am Lydia
Guy that was. Life gives strange histories, Doctor."

" Strange indeed ! But why did you not tell me
this last night ? "

" The time had not come. Something stood in the
way, and held me back. It may have been pride ; but
I cannot tell. I sent for you, because fear lest my
child should die overcame all reluctance. I knew that,

if human skill could save him, you would not fail. It did not save him. You came too late. Not for my own sake, nor even for my children's have I now lifted the veil that concealed my identity ; but for my husband's. Oh, Doctor! have regard for him. He is one of the best of men. For his sake, I now crush back the native pride which would have let me die, alone, with sealed lips, and tell you who I am. Don't fear that my husband will burden you in any way. He is neither a drone nor an incapable. You have skill as a physician, and influence as a man. Restore my husband's health — you have already promised that — and then help him to some position where his education, his talents, and his industry will make both him and his family independent. Oh, Doctor ! " Mrs. Ewbank laid her hand on his arm, and spoke with increasing fervor. " Help us now ! Help my husband. He is a good and a true man. I, his wife, say this, knowing what I say."

. " Be of good courage, Lydia," answered Doctor Hofland. " I will do for your husband all in my power."

" God bless you ! " As she said this, sobbing, Mrs. Ewbank caught the Doctor's hand and kissed it.

" Mrs. Hofland will be here in a little while," were the assuring words spoken by Doctor Hofland, as he turned from the daughter of his early friend, and left her with tears flooding her face ; tears of hope —

sweet, not bitter, even though she stood in the death-chamber of her latest born.

Since the Doctor's entrance, a load of wood had been left at the door, and a sawyer was cutting it. Little Esther had brought in an armful, and was kindling a fire in the room below. She paused in her work, looking up at the kind-hearted physician as he came down stairs.

"That's right," he said, in a voice of encouragement. "Make up a good warm fire, and drive out the winter." And he passed on, leaving the house and hurrying homeward.

"I have a strange story for your ears," said Doctor Hofland, on meeting his wife. "The sick child I visited last night is dead."

"The child, whose parents you found in such destitution, and to whom we sent a basket this morning?"

"Yes."

"Better in heaven than with them."

"Not that love failed in the parents' hearts; but, all God's providences are right."

"What is your strange story?" asked Mrs. Hofland.

"You remember Lydia Guy?"

Mrs. Hofland gave a start.

"She is the mother of this dead babe."

"Why, husband?" The color went suddenly out of Mrs. Hofland's face.

" It is true. From the moment I looked at her last evening, and heard her speak, I was impressed with something familiar. The same thing struck me this morning. But, I had not thought of Lydia. You may imagine my surprise when she revealed herself."

" So much for an imprudent marriage! I had little hope in her future; but, I did not think of a fall so low as this."

" She may be rising instead of falling," returned the Doctor; " and from something I observed and heard this morning, she is standing in a higher place than when you saw her last."

" Internally higher, you mean."

" Yes; and that, you know, is the only true and permanent elevation."

" What is her name? "

" Ewbank."

" Brady was the name of the man she married. I remember that. She must be living with a second husband."

" Yes, that is probably so; and he is a very different man from the first husband. Educated, refined, religious — so, in a brief observation, I read him; and Lydia said to me — ' he is one of the best of men,' with her heart in her voice. Lena, for the sake of your old friend, her mother, as well as for humanity's sake, go to her without delay. I will see that all things are

5

fittingly arranged for the child's burial. In the ways
of Providence, this family has come to our door, and
we must not fail in duty. It is my intention to see
her brother, Adam, this morning, and advise him of
her extremity. He cannot know the state of destitution in which she is living."

"It might save you an unpleasant interview to send
him a note. I've heard that he is a cold, haughty
man," said Mrs. Hofland.

"I shall not regard my own feelings in the matter,"
replied the Doctor. "A personal interview will best
serve Lydia, and I shall seek it without delay. If he
will yield nothing through kindness, or humanity,
shame must extort unwilling benefaction. I hold a key
that will unlock his money chest, and must use the instrument, be the gain to his sister ever so small."

CHAPTER VIII

DAM Guy's " Lottery and Exchange Office" was on Baltimore street, in an old, dingy, two storied brick house, built in the preceding century. In each of the lower windows was a painted screen ; — one bore a figure of the goddess Fortune, blindfold, standing on an immense cornucopia, from which gold and silver coin were pouring, as from a fountain ; the other screen had, under the words, " *Prizes sold at this Lucky Office*," the tempting figures, $100,000 ; $50,000; $30,000 ; $20,000; $10,000; $5,000 ; $4,000 ; $3,000 ; $2,000 ; $1,000 ; $500— arranged in lines one under the other, so as to fill the whole window. Standing on each side of the door were other canvas screens, on which the early drawings of Virginia, Maryland, and Delaware Lotteries were announced, and the prices of tickets, half tickets, quarters, and eighths, made alluringly prominent.

It was about eleven o'clock in the day, when Doctor Hofland entered this office. Three persons were behind the counter, busy in the work of exchanging uncurrent money for coin and city bills, or in selling tickets to covetous men and women, who had more faith in luck than work. One of these persons he recognized as Mr. Guy, and waited until he was disengaged .

" And now, what can I do for you, Doctor ? " said the man of money, a business smile on his face, as he turned to Doctor Hofland.

" Can I have a few words with you in private ? " asked the Doctor.

" Certainly. Walk back," and Guy came from behind the counter. But the smile had gone suddenly out of his face, which now wore an aspect as cold and as hard as iron. The two men retired to a small room, which was used for private and confidential purposes.

" Take a chair, sir." It was as if another man had spoken, so changed was the broker's voice from what it was, when he said, blandly, " And now, what can I do for you, Doctor ? "

The offered chair was accepted, and the two men sat down, at a small table, covered with baize.

" Are you aware," said Doctor Hofland, coming at once to the business in hand, " that your sister Lydia is now in the city."

" No, sir. I am not aware of the fact." Guy's manner showed both annoyance and indifference; and his hard mouth grew harder.

"It is true. I discovered her this morning, under circumstances of a distressing character."

"I am sorry, but I can have nothing to do with her. She took her own way in life, and must walk in it to the end. She is no more to me, Doctor, than any other woman."

"She is your sister," answered the Doctor, speaking firmly.

"As you choose about that." The man showed irritation.

"No, it is not as I choose, Mr. Guy. The fact stands by itself, and words cannot change it. But, I did not come here to annoy you; only, as in duty bound, to inform you, that your sister is in a very distressed condition. Her husband is too sick to leave his room; one of her children died this morning; and she is without money to buy food, or even to bury her dead."

"Did you come here at her instance?" demanded Guy.

The Doctor answered: — "No, I came at my own instance. She did not mention your name."

"Very well." Guy spoke in a short, off-hand manner. "Let it be so. And now, Doctor, we must understand each other. I'll give you one hundred dollars for her use on this express condition :— She is not to know from whence it comes. Spend it for her in your own way. I leave that to your discretion. But, I enjoin this obligation — be silent in regard to me."

"Just as you please about that, Mr. Guy," returned the Doctor. "I will be your almoner, and keep your secret."

Guy arose, in a quick, nervous manner, and went into the front office. In a few minutes he came back, clasping some bank notes in one of his hands.

"There," he said, almost impatiently, as he thrust them towards Doctor Hofland.

"I will see that the money is spent so as to do the largest service," remarked the latter, as he took the bills.

"And don't mention my name. I must repeat that injunction."

"I have already promised, Mr. Guy," answered the Doctor, with just enough decision in his voice, to make himself felt as a man above trifling or double dealing. "And," he added, permit me to remark, that whatever you may feel inclined to do for your sister in her present painful extremity, may be effected without fear of intrusion or annoyance for the future. I do not believe that either Lydia, or her husband, will ever, of their own motion, cross your path."

"Tell that to the marines!" was half lightly, half gruffly responded.

"The old pride is not crushed out of your sister, Mr.

Guy. She has something of her father's spirit left. She can suffer but not humiliate herself."

"May be so," was returned. But the fellow, her husband, is, no doubt, of a different kidney." He said this with an air of heartless indifference, moving, as he spoke, towards the front office, and showing his desire to get rid of his visitor.

"You will find yourself mistaken in him also," said the Doctor.

"It doesn't matter to me what he is, Doctor Hofland," replied this man, facing squarely around in a resolute way. "And I want you to understand once for all, that, so far as I am concerned, he belongs to the undistinguishable mass of paupers, beggars and adventurers. I don't wish to hear about him — don't want to know him — don't care whether he starves to death, hangs, or is drowned." Mr. Guy wrought up, suddenly, into a state of passion, and betrayed more than seemly intemperance of speech.

"Good morning," said his visitor, with contrasting calmness, and bowing low, retired. There was a degree of unfeeling brutality about Mr. Guy that shocked, painfully, the feelings of Doctor Hofland; and it was some time before he could shake off a sense of humiliation produced by the interview. He felt like one who had extorted for himself an unwilling favor.

As in nature, so in life; peace and tranquillity ever

succeed to stormy periods — and, usually, the sky is clearer, and our vision penetrates farther into its heavenly depths. Winter breaks, often, amid lightning and thunder. The season which followed closely upon that stormy and wintry period, wherein it seemed to Mr. and Mrs. Ewbank that everything was about perishing, was full of calmness and hope. Lydia had unbounded faith not only in Doctor Hofland's willingness, but in his ability to aid her husband; and she inspired Mr. Ewbank with a like confidence. The money received from Mr. Guy was not placed in their hands, but expended in such ways as the Doctor thought most useful, and least calculated to wound a native sense of independence, which he was pleased to see existed. There were tender incidents connected with little Theo's burial, that gave to Doctor and Mrs. Hofland new opportunities to read the stricken hearts, laid, almost bare, before them. Every changing aspect of character, presented by Mr. Ewbank, increased their respect. There was a basis of high moral qualities — a sensitive honor — and a love of independence, that marked him as a true man. They found him under a cloud; but, already, the cloud was breaking. It seemed as if, for discipline and use to others, he had been kept for this time, perfecting in trial and suffering. Supplied with all things needful to health and strength; and with hope beginning to rest on a fairer promise in the future, Mr. Ewbank found himself rapidly gaining his lost vigor of mind and body. One thing was especially pleasing to Doctor Hofland, whose interest in Lydia and her husband daily increased. There evidently existed a very tender attachment between them; and it grew plainer, the more he observed and studied Lydia, that she regarded her husband not only as a good, but as a wise man, and leaned upon his judgment of things as conclusive. The union was one of hearts; and the wife had found in her husband a man whom she could implicitly trust and deeply love — a man, who, standing far higher than she had stood, was steadily raising her to his serener level. It was only a part of needed discipline, that they should pass under the cloud; but, now that it was lifting itself, and the sun beginning to fall through — now that winter had broken, and the air become milder — the motions of a true life were pervading their souls with a promise of another spring time, another summer, and an autumn rich in fruitfulness. So Doctor Hofland read the signs.

CHAPTER IX

N a few weeks, Mr. Ewbank was so far recovered, that he was in condition to take almost any light employment. Through the influence of Doctor Hofland, three or four scholars in Greek and Latin were obtained. So favorably were these impressed by their new teacher, and so warmly did they report at home and elsewhere, in regard to him, that others were led to join the class, which was preparatory to a college course, and made up of the sons of rich men, who could afford to pay liberally.

Having recommended Mr. Ewbank to some of his friends, in the beginning, Doctor Hofland felt a certain degree of responsibility, which caused him to drop in, now and then, upon the teacher, in order to see how he conducted himself among his scholars. With each visit he became more and more impressed with his superiority as a man. There was nothing small or weak about him ; nothing of that petty assumption which we see in the mere pedagogue. Yet, he was wholly in earnest with his pupils, giving himself to them in such wise and sympathetic communications, that they were held by the very pleasures that attended reception.

" You do not seem to have any dull boys here," said the Doctor, one day, after listening to some brief exercises.

" They are not all bright, as that word is commonly understood," answered Mr. Ewbank. " Among a dozen lads, such as you have now before you, will always be found the usual differences. Some are quick of apprehension, responding, like polished surfaces, to the first glances of light, while others must dwell for a portion of time in the sunbeams, until their warmth is felt, and then there is motion within. It is the teacher's business to distinguish between these two classes, and to develop each according to its mental peculiarity. Often it will be found, that, as to intellectual power, the latter is superior to the former. The machinery is on a grander scale, and takes more heat to set it going."

" It requires faith and patience to deal with them aright," said the Doctor. " And how few of us possess these essential qualities ! All is so plain to the teacher, that he looks for flashing responses, when his pupils are before him. If any hesitate, or falter, or stand dumb, he is too often annoyed, impatient, or angry — thus

closing their minds. And so, instead of helping, he
hinders them. If you have learned the better way,
Mr. Ewbank, happy are the dull boys who come under
your rule."

" I see the better way," was returned, " and am trying to walk in it; but I fail, in some things, continual-
ly."   .

" As we all fail. Imperfection is stamped on human
things. But, always, right effort in any direction gives
right results. These may be very small, but the smallest gain is something."

" True, Doctor; and in that I have a never-dying
incentive. If I make a single step in the right direction,
I am just so much nearer the result. A step to-day, a
step to-morrow, wearily though each may be taken, advance me towards the goal. And if I so press onward,
in each day as it it is given, shall I not look back, after
many days, and see the winding path of an accomplished
journey stretching afar off in the fading distance ? In
my experience, Doctor, the gain of each day, in any
given direction, is small. We must work and wait.
We must advance one single step at a time, and take
hope from even the smallest signs of progress."

" So you deal with your pupils, as well as with yourself ? "

" So I try to deal with them, Doctor."

" Have you trouble with any ? There are the in-

different, as well as the dull.   A dozen boys in school,
represent almost as many dispositions."

" I first gain my pupil's respect and good will."

" How ?   That is a secret hidden from the many."

" There is no rule applicable to all cases, unless it be
this — kindness of feeling towards the lad, and a sincere
desire to do him good.   Feeling is magnetic, and com-
municates itself by laws peculiarly its own.   If there
be genuine good will in your heart for any with whom
you are in contact, it will be known without the intervention of language.   Frst, I try to feel right towards
my pupil — to forget all about myself, and think how I
can best serve him.   In regard to education, I have
views not held in common by all teachers; or, if held,
not acted upon, except in rare instances.   My effort is,
not to move the machinery of a pupil's mind by outside
pressure, but to set it going by virtue of a force gene-
rated within, and to direct my effort chief to the work of
feeding that force.   To this end, I do not make the
memory a storehouse, cumbered with an excess of material; but give chiefly such things as are wanted for
present use, knowing, that in such use comes appropria-
tion and incorporation into the mental substance.   Plants
grow from within — animal bodies grow from within —
each by a law of life that takes and assimilates nutrition,
particle by particle.   By the same law, mind grows.
Its food is knowledge.   But knowledge, when present-

ed, is crude. The mind's digestive organs must pass it
through processes exactly corresponding to those which
take place in the animal economy, before its nutrition is
found and taken into the soul's substance. I cannot
digest for my pupil. The mere transference of things
from my memory to his, cannot give him intelligence.
He must be led to think for himself — to take the food I
give and pass it through all the digestive processes for
himself. Then he has healthy life — then he grows.
But, to weigh down his memory with a great burden
of things not comprehended, is to impede growth, and
make all educational processes laborious, distasteful and
imperfect.   Holding, as I do, to a perfect correspondence
between the mind and the body, as to functions and
laws of life, I take it for granted — science and knowledge being the mind's food — that, if this food is given
in right proportions and of right quality to children, they
will receive it with eagerness and delight ; hunger and
thirst always succeeding digestion and assimilation, and
calling for new supplies of food.   You see how much,
regarding education, is involved in all this."

"Your ideas and mine run parallel, at least on this
subject," said Doctor Hofland. "It is one on which
you seem to have thought deeply." .

"Yes."

"But, neither your duties nor mine will permit its
further discussion now," and the Doctor made a motion

to retire. " We must compare notes, however, at some future time, and when we can get down deeper into the subject. I see that your theory is right ; and, I trust, your practice also — though, in my observation, Mr. Ewbank, men of theory almost always fail in application. Why should this be ? "

" Because, the thought is usually above the life," answered Mr. Ewbank.

" Give me your meaning in other words," said the Doctor.

" Because our intellectual states are higher and more progressive than our affectional states. We can see more than we are willing to do. The mind, as you are aware, is two-fold."

" Yes."

" There is will and understanding."

" Yes."

" Feeling being predicated of the one, and thought of the other."

The Doctor assented as to a familiar proposition.

" Thought has power to rise above the actual state, which is governed by what we love. It can go up into clear skies and serene atmospheres, and make to itself a dwelling place, all beautiful and symmetrical. But, it must descend again to its companion, love ; and then, it too often happens, that love refuses to abide in the new dwelling which thought has made, and holds her companion down to the old mean level. And so, the man, though he sees what is right, does not always do what is best. His theory is true; but, when he comes to the work of application, he fails for lack of that self-compulsion which takes the grovelling affections up to the nobler heights which thought has power to gain."

"Judging from what I see," remarked the Doctor, "you are able to go up and dwell in the house you have builded. In other words, to make theory and practice one."

Mr. Ewbank's face did not brighten as we see the face brighten, sometimes, under a compliment that gives pleasure. If there was any change, it was towards a graver aspect.

"No man knows better than I do," he replied, "how hard it is to force the lagging spirit into right ways. Success, in any case, is too intimately associated with memories of possible and impending failure, to leave much room for self-gratulation. For all gain of good, I am profoundly thankful; but, the gain is ever so hardly won, that no room is left for pride. With every enemy we conquer, ten come into view, marshalling themselves for battle."

The two men stood silent for some moments, under the pressure of thought.

"Good morning," said Doctor Hofland. "We must talk about these things again."

" Good morning, sir."

The physician departed on his mission of healing, and the teacher remained with his pupils, strengthened for his work through the Doctor's kind manifestation of an appreciative interest, so rarely met by persons of his peculiar mind.

CHAPTER X

NLY a few houses had been erected in the immediate neighborhood of that spotless shaft, springing two hundred feet in the air, so wonderfully emblematic of the strength, purity, and exquisitely harmonized proportions of the man it was designed to symbolize and honor — WASHINGTON. In one of these, Mrs. Larobe, the wife of Justin Larobe, resided. Let us look in upon her. Time, evening.

Mrs. Larobe was alone, sitting before the parlor grate, looking dreamily into the fire. Over twenty years have passed since her first introduction to the reader ; and these years have wrought seriously with the woman. She has gained much through a subtle force of character, united with an unscrupulous will — much as to things external. But, with every gain, was suffered some loss that touched the inner life — some disappointment that left an aching void — some painful sense of inadequacy or short coming — some startling discovery, that what seemed gold in the distance, was only tinsel and dross. She had destroyed a goodly temple, in order that, with the costly materials thus gained, she might build for herself. Alas! The building, as stone on stone, and timber on timber, went into their places, did not grow out into proportions of wonderful beauty, such as imagination had pictured. It was weak here, unsightly there, and mean, rather than magnificent, in her eyes.

At fifty-five, Mrs. Larobe had the same light, compactly built form, and the same cleanly cut features, that marked her as Mrs. Harte, the Housekeeper of Adam Guy, more than twenty years before. The cold, light blue eye was as steady and as closely veiled to common observers as then. Her dress was scrupulously neat and in good taste. She wore a small cap, ornamented with a sprig of half blown roses; and at her throat, pinning a lace collar of rare fineness, sparkled a diamond of considerable value. The furniture of the room in which she sat, corresponded with the woman. Everything was in good taste. There was no excess of articles; no flaunting display; no incongruity. In quality, all was of the best and the costliest.

Though we find in this woman the same light compactly built form, the same cleanly chiselled features, and the same cold, mysterious eyes, we do not find the same expression of face. The inner experiences have cut their sign of suffering and disappointment on every lineament, and as she sits alone, dreamily, before the fire, you see that time has not fulfilled the promise of other years.

From a bronze time-piece on the mantle, the hour of eight rung out. Mrs. Larobe started at the sound. At the same moment, the door opened, and a girl came in. She was between fourteen and fifteen, had a vacant, repulsive face, and was slovenly dressed.

" Go out, Blanche ! " said Mrs. Larobe, in a short, cold manner, nodding her head towards the door through which the girl had just entered. But the intruder took no heed of this injunction.

" Blanche ! Go out, I say ! " The cold eyes of Mrs. Larobe flashed, and her thin lips showed signs of feeling.

" Why can't I stay here ? " answered the girl, commencing to draw a chair towards the fire.

" Because I don't want you," was sharply replied.

" Nobody wants me," said Blanche, in a tone that should have touched the mother's heart. " Leon snaps and snarls at me like a dog, and Herman says I'm a fool, and pushes me out of the room. Can't I stay here, ma ? "

" No ; I said no at first."

" I'll lie on the sofa, ma. I wont do anything, " plead the girl.

Mrs. Larobe, whose will ever sought to have its way, arose with a quick impulse, and catching Blanche by the arm, endeavored to lead her from the room. But the girl, if she did not inherit her mother's clear intellect, had something of her stubborn will.

" I'm not going out," she said doggedly, and with resistance.

Mrs. Larobe's mind happened to be in a chafed condition, and she grew very angry at this opposition.

" Go instantly ! " she exclaimed, throwing her full · strength into her arms, and pushing Blanche towards the door. Madly the girl struggled against her mother. Finding herself borne along in spite of every effort to remain in the room, she suddenly relaxed every muscle, and gliding down from her mother's grasp, sunk upon the floor like an inanimate mass.

Almost blind with passion, Mrs. Larobe stooped over her child, and catching her two hands, commenced dragging the prostrate body towards the door.

" I'll scream if you don't let me go," cried Blanche, passionately.

But Mrs. Larobe did not heed this warning. Then there leaped out upon the air such a strange, wild, quivering cry that even Mrs Larobe, mad as she was, started in surprise, and half relinquished her hold. It was repeated again and again, more like the shriek of an animal than the cry of a human being.

" Hush ! " said Mrs. Larobe, in stern command.

But the cry went on.

" Hush, I say ! "

She might as well have spoken to the wind. Through
her own cruel blindness, she had betrayed this weak
and disordered human soul into the temporary possession of evil spirits, who were now tormenting them
both. Finding no abatement in the loud, unearthly
screams, Mrs. Larobe endeavored to close the mouth of
Blanche with her hand, and had partly succeeded, when
she heard the ringing of the street door bell.

" Blanche ! Blanche ! Stop this instant ! Hark !
Somebody has rung the bell. Get up ! Get up !
Quick ! "

As the servant passed along the hall, on her way to
the door, Mrs. Larobe, in despair of forcing her daughter to cease screaming and rise, changed instinctively
her tone and manner, and addressed Blanche coaxingly.
This had the better effect.

" Come, dear ! Get up ! Some one is coming in.
Don't let them see you lying here. Hark ! There's
a man's voice. Get up, and run out, quickly."

So far as to cease screaming, and to rise from the
floor, Blanche obeyed her mother. But she did not
stir from the room. While the two were yet in con-
tention, a man's heavy step was heard along the hall.

The door of the front parlor was opened by the servant, and the visitor entered.

"A gentleman wishes to see you," said the servant, looking into the back parlor from the hall.

"Who is it ? " asked Mrs. Larobe, in a low tone.

"He did not give his name."

"Did you turn up the gas ? "

"Yes, ma'am."

"Here, take Blanche with you."

The servant advanced a step or two, but Blanche retreated towards the grate, frowning and distorting her face.

· I'm not going out," she muttered.

"But you must go, dear. I have a visitor, and you are in no condition to be seen," urged her mother, crossing the room to where the girl had retired, and again taking her by the arm.

"I'll scream," said Blanche, with a threatening look.

Mrs. Larobe dropped her hand, weak and baffled, before this imbecile girl. A moment or two, she stood in painful resolution; then ordered the servant to retire.

"If I permit you to stay," she said to Blanche, "you must hide yourself away in that arm-chair, and not speak a word. Do you understand ? "

"Yes."

"Very well. Now sit down, and keep perfectly quiet."

Blanche took the chair in which her mother had been seated, and was wheeled to some distance from the grate, towards a corner of the room, the back of the chair being turned towards the grate. After repeating the injunction for Blanche to remain quiet, Mrs. Larobe crossed to the folding doors, which, until now, had been closed, and throwing one of them open, advanced into the front parlor, where a fire also burned in the grate. Before this, with his back to the folding doors, stood a man, who turned at the moment of her entrance. Mrs. Larobe stopped suddenly, a frown of displeasure, not unmingled with surprise, crossing her face. The man bowed, with a cold formality, that had in it something of mockery. His eyes were sinister in their expression.

"Edwin!" Mrs. Larobe uttered the name like one both displeased and confounded.

"Madam!" And the formal bow was repeated.

"To what am I indebted for this visit?" demanded the woman, retiring into the placid exterior, with which she had all her life veiled so much of passion.

"That question is not to be answered in a single sentence, madam," replied the visitor. "But you may be very sure that except for a matter of serious import, I would not be here."

The young man's eyes were fixed intently on Mrs. Larobe's face, and he saw there what she would have given much to conceal — a sign of alarm.

"Be seated, Edwin." There was a change in Mrs. Larobe's manner.

The young man drew two chairs in front of the grate, and motioned Mrs. Larobe to take one of them. Almost passively, she obeyed.

"Some things have recently come to light, ma'am, that have a bad look." The visitor spoke slowly, dwelling upon one or two of his words with marked emphasis.

Mrs. Larobe's eyes were fixed intently on his countenance. She did not, however, trust herself to remark upon a sentence, the whole meaning of which it was impossible for her to guess.

"A very bad look," repeated Edwin Guy, the woman's step-son, for he it was.

"Whom do they concern?" Mrs. Larobe asked, feigning indifference, and veiling the uneasiness which fluttered around her heart under an icy coldness of manner.

"They concern you, and me, and every member of the family!"

So quickly and emphatically was this thrown out, that it gave Mrs. Larobe a visible start. Edwin saw

6

her face blanch, and the expression of her steel-cold eyes change.

"Concern me, Edwin?" The woman tried to regain her self-possession, but only with partial success.

"You, perhaps, most of all," said Edwin.

"What about my mother?" Here broke in a thin, sharp voice, and looking past his step-mother, Edwin saw the half wild, half vacant face of Blanche, thrust eagerly out in a listening attitude, only a few yards distant.

Springing up, with an almost cat-like bound, Mrs. Larobe turned towards Blanche, and catching her by the shoulders, swept her from the room, ere the girl had time to collect herself for resistance, and bearing her back to one of the rear rooms, gave her in charge of a servant, with an injunction and a threat so fiercely uttered, that both child and servant were left, on her departure, in no mood to disregard her will.

For a few moments, Mrs. Larobe stood in the hall, near the parlor doors, smoothing down her ruffled feelings, and schooling her countenance into an aspect of indifference. Edwin was pacing the floor as she entered. Pausing, and folding his arms, he fixed his eyes keenly upon her, and stood thus regarding her until she reached and resumed the chair from which she had arisen so abruptly a little while before.

"You, madam, perhaps, most of all," said Edwin, as

he also sat down, yet not removing for an instant his gaze from Mrs. Larobe's countenance.

"Say on." She spoke with assumed indifference.

"My father!"

The tone in which this was uttered, more than the reference itself, caused Mrs. Larobe to start.

"What of him?" she asked, with a slight betrayal of uneasiness.

"Has had foul play."

"I was not aware of it before." The sentence did not come with a free breath, which Edwin, all on the alert, perceived.

"Murder will out, ma'am! Wrong does not sleep forever; sooner or later it cries up from the earth."

"So they say." There was a slight expression of irony in Mrs. Larobe's voice; but it not hide completely her true state of mind.

"And it has not slept in this case. You are betrayed, madam!"

The covert defiance in Mrs. Larobe's tones had pricked the feelings of Edwin, and led him to this outspoken sentence.

"Betrayed!" Guilt revealed its terror in the woman's white face and quivering lips.

"Yes, you are betrayed, miserable woman!"

"Betrayed in what?" she asked, seeking to regain her self-possession.

" As an accomplice in the death of my father."

Mrs. Larobe took a long, deep breath. She did not respond for some time. Edwin waited for her to reply. At length she said, speaking calmly —

" His death was wholly accidental. In trying to escape from the confinement made necessary by insanity, he fell from a window, and was killed. I was not there."

" But my father, a sane man, was there through your wicked contrivance. I have the whole story, ma'am; from the drugging to the forced removal to an infernal prison on Long Island. Doctor's evidence, keeper's evidence, and subordinates' evidence — all written down in due form, and attested, and in the hands of counsel. Doctor Du Pontz will be in court, and you know what he can tell."

" Doctor Du Pontz!" exclaimed Mrs. Larobe, paling again.

" Yes, Doctor Du Pontz, of the mad house on Long Island. Accomplices in crime are never safe depositories of our secrets, madam. When the courts take hold of them, self-preservation becomes the first law of nature."

" Edwin," said Mrs. Larobe, her whole manner changing, " let me understand you fully. Why are you here ? "

" To obtain my share of my father's estate, wrongfully withheld by you, under a forged or forced will, which I have sufficient evidence to break, and will break, if no easier road is opened to the end I am sworn to reach. I have spoken plainly, madam ; do you comprehend ? "

Mrs. Larobe took thought before answering.

" I think I understand you, Edwin," she said, speaking with deliberation."

" Say on."

" You are here to extort money from a woman imagined to be in your power."

A deep flush of anger darkened the face of Edwin, even to the temples.

" I am here," he answered, sternly, " for justice ; and it must come, easy-handed or hard-handed. The choice lies with you. Through fair concession, or open force — just as *you* will, madam. If you can show a fair record in open court, defy me to the contest ; if not, beware ! There is bad blood between us, as you know ; and I shall not scruple to destroy you, if my interest goes wholly over to the side of feeling."

" What do you want ? " asked Mrs. Larobe.

" I have said what I want."

" Say it again."

" My share in my father's estate."

" What is your share ? "

" Twenty-five thousand dollars ; and I received but ten."

" You largely over-estimate your father's property."

" No; I have told the sum of its value to the last
dollar; and my share is twenty-five thousand, which I
am bound to realize, principal and interest. Having
taken the best legal advice our city affords, I knew just
where I stand."

" Who is your lawyer ? "

Edwin shook his head, and smiled in a sinister way.

" Does Adam know of this ? " asked Mrs. Larobe.

" Not yet."

" Or Frances ? "

" I have not seen her for two years."

" You are moving alone, then ? "

" Alone for the present. But when the matter comes
into court, I shall not, of course, stand alone. The case
will be open to all eyes. Adam has received his share ;
but Frances, and Lydia, who will no doubt be at once
forthcoming, have claims to an equitable division, parallel with mine. Lydia, having only received one thousand dollars under the extorted, and therefore void will,
must have the largest award."

Mrs. Larobe dropped her eyes to the floor, and sat
for a long time in deep thought.

" Come and see me again to-morrow night, Edwin.
I must have time to think on this subject. It involves
too much for any hasty decision."

" It has narrowed itself down to very simple posi-
tions," answered the young man, " and may be settled

in three minutes. You can have a law suit, with its consequent exposure and certain disaster ; for, as I have told you, I am in possession of evidence clearly establishing the fact, that you and your present husband conspired to murder my father, and succeeded in effecting your hellish design through the intervention of a villain named Du Pontz ; or, you can have immunity and security through concession to my just claim. I am poor, because your and your husband robbed me — I speak a plain language, madam — and am in pressing need of money. Necessity offers us stern and conclusive arguments, and, yielding to these, I am ready to forego justice and vengeance for the present good I seek. But, if this be withheld, then for the long and sterner task of dragging iniquity into light, and gaining my ends by force. I have but to cry this game, and a pack of hounds will be on the scent. Now, madam, you understand me ; and you must elect accordingly."

" What security have I that you will keep the secret you profess to hold ? " said the pale-faced, agitated woman — agitated in presence of an appalling danger, beyond all power of concealment.

" Only my word," answered Edwin. " No other security is possible in a case like this."

" Only the word of a bitter enemy." Mrs. Larobe spoke partly to herself.

" Better trust to him, than to the law's tender mer
cies. Better conciliate one enemy, than defy a score."

Mrs. Larobe's figure shrunk in the chair, as if under
the pressure of a heavy weight. Her mind seemed par-
alyzed by crowding fears.

" Edwin I must have time to think," she said almost
fretfully.

" Madam, I cannot wait. To-night you must decide,"
was answered, sternly. " When I leave here, I take
your yea or nay."

" And if nay ? "

" To-morrow the case will go to court. My lawyer
has everything ready, and the town will be startled by
revelations of an astounding character."

" If yea ? "

" And your word is kept, ruin and disgrace are turned aside."

" What will yea involve? " The woman's face was
still very pale, but she was now speaking calmly.

" I call my share of the estate, twenty-five thousand
dollars, of which I received ten thousand. My claim is
for the balance, with interest since the period of my
father's death. I demand nothing more, and will take
nothing less ; so chaffering as to the sum will be just so
much lost time, to say nothing of the irritation and ill-
blood it will create. I am in a position to name my own

terms, and I shall not abate one jot or tittle of the full demand."

Again the woman was silent, thought beating around on every side in a fruitless endeavor to find a way of escape from impending danger. To yield even a small part of Edwin's demand, under almost insolent threats, was so deep a humiliation, that the bare idea revolted her soul; yet, to brave what lay beyond was more terrible still. She could measure the evil on one side, with some degree of accuracy; but on the other, it swelled up vaguely to almost illimitable proportions. It was a mountain which, if it fell upon her, must grind her to powder.

"You will not give me time for reflection or consultation," she said, in a weak way, for the bold, defiant spirit had gone out of her.

"Consultation! Madam, the secret is yours, and mine, and my lawyer's to-night," said Edwin, in a warning tone. "I did not come here until the mine was ready and the train laid. Let me admonish you to circumspection. If there is to be consultation, our parley closes. I will not wait for your subtle villain of a husband to calculate the board, but checkmate you all in a single move. I hold the advantage, and will not let it pass. When I leave here to-night, I must take, as already said, your yea or nay. If nay, to-morrow morning, when the court opens, our proceedings will

6*

commence. · And then, you know what must follow. The indictment will be for criminal offences, and when the trial closes, you will hardly escape a prison."

Edwin saw a shiver run through the frame of his step-mother.

" You have me in your power," she said, slightly rallying, " and are taking a base advantage."

" Yes, I have you in my power," answered the young man, " as you once had my unhappy father in your power. But, I will not take the base and wicked advantage you took of him. A simple act of justice, and ' you are safe and free. Withhold that, and I wrench from your hands what I claim of right, and in the act, destroy you. A wise and prudent woman cannot hesitate long as to a choice between these evils."

" The sum you demand is large, Edwin. It is impossible for me to control such an amount," said Mrs. Larobe.

" Your misfortune, if you cannot do so," was coldly replied.

" Real estate cannot be sold or mortgaged except through my husband."

" You have stocks. But, I am not here to discuss questions of this nature. If you will not, or cannot, satisfy my just claims against the estate, say so, and I will trouble you with my presence no farther," and he moved a pace or two towards the door.

" I have eight thousand dollars in Union Bank stock."
A sense of most imminent danger extorted this.

Edwin returned a pace or two into the room.

" For the present, anything beyond that is hopeless,"
added Mrs. Larobe.

Eager as the young man felt to grapple after this
large sum of money, and secure its possession, he was
politic enough to affect scarcely a sign of interest.

"Only a third of my claim.   It will not do, madam," and he shook his head.

" If you will take this stock and give me time."

" How much time ? "

" It is impossible to say.   Three, six, or even twelve
months may intervene, before I am able to arrange for
the balance."

Edwin stood for some time with his eyes cast down.
Then he crossed the room ; wheeled sharply and came
back again — crossed once more, and then returned.
Meantime, Mrs. Larobe was in a tremor of suspense.
She had made the best offer in her power ; for her unscrupulous husband had so managed her property as to
place the control of it almost entirely out of her hands.

" Madam," said Edwin Guy, pausing before his step-
mother, " let me understand your proposition.   Say
the best you can do, and I will answer, in less than five
minutes.   The sum of principal and interest due me, I
will call, in round numbers, twenty thousand dollars.

A net calculation of interest would make it exceed that amount. You can pay eight thousand down."

" Yes," faintly murmured Mrs. Larobe.

" And the balance when ? "

" Not sooner than within a year."

Edwin shook his head. Mrs. Larobe's face was pale, her lips colorless, her nerves in a tremor. She had taken fear, as a guest, into her bosom, and fear had gained the mastery over her.

" If within six months, I might accept your offer." Edwin spoke as one whose mind was only half made up.

" In three-quarters of a year, I may succeed in getting so large a sum together," said Mrs. Larobe.

Again Edwin walked the floor, and his step-mother still sat in her agony of suspense. Here was the only door of escape, and she was ready to fly through it, when opened wide enough, shuddering with terror.

" This I will do," said the young man —" this, and only this." He spoke as one dictating terms to an enemy wholly in his power. " I will take your two checks for four thousand dollars each, dated on to-morrow and the day after. This will give you time to sell your stock. I will not present the check dated to-morrow, until after one o'clock, in order that you may get in your deposit. For the balance of twelve thousand dollars, I will take your three notes at three, six, and nine months, each for four thousand. In return for them, I will write you out a receipt in full for all claim against my father's estate, thus removing every legal basis for a suit. Furthermore, I will take the most solemn oath you may prescribe never to move myself, or in any way instigate others to move against you in regard to your foul dealings towards my father. To-night, not a living soul, beyond my lawyer, knows of the well linked evidence I possess bearing on this subject. It shall sleep with us, safe as in a tomb."

What was left for the frightened, confounded, bewildered woman! She was in the hands of one who had, she verily believed, the power utterly to destroy her, and she dared not defy him to the worst. It was in vain that she pleaded for time to consider — for a single day. Edwin was inexorable. Now, he felt, that he could work his will. To-morrow might be too late.

"Now or never," was his stern answer to all pleadings and remonstrances.

"Edwin Guy," said Mrs. Larobe, as, half an hour afterwards, she handed her step-son the checks and notes he had demanded, and received his receipt in full against the estate —"Edwin Guy, this is a hard necessity." She had regained much of her old, self-poised manner.

"You have still your option, madam," answered the

young man, holding the papers so that she might receive
them back.

"I have made my election," she replied, "and it
must stand. In your honor, Edwin, I confide."

"My honor is sacred. I will be as silent as the grave;
yet, only on one condition."

"What?" Mrs. Larobe's face paled a little.

"You are to be as silent as the grave also. If you
betray anything of this transaction to a living soul, I
shall hold myself free of all pledges. I warn you to be
discreet!"

"Fear not my discretion," was answered; "I, too,
will be as silent as the grave."

"Be it so, madam — and silence shall be your pledge
of safety. Good night!"

And ere the miserable woman, on whom the son of
Adam Guy had wrought this sharp retribution, had
time to rally herself, Edwin was gone.

CHAPTER XI

HE scene described in the last chapter, took place nearly three months after Edwin Guy's first interview with Doctor Hofland in regard to his father. Larobe had proved himself a more skilful strategist than either Edwin or his lawyer, Glastonbury, had anticipated, holding off his assailants, now by a bold, and threatening front, and now deceiving them by feigned movements, day after day, and week after week, all the while endeavoring to entrap Guy into some false position, where he could cripple or destroy him at a single blow. Not once, after his first interview with Guy, did he betray to that individual the smallest sign of apprehension, concern, or concession. Forewarned, forearmed. At the second interview, he was self-possessed, and very reticent. He listened, coldly and patiently, to all the young man had to say, leading him on by casual questions, made in a tone that was almost indifferent, and get-

ting deeper and deeper into his thoughts and purposes,
while he closely veiled his own.

The threatened suit was, in the mind of Edwin, only
a last resort.   All he wanted was money, and the shortest way to that end was the way in which he meant to
walk.   The foul play to his father, of which he was only
in possession of dark hints, notwithstanding his pretence of knowing so much, might go unavenged, so that
he could clutch a fair portion of the devised estate.   The
longest and most doubtful way to reach the object of
his desire, was through the courts.   In the beginning,
it had seemed the surest, and, probably, the only way;
but the alarm and anxiety betrayed by Larobe at the
first interview, left a strong conviction on his mind, that
the lawyer would, to avoid the perils and disgrace of a
suit, yield to almost any demand he chose to make.
He felt certain that he had him in his power; and began to count over, in fancy, his thousands of dollars,
as already in possession.

But, his second interview with Larobe, dashed, with
a chill, the young man's rosy anticipations, and removed
to an uncertain distance that fruition on which he had
just seemed entering.

" I understand," he said, rising to withdraw, after an
hour's unsatisfactory skirmishing with the lawyer, " that
you wave all arrangements, and mean to accept the perils
of a suit ? "

"I did not say so." The tones of Larobe were almost indifferent.

"So I read the meaning of what you have said tonight, and, accepting that meaning, I shall proceed to act accordingly."

Something like a suppressed cough in the room adjoining, reached at this moment the ears of Edwin Guy, and, glancing towards a communicating door, he saw that it stood ajar. He did not observe the wary, almost anxious look fixed on him by the lawyer, as his attention was turned for an instant on this door.

"I-cannot limit your actions, of course," evasively answered Larobe. "All I can do, is to govern my own."

There succeeded a silence of nearly half a minute, when, no further remark being offered by the lawyer, Guy commenced crossing the room, with the purpose of retiring. His hand was on the door.

"Edwin," said Larobe.

The young man turned partly around.

"Take a word of advice in this matter."

"Say on."

"You are a little too eager — are trying to move too fast." There was just a shade of irony, or sarcasm, in the lawyer's voice.

Guy stood still, looking at him, but not venturing a reply.

"And may get thrown from the track. So, I counsel prudence."

"When the devil offers good advice," said Guy,
stung by something like contempt in Larobe's manner,
"we may safely assume that he is altogether disinterested, and has our good at heart."

Larobe only shrugged his shoulders.

"Good evening."

"Good evening, Edwin. If you wish another interview before commencing your suit, make free to call.
As I have already said, I am still your friend. It will
be for you to set me over to the enemy's side ; and it
is but fair to warn you, that, as an enemy, I am never
scrupulous. You are treading on dangerous ground, as
your own lawyer, if he be honest, will tell you. An
attempt to extort money, under threat, is a crime in law ;
and you will be a sharp man at the business, if you get
through without punishment."

"Justin Larobe !" said the young man, flashing out
in sudden anger, "I know the length and breadth,
even to the thousandth part of an inch, of your friendship for me — it is that of the wolf for the lamb. You
cannot, under any provocation, be more my enemy
than you are to-day."

"Be it so, if you will. Only take heed that, in pro-
voking me to strike, you are not altogether at mercy of
the blow."

" I will take heed," said Edwin, and, opening the
door, he passed out, painfully aware that in this second
interview with the lawyer, he had gained nothing, and
probably lost all his first seeming advantage.

" You must not call on him again — at least not for
some weeks," said Glastonbury, to whose office Guy
went immediately after his conference with Larobe.

" Not for weeks! " Even the interval of weeks, before getting to where he could lay his hands on the
money which had seemed so near his grasp, appeared
a long time to the eager young man.

" As before said," answered Glastonbury, " this is
a business in which we will have to make haste slowly.
Every inch of the ground we take must be well considered, lest it prove unsafe.   There is not a man in the
city, against whom an affair of this kind might not be
more safely conducted.   It is evident, that he has recovered from his first surprise, and now stands on
guard."

For over two weeks, no sign of invitation or approach on either side was apparent.   Twice Larobe
and Edwin had met in the street, passing with a cold
nod of recognition.   Both were but acting, however;
and both on the alert.   Towards the end of the third
week, a note came from Larobe, asking for an interview in the evening at his rooms in the City Hotel.
At this meeting, the lawyer gained what he desired —

information as to the progress Edwin was making towards the initiation of the threatened suit. Nothing had
really been done, and he was, thus far, satisfied; he
was, also, becoming assured that nothing would be done,
so long as there was any hope of driving him, through
fear, to the payment of the sum Edwin had demanded.
This payment he had, from the first, resolved to make,
rather than risk the consequences of a legal search into
all the circumstances of Adam Guy's illness, and removal to an insane asylum. But he was not the man
to yield anything without a struggle. Moreover, in
the very fact of this yielding, was an admission that
wrong had been done; an admission that placed him in
the power of Edwin, and he was too unprincipled and
unscrupulous himself to have any faith in another's
pledges or promises. How was he to be in safety, after
buying off with money this dangerous foe. What
guarantee could he have that the contract would remain unbroken? Is the tiger rendered docile by a
draught of blood?

Two or three more weeks were suffered to go by, in
a mutual wariness. Then Larobe received a communication from Mr. Glastonbury, Edwin's lawyer, in
which he was notified, in formal manner, that he had
been instructed to bring suit for the purpose of breaking the will of Adam Guy. This brought the two
lawyers into communication, and they spent several

weeks of skilful manœuvering, each trying to get such a position as would be impregnable in defence, or possess superior advantage in assault. So much was involved on both sides, that great circumspection was demanded. Enough, however, was gained by Glastonbury, to assure him that Larobe would scarcely risk the suit. But there were difficulties in the way of a compromise, almost insuperable. What were the guarantees for future immunity? What surety could be given, that similar attacks would not come from other members of Mr. Guy's family, even if Edwin were, ever after, to remain quiet?

The one position taken by Larobe, in his interviews with Glastonbury, was, that the movement against him on the part of Edwin Guy, was simply for the purpose of extorting money; and that his only cause of hesitation in the matter grew out of an unwillingness to be dragged into court on such gross charges as were assumed, and put on the defensive against bribed witnesses whose false statements might not only have weight with a public too apt to believe the worst, but with a prejudiced or stupid jury also.

"But, in avoiding one danger," he said, "I am not disposed to risk another and greater."

"It is for you to make the election," replied Glastonbury. "My client has become impatient of delay, and insists that proceedings at once begin."

" He may find himself checkmated in the third or
fourth move," said Larobe. " I have not been passive for nearly three months."

" It is for you to conduct your own side of the game,
and I doubt not it will be skilfully played," answered
Glastonbury, his lip twitching, and lifting back over
the canine teeth, in a way peculiar to himself.

" I have secured evidence already, and shall meet
you with a counter suit."

" Ah ? "

" Yes. Your client has been several times in my
rooms, blustering and threatening. All that he said
might not favor your side materially, if produced in
court. Nevertheless, I have it, word for word, written
out, and by a witness who will take the stand. I did
not choose to be alone, you see."

Larobe's small brown eyes looked forth keenly from
their deep coverts, and scanned the face of Glastonbury.
There was no change in its expression ; but the upper
lip twitched oftener, with its nervous motion, showing
the fangs, first on one side and then on the other.

" And prove what ? "

" An attempt to extort money," replied Larobe.
" An open demand for a certain sum, as black mail ; so
giving me immunity against prosecution for an alleged
crime. There are two points here, as you will perceive ; two criminal offences punishable under the law.

An attempt to extort money by threat, and the compounding of felony."

Glastonbury simply answered, and without apparent change of feeling, though he saw that Larobe had gained an advantage over his client.

" Guy has little to lose, and all to gain in this matter; you have nothing to gain and much to lose. Let the case go as it will, should it come into court, you cannot escape without serious damage. We are prepared with evidence that will show darkly against you, Mr. Larobe. It is possible that you may have testimony running parallel, which will complement ours, and give a different signification to many things veiled in mystery. I trust, for your sake, that it may be so. But, I would not advise you to accept all the risks. Settle it with the young man, if it be within range of possibility. He is, at the present time, believe me, in possession of facts touching some things in your past life, that make him a dangerous enemy."

Whatever impression this had on Justin Larobe, he was skilful enough at concealment to hide from even as keen an observer as Glastonbury, and the two men closed the interview and separated, neither satisfied in regard to the other.

" You have well nigh ruined your case !" was the salutation received by Edwin Guy, when next he appeared in Glastonbury's office. The lawyer's upper lip moved nervously, and his eyes looked sternly at his client.

"Ruined my case! How?" Edwin's face paled.

"I warned you, over and over again, to be prudent in what you said to Larobe."

"And I have always been prudent," replied the young man.

"As prudent as though a third party, your enemy, were present?"

"Not so guarded as that. Why should I have been?"

"A third party was present."

"What?"

"A third party, concealed, and noting down, for evidence, every word to which you gave utterance."

"How do you know?"

"I have it from Larobe himself; and he is now preparing to set off our suit with one for the two crimes of attempting to extort money by threat, and for compounding a felony."

Edwin's face grew paler still.

"Then he will abide our movement against him?" he said.

"I am not sure; but it looks that way. I told you, in the beginning, that we had an antagonist to deal with of the most wary and determined character, and one who would seek an advantage against you, and press it to tho death when gained. If, as he alleges, he is in possession of evidence going to show that you threatened him with this suit, unless he paid you a certain sum of money, your chances of gaining it are not good ; and you may be so thrown at disadvantage as to be visited by serious legal consequences. I'm afraid you are far ther away from your object to-day, than you were two months ago."

There was a silence between the two men for three or four minutes. Then Glastonbury said —

" Other heirs are living ? "

" Yes."

" Where are they ? "

" My sister Frances may be in the city. I am not certain, however."

" No matter. We can use her name ; and that, I think, will be our tower of strength."

" I do not understand you," said Edwin, looking perplexed.

" Larobe does not, I think, really mean to risk a suit ; but, with his present advantage, he will hold us off indefinitely. We do not want a suit. For, if prosecuted to the end, and successful, years must elapse before anything can be realized, and then so many other claimants to the estate may come in, that our share will hardly be worth fighting for. If, however, Larobe is satisfied that we mean to bring the suit in your sister's name, against

7

whom he can threaten nothing, my opinion is, that he
will yield."

Edwin did not see much to hope for in this view of
the case. Delays had already wearied him. He saw,
in Larobe, an antagonist so skilful, so guarded, so wary,
that victory seemed more and more doubtful every day.
Nearly three months had elapsed, and he saw himself
farther off from the end he sought to achieve than in
the beginning. It was while in this state of mind that
he determined, without consulting his lawyer, to have
an interview with his step-mother, Mrs. Larobe, now
living separate from her husband, and try what was to
be done with her. His success, in that interview, is
known to the reader.

CHAPTER XII

EN minutes after one o'clock, on the day after his interview with his step-mother, Edwin Guy ascended the steps leading to the Union Bank, holding a check of four thousand dollars clench-ed tightly in his hand. He had many doubts and misgivings in his heart, and glanced about him uneasily. In-stead of meeting a prompt payment of his check, might he not encounter an officer? That was in the range of possibilities. More probable than this, he thought, might be the answer —

" No funds."

As he entered, a lady swept past him, moving with quick steps. She was in the act of drawing down her veil; but he saw a portion of her face. It was Mrs. Larobe. If she saw him, she had no desire to make recognition of a detested persecutor — of one who had forced on her the bitterest necessity of her life; and that

life, in these later years, had not been free from bitter
necessities.

Had she made the required deposit? That was still
the doubtful query. Edwin was in no state to linger,
but moved on with a desperate hope that all was right,
and, standing at the counter, presented his check. The
teller glanced down at his face, let his eyes dwell upon
it for a moment, and then looked across the counter at
Edwin, regarding him with apparent scrutiny. Then
turning to a book-keeper, he asked a question, and the
book-keeper referred to an account on his ledger.

The teller came back, and handing the check to Edwin, said,

"No funds."

"Are you certain?" The young man lingered.
"The drawer of this check said that funds to meet it
would be on deposit by one o'clock, and it is past that
time now."

The teller again reached his hand for the check and
stepped to the counter where the receiving teller stood,
asked a question, and received, as Edwin saw, an affirmative reply.

"How will you have it?" The teller's hands were
over his money drawer.

"In hundred dollar bills," was answered.

Forty bills were counted out. Clutching them with

ill-suppressed eagerness, Edwin Guy left the bank and hurried into the street.

As Mrs. Guy left the bank, only a few minutes before, she removed the veil which had been drawn quickly, on seeing Edwin, in order to get full draughts of the fresh air, for she felt like one about to suffocate. Slowly she moved up Charles street, on her way homeward, weak in every limb, the effect of nervous exhaustion. As she came near St. Paul's Church, she saw, on the corner, an old man of such singular appearance, that he was attracting the attention of passengers on the street, some of whom stood still to observe him more narrowly. His dress was meagre, worn and incongruous ; his hair, of iron gray, was long and uncombed, his face covered with a white beard, that fell down from his chin to a distance of six or seven inches. He stooped considerably ; and his garments hung loosely around an emaciated body. The upper part of his face, which could alone be seen, had a pale and sickly hue ; but his deep set eyes, looking out of almost bony orbits, had a glitter and fire in them too bright for reason.

Mrs. Larobe had advanced along the pavement to within a few paces of this old man, whose appearance was that of an escaped pauper or lunatic, before he observed her approach. The sound of her footsteps, or the rustle of her garments, reaching his ears, he turned and looked into her face. As their eyes met, the old

man gave a start, moving back, a pace or two, and muttering some incoherent ejaculation. Then advancing,
he leaned forward, with his wild and fiery eyes fixed
eagerly on Mrs. Larobe's face. Frightened at this unexpected encounter with what was evidently an insane
man, Mrs. Larobe drew down her veil, and sweeping in
a wide circle around him, hurried onward, without glancing back, lest her doing so should lead him to follow her.

He was following, nevertheless; but at so slow a
pace, that when Mrs. Larobe reached Franklin street,
and looked back for the first time, he was not visible.
Still excited, and inwardly trembling with a vague alarm,
she kept on, without checking her speed, until she arrived at home.

Not for a long time had Mrs. Larobe felt so completely unnerved as now. The conviction which, for a year
or two, had been haunting her mind, that the foundations
of her peace were wholly insecure, and that it was too
late in life to commence building again, if the present
house fell, was now gaining confirmation. Edwin's visit
and imperious demand, which she dared not refuse,
though compliance did not remove all fear of the terrible
consequences threatened, was an event of such a disturbing and depressing nature, that she could not rise above
its influence. The night that followed this visit had
been almost sleepless. A dozen times she repented of
compliance; yet, as often, in going back over her past

life, and dwelling on certain events, a knowledge of which Edwin claimed to possess, she felt a sickening sense of the imperious necessity that was upon her, and saw that no other way of escape remained. She had found no difficulty in selling her stocks, though, in the negotiation with a broker, she was compelled to make a loss of three per cent., besides commissions. Five thousand dollars were paid down, and she was to receive the balance next day, in order to make good the second check of four thousand dollars held by Edwin. Parting with these large sums, was like wringing drops of blood from her heart ; not that she had a miser's love for money — she valued it for the position and power it gave her. The hardest thing to bear in this hard necessity, was the triumph gained over her by Edwin, whom she had hated with that implacable hatred, the wronger cherishes for the wronged. Suddenly the tables were turned, and she found herself at his mercy. This was too hard for endurance. It seemed, at times, as if it would drive her mad.

How could she get him out of her way ? For hours, in the darkness, she pondered this dark question, the will to compass murder full-formed in her heart. There were no doubts, nor hesitations, nor weak tremors at thought of steel or poison ; only at thoughts of safety to herself. If the power of invisibility could have been the gift of a demon, she would have accepted the boon, and, with her own hidden hand, sent death to the heart of her step-son. But, certain immunity was impossible. She could not venture into this path of crime, without the encounter of risks too great to be accepted. And so, the question of how he was to be removed from her obstructed path, was pondered in vain.

The visit and extortion of Edwin, made in the face of terrifying threats, the wild thoughts and heart-struggles of the night, and the constrained work of the morning, left Mrs. Larobe in that sensitive, nervous condition which is liable to disturbance from the most trifling causes. When she left the bank, after handing in the deposit which was to make good the extorted check, she was, as we have seen, in a state of nervous exhaustion. Except for this, her encounter with the strange looking old man, would have been an incident to be forgotten in a moment. But, trifling as the incident was, it added largely to the disturbing forces by which she was now assailed.

As the street door of her own house closed behind her, Mrs. Larobe moved slowly and with weak steps along the hall, entering one of the parlors, and sinking in tremor and exhaustion upon a sofa. Over ten minutes elapsed, before rising to go up stairs. A few moments she stood in front of a large pier glass, stretching from floor to ceiling, scarcely recognizing her own pale, troubled face. How had less than twenty-four hours

of baffling contest with superior forces, marred the
smooth repose of her countenance. Turning from the
mirror, she stood, for an instant, among the curtains
that drapped the long low windows; but, only for an
instant. Back, as if a strong arm had drawn her away,
she moved suddenly, catching her breath, and clasping
her hands over her bosom. The strange old man had
glanced up to her from the pavement, starting, as before,
at her sudden apparition, and then bending towards her
with a wild, eager look.

Mrs. Larobe shuddered, and sat down, again; sat
down and listened breathlessly. Every moment she expected to hear the bell ring. But, five minutes passed,
and no hand pulled at the wire. Then she breathed
more freely. A stealthy reconnoissance from behind
the window curtains, satisfied her that the insane man,
for so she regarded him, was no longer in front of her
house. This added excitement finished the work of
exhaustion. When Mrs. Larobe reached her chamber,
she had only enough strength left to remove her dress,
and loosen her under-garments. For more than three
hours she lay in such apparent stupefaction, that both
her children and servants became alarmed, and made
efforts to arouse her. She gave no heed to them, beyond expressing a desire to be left alone, until an under-
toned conversation about sending for a physician, aroused
her to the necessity of regaining a portion of her lost

7*

mental and bodily equilibrium.   So she spoke in firmer tones, saying that she was better, and would be down at tea time.

In this she kept her word.   At the tea table she appeared with little change from her ordinary manner, but was paler than usual, eat scarcely anything, and spoke but few sentences during the meal.   After tea, she retired to her own chamber, into which only Blanche intruded.   Mrs. Larobe sent her away, but she soon came back and insisted on remaining.   Her presence, considering Mrs. Larobe's state of mind, was not now to be endured; so she was thrust violently from the room, and left to scream and beat the door in passion, until she grew tired.

About eight o'clock, a servant tapped for entrance, and was directed to come in.

" There's a gentleman in the parlor," she said.

" Who is it ?" Mrs. Larobe knit her brows and looked annoyed.

" He didn't give me his name, ma'am," replied the servant.

" Why didn't you ask him ? "

" I did, ma'am, but he said it was no difference."

" Was it the gentleman who was here last evening ? "

" O no, ma'am.   It isn't him."

" Very well.   Say I'll be down."

The · servant withdrew. Mrs. Larobe felt herself yielding to returning nervous tremors.

" Who can it be ? " she asked herself. " I wish visitors would send up their names." She was about recalling the servant, and insisting on the person's name, when she altered her mind, and making a few changes of dress, went down to the parlors. She had been there for scarcely a minute, when a loud cry was heard, followed by a jarring sound, as · if a heavy weight had fallen. Children and servants ran down stairs in alarm, and on entering the parlor, found Mrs. Larobe on the floor, inensible, and alone. The visitor had made good his escape.

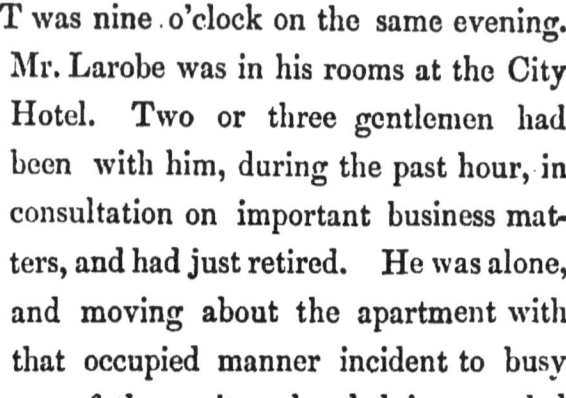T was nine o'clock on the same evening. Mr. Larobe was in his rooms at the City Hotel. Two or three gentlemen had been with him, during the past hour, in consultation on important business matters, and had just retired. He was alone, and moving about the apartment with that occupied manner incident to busy thought, when one of the waiters handed in a sealed note. A glance at the superscription, wrought an instant change in his countenance. There was an expression of surprise, followed by a half angry knitting of the brow. Sitting down at the table, over which a gas light was burning, he unfolded the note with a perceptible nervousness of manner, and read —

"I must see you to-night. We are in the most imminent danger. All is at stake. Come instantly.

"JANE"

The hand by which these alarming sentences were penned had trembled with every stroke; not more, however, than the hand now holding the small piece of paper on which they were written. The lines were more deeply cut on Mr. Larobe's already knitted brow. He knew the writer too well, to disregard her injunction. If she said there was imminent danger — that all was at stake — it was so!

"Come instantly!" Mr. Larobe read the closing sentence again, crumpled the note in his hand, and threw it into the fire. As it blazed up, he arose quickly, and taking his hat and overcoat, started for the residence of his wife. A rapid walk of less than fifteen minutes brought him to the vicinity of Washington's Monument, where Mrs. Larobe resided. The servant who admitted him, opened one of the parlor doors; passing in, he found himself alone with his wife. She was sitting in a large chair, but did not rise nor speak. Her face looked shrunken and older by years than when, only a few weeks since, he had seen her go past him in her carriage. All the calm, resolute firmness of her mouth was gone. It was almost pitiable to see how feebly her lips were dropped apart; how utter exhaustion was expressed in all the lines of her countenance.

Mr. Larobe took a chair, and drawing it up close, sat down. If his heart had trembled on reading her note, it shivered now.

growing clear."

In ten minutes, as Mr. Larobe had said, he came back with a policeman, and left him in thehouse, promising his wife, on retiring, that he would see her early on the next day. Mr. Larobe was not in his room in the hotel that night; nor was he to be found in his office, or in any of the court rooms on the following day.

At one o'clock Edwin Guy was at the counter of the Union Bank.

The teller handed back his check, with a firm shake of the head.

"What's the matter?" asked the young man, in a tone of feigned surprise.

"No funds," said the teller.

At half-past one, Edwin called again.

"No funds," was repeated.

At two he was there, and got the same reply.

"Are you certain?"

"Certain," answered the teller, coldly.

Half-past two saw Edwin at the counter again with his check. The teller recognized him and shook his head. At ten minutes of three he was there once more. Now, as he offered the check, it was taken by the teller, who stepped back from the counter, and spoke with the cashier, who was standing at a desk. The cashier came forward, with his eyes fixed keenly on Edwin.

"Is your name Edwin Guy?" he asked.

"That is my name, sir." The young man's eyes fell under the cashier's gaze.

" We are instructed to retain this check," said the bank officer.

" By whose authority?." demanded Edwin.

" By authority of the drawer."

" It is my property, sir, you have no right to retain it. If you will not pay the check, hand it back," said Edwin, partially recovering himself.

" Our orders are imperative, and we take the responsibility," said the cashier, coolly, at the same time handing Edwin a letter, bearing his name on the envelop. He knew the writing to be that of Justin Larobe, and so, without further remonstrance, left the bank in order to get at the contents of this letter, and thence at some fair estimate touching the new difficulties, if not dangers, that were in the way before him. They were in few words.

" EDWIN GUY, SIR.— I have seen your step-mother, and the payment of her check is stopped. It will be safest for you to see me to-night. If you don't call at my rooms, I will order your arrest to-morrow.

JUSTIN LAROBE."

Edwin did not go to his lawyer, for he had acted in this matter without consultation. During the remainder of the day, he considered the question of calling upon Larobe, regarding it on all sides. The decision was in favor of calling. He understood very well the business on which he was so peremptorily summoned. Larobe would demand a return of the four thousand dollars, and also of the notes for twelve thousand which he had extorted from his step-mother. Touching this demand, he was in no vacillating condition of mind. " A bird in the hand is worth two in the bush." This adage expressed his state precisely. He meant to hold on to what he had, and defy Mr. Larobe.

At as early an hour as eight o'clock, he was at the City Hotel. He found Mr. Larobe alone, and was received with almost angry sternness.

" Well, sir! for what am I wanted ? " demanded Edwin, in a tone of defiance.

" Sit down," said the lawyer.

Edwin sat down.

" It seems," remarked Larobe, suppressing his feelings, and speaking in a low, rather threatening voice, " that you will not be at peace until you find yourself in the state's prison."

" I shall at least have good company," was answered, with a cold, sneering manner · " which will be some consolation."

It was plain that Larobe had not anticipated just such a response ; for he turned his head with a slightly baffled air.

"You must restore the money paid you on Mrs.

Larobe's check, and also the notes you extorted from her under threat," said the lawyer, in a firm voice.

" Never ! " was the resolute answer.

Larobe turned to the table by which he was sitting, and taking up a slip of paper, handed it to Edwin. It read thus : —

" CAUTION. — All persons are cautioned against receiving three promissory notes, each for four thousand dollars, at three, six, and nine months, respectively, and bearing date March 27th, 18 —, drawn by Jane Larobe in favor of Edwin Guy. Said notes having been extorted, under threat, by said Guy, and without equivalent, will not be paid at maturity."

After reading this advertisement, Edwin coolly handed it back, with the monosyllable —

" Well ? "

" Unless you restore the money and notes to-night, that advertisement will appear in to-morrow morning's papers."

" What then ? "

" In the first place, the notes will be rendered valueless. In the second place, you will find yourself under arrest."

" And in the third place," added Edwin, speaking as coldly and as resolutely, " you will find yourself under arrest, also, charged with the crime of murder ! Were you fool enough," he added, flushing with excitement,

" to imagine that I was to be frightened by a puny threat like this, when I had my hand on your throat, and could strangle you at a moment's warning. Beware, sir, how you cross my path ! Publish your advertisement in the morning papers. Good ! Ere twelve o'clock, you will find yourself over the Falls. And hark'ee, my friend ! Don't for an instant flatter yourself with the notion that I am hare and you hound. The hunt, I fancy, will be in the reverse direction. So, get out of my course, or you will find, when too late for succor, my fangs in your side. To-morrow morning, I shall expect to receive, by ten o'clock, at my office in the Custom House, the check withheld at your instance to-day ; and by twelve o'clock, the money to make it good must be in the bank. In default of this, I swear by all that is sacred, to drag you and your guilty wife, stripped of your infamous disguises, into open day. Maybe you have a concealed listener — a witness, writing me down, word for word ! Ah, ha ! I trust he will omit nothing."

All this was so far from what Larobe had anticipated, that he sat like one confounded, not knowing what answer to make. Seeing his advantage, Edwin Guy receded towards the door, and with his hand on the knob, added these brief sentences —

" Make your own election., I am prepared for you at all points. Thwart me a step farther, and your ruin be on your own head ! "

And not giving time for Larobe to recover himself, or reply, he swung open the door, and passing out, left the astonished and discomfited lawyer to his own troubled and deeply anxious thoughts.

CHAPTER XIV

DWIN GUY was not, usually, an early riser, but the next morning he was abroad a little after daylight. The object was soon apparent. Taking a position at the corner of one of the streets crossing Baltimore street, he waited for a short time, when the carrier of a newspaper came by, from whom he bought a copy of the " American," which he thrust into his pocket.

" Am I too late for the ' Chronicle ? ' " he asked of the carrier.

" Too late, sir." And the carrier hurried on his way.

" No matter for that, a " Chronicle" must be had, and it was obtained from a door knob at the expense of a subscriber. There was no difficulty in getting the " Sun." Returning to his home, Guy commenced an examination of the three morning papers, in a hasty, nervous manner, confining himself to the advertising columns. Nearly a quarter of an hour elapsed before he was fully satisfied.

"As I thought," he then said, speaking aloud, and with the air of one relieved from an uncomfortable suspense. "A man in his position will think twice before endangering the mine over which he stands."

At ten o'clock, Edwin was at his desk in the Custom House ; not employed in his usual duties, but waiting. He waited in vain. The check which had been demanded of Larobe, was not restored. If the lawyer hesitated, and held off from attack, he was not to be driven from an assumed defensive. The check for four thousand dollars being in his possession, he did not mean to give it up.

Having acted in the matter of extorting money from Mrs. Larobe without consulting his lawyer, Edwin Guy found himself standing alone amid dangers, difficulties and temptations, with no counsellors but cupidity and desperation. The one quickened into life all his mental resources adapted to the occasion, while the other made him bold and unscrupulous. He had grown impatient of legal strategy and delay, and abandoning his covered position, dashed in upon the enemy, gaining a single advantage ; but, already, the enemy, rallying in force, had recovered a portion of its losses, and was pressing down upon him with a vigor that threatened his safety.

The question which, for the time, most perplexed Edwin, was in reference to his legal adviser, Glastonbury. To brave, alone, the perils of his new position, in face of an enemy so full of resources as Larobe, left the issue very doubtful. But, on the other hand, to inform Glastonbury of what he had done, would involve not only a division of the spoils in hand, but a return to strategy and delay, which he could no longer brook. He had moved upon the enemy, and at a dash discomfited and weakened him; and, now, all his impulses were in favor of trusting to his own counsels, and his own weapons. Acting under legal advice, he would be in a straightjacket; but free, alert and vigorous, while his own will and thought gave sole direction to every movement. From ten o'clock, the time he had fixed for the return of the four thousand dollar check, until twelve, Edwin Guy debated this question of consultation with his lawyer, but without coming to a final decision. The threat he had made, at parting with Larobe, could not be executed without legal process; therefore, not without Glastonbury. But, it was only a threat, meant to intimidate. That it had been, in a degree, effective, was seen in the fact that no advertisement of the notes extorted from Mrs. Larobe had appeared. It had not been effective, however, in recovering the check which had been retained by the bank officers.

At twelve o'clock, with this perplexing matter still

unsettled in his mind, business connected with his duties in the Customs, required Edwin Guy's presence in a remote part of the city, whither he repaired. It was night before he returned, and then the Custom House was closed. If any communication from Larobe had found its way to his desk, he could not know it until morning. This left him in a state of suspense and uneasiness. Conjecture was busy ; but, conjecture increased instead of allaying uneasiness. Nothing was left but to wait for the next day, and whatever it might bring forth. In the morning, he again arose before the sun, and again made diligent search through the morning papers for the threatened advertisement. But, Larobe had not yet made good his word. Like Edwin, he regarded a defensive attitude, just now, as safest.

Days went by, without further communication between the belligerent parties. Guy felt a painful sense of uneasiness, for, while he remained idle, he understood enough of Larobe's character, to be well satisfied that preparations for assault and meditated destruction must be in progress. Still, he hesitated on the question of consulting Glastonbury.

One, two, three weeks elapsed, without the sign of a movement on either side. Guy had dwelt on the relation he now held to his step-mother and her husband, until his mind was completely bewildered. He could not see clearly in any direction. Whatever he proposed to do, was met by the apparition of some suggested consequence that it seemed folly to brave. He had about concluded to make a clean breast of it to Glastonbury, when he received a note from that individual, desiring him to call. Guy repaired to his office, anticipating an almost angry interview with his lawyer. In this, however, he was disappointed. Glastonbury received him with a composure that amounted almost to indifference, and after he was seated, said, with a quiet smile, and in a tone that betrayed hardly a pulse of interest,

" So, you have undertaken to manage this case yourself."

The young man colored, and, in some embarrassment, which he vainly tried to cover, replied —

" No; I have only ventured a movement or two, by way of experiment. That is all."

" Successful ? " Glastonbury drew a cigar from his mouth, and turning his head on one side, slowly blew the smoke from his lips. He looked the picture of cool indifference.

" Yes." Edwin tried to absorb a portion of the man's coolness.

" Ah ? To what extent ? " There had been a draft on the cigar, and now the blue smoke was again curling lazily about his head.

" I have four thousand, dollars in cash, and notes to the

8

valuo of twelve thousand, all payable within nine
months."

"From Mrs. Larobe?"

"Yes."

"You'll hardly get beyond the four thousand, my
young friend."

"Why not?"

"Because, in this dash upon the enemy, you havo
given up a strong position, which cannot be regained.
In the open field you are no match for him. I'm sorry
for this imprudence. It has given Larobe the power of
effectually barring you against any further interest in
your father's estate."

"I am not able to see that, Mr. Glastonbury," answered the young man, growing serious.

"It is nevertheless true. The law does not recognize
as legitimate these forced transactions, and goes on the
assumption that right is weak where might is umpire.
If it had been settled, that legal redress was scarcely
possible, and that right must be had through extortion,
then your desperate course would have justification on
the ground of a last resort. It was not well, I think,
to throw away the advantage you possessed, in this
doubtful venture. But, the deed is done, and there is
no help for it now."

"Still, you do not explain how I am barred thereoy
from legal action," said Edwin.

" You gave Mrs. Larobe some kind of a receipt ? "

" Yes."

" Of what tenor ? "

" In full of all claims against my father's estate."

" Will not that bar you against recovery ? "

" If the notes and checks are paid, yes."

The lawyer shook his head. " Your receipt is in full of all demands against your father's estate."

" For a consideration. In default of the consideration the original claim becomes good," said Edwin.

" You were not dealing with an executor, or legal representative of your father's estate, remember," answered Glastonbury, " whose failure to abide by the contract restored' your legal claim. The transaction was with an individual, whose promises to pay you accepted in lieu of all interest in the estate. It will be hard, I think, in the face of that receipt, and also in the face of your extortion of terms under threat, to obtain from any court a favorable decision. Very sure am I, that no lawyer of any standing at the bar could be found willing to undertake the case on a contingent fee."

" Which means," said Edwin, " that you abandon it ? "

" To waste time and labor in attempting to reach an impossible advantage, would be an act of folly," softly answered the lawyer. " A new line of warfare having been adopted, it becomes necessary to abandon the old.

We must now see what advantage lies in the assumed position, and make the most of it.   You have four thousand dollars ? "

" Yes.".

" And notes for twelve thousand more ? "

" Yes."

" To whose order are these notes drawn ? "

" To my own."

" Ah !   That was a mistake ! "

" They should have been to Mrs. Larobe's order ? "

" Assuredly."

" Right.   I was a fool not to have seen that.   But there's no help for it, now."

" You must realize on these notes as quickly as possible," said the lawyer.

" Sell them !

" Yes.   Get then off of your hands at once, for any sum they will bring, and leave the purchaser to collect at maturity.   They will not be paid ; you may rely upon that.   A third party can sue them out with fair prospect of recovery against Mrs. Larobe ; but any such attempt on your part would certainly fail of success."

" I have thought of that," replied the young man, " but hesitate about offering the notes.   I cannot feel that it would be safe to trust them in the hands of a broker."

Glastonbury answered, "No, not by any means," speaking with decision. "We do not know to what extent a knowledge of their existence may prevail, secretly communicated to brokers and money-lenders."

"What then is to be done? How are we to sell the notes?"

Glastonbury's indifferent manner had quite passed away, and he looked serious and business-like. Nearly half a minute elapsed before he answered, with a thoughtful air —

"You have put the question most difficult to meet. The thing must be done; but how to do it? — there lies the problem."

And the lawyer went to thinking again. "There is a man with whom something might be effected. He has the money, and likes large slices in the way of discounts. I don't know about him, but he may be induced to advance on this paper." Glastonbury talked as if to himself.

"Are you personally acquainted?" asked Edwin.

We see each other now and then, in a business way."

"Could you approach him on this subject?"

"That is just the question I am debating. It will not do, my friend, to trust this paper with any third party. Either you or I, must negotiate direct. Again, its value is in jeopardy every hour it remains in your

possession.   Suppose a caution appear in the ‘ American’
to-morrow morning, giving notice that it has been
fraudulently obtained and will not be liquidated.   Its
market value is gone ; for no capitalist will touch it.
It should be endorsed to make it negotiable, and then
pass from your immediate possession.”

Edwin Guy put his hand, almost mechanically into
his pocket, and drew out his wallet.   Removing the
three notes, he unfolded and laid them on the lawyer’s
table.   Glastonbury took, and carefully examined them.

“ Perhaps I had better see the person of whom I
spoke just now,” continued the lawyer, “ and try him
with the shortest note.”

“ Very well.   You understand the matter entirely,
and will act, I know, with all needed prudence.”

“ He’s another Shylock in his greed of money,” said
Glastonbury ; “ and will demand a heavy discount, seeing that it is a woman’s note, and the endorsement of
no value.”

“ A bird in the hand is worth two in the bush, Mr.
Glastonbury.   Sell the paper for whatever it will bring.
I leave all in your discretion,” was Edwin’s prompt re-
ply.

“ Put your name on the notes.”   And the lawyer
pushed his pen towards Guy, across the table.

The endorsement was made.

“ A third party holds them now.   Legally, they have

been negotiated, and are no longer your property," re-marked Glastonbury, as he took possession of the notes. " Their value is simply commercial, like any other article bought and sold in the market, and good against Mrs. Larobe in the face of all allegations. You under-stand me ? "

" O yes."

" Very well. To-day, if possible, I will see my man, and try what can be done with him. I do not think he will bite on the instant — he isn't that sort of a fish ; but generally surveys the bait from all sides. When he does take hold, however, it will be with a will."

" Shall I see you to-morrow ? " asked Guy.

" To-morrow ? — to-morrow ? " He questioned in a doubtful way. " Yes, you may call in ; but I have a case down for argument, and shall, most likely, be in court all day."

" In that event," said Edwin, with some anxiety of manner, " you will not be able to see our capitalist. Of all things, we have most to fear from delay. Too much time has already been lost. An advertisement, such as you referred to, is likely to appear at any mo-ment."

" Very true, and it is, therefore, my intention to open the matter of negotiation at once. I shall not wait until to-morrow. Still, two or three days may in-

tervene before a transaction can be effected. He will
demand too large a slice. One half, at least."

" One half ! " There was no feigned astonishment
in the voice of Edwin Guy.

" He's another Shylock, as I told you," said Glastonbury, coolly.

" So I should think," replied Edwin.

" But, of course, I shall not yield to and such demand."

" Of course not." Edwin was far from being altogether satisfied, or from feeling altogether safe in this new
relation to his lawyer. Something in the man, never
observed before, stirred a latent suspicion of unfairness
in his mind. There was nothing clear upon which his
thoughts could rest ; only a vague impression that disturbed his confidence. And this dwelt with him for all
that day, and kept him wakeful through the succeeding
night.

CHAPTER XV

O N the next day, Edwin Guy made over half-a-dozen ineffectual attempts to see his lawyer. Glastonbury was occupied in court until a late hour, and then, instead of returning to his office, where Guy sat impatiently waiting for him, went home to dinner. Twice during the evening the young man tapped at the office door, but found the room tenantless. Until nearly ten o'clock, he lingered in the neighborhood of St. Paul's and Fayette streets, but did not meet the individual he was so anxious to find. The vague uneasiness felt on the day before, had increased. Suspicion crept into his mind. Doubts oppressed him. If Glastonbury chose to keep the notes, or return them to Mrs. Larobe, what redress had he?

On the morning that followed, Edwin was at Glastonbury's office by half past eight o'clock. The lawyer

8*

had not yet arrived. Nine o'clock, and he was still absent. The young man became too restless to sit still.

"Ah! here you are!" he exclaimed, at last, as a form darkened the door, and he looked into Glastonbury's cold, still, unreadable face.

"Anything new happened? You look flushed, my young friend." A single glance from the lawyer's searching eyes, left with Guy the uncomfortable impression of having been read through and through.

"Nothing," he answered. "Only, I am naturally anxious to hear whether you have succeeded in that negotiation. There are always so many slips between the cup and lip, that I shall be nervous until all is safe. Have you seen the person of whom you spoke?"

"Not yet, I called at his office twice on the day you handed me the notes, but did not succeed in finding him. Yesterday, as I said would be the case, I was in court until a late hour. This morning, I determined to make sure of him, and called at his office on my way down. Unfortunately, he left in the early train for Washington, and will not be home for a day or two."

Edwin made a gesture of disappointment.

"Sit down." And the lawyer blandly waved his client to a chair, himself taking one at the same time.

"I have thought of another party," he said, "with whom something may be done. But I want first, to see my man, who has slipped off to Washington. He's close-mouthed, and will never speak of the paper, should he decline to purchase; and that, you know, is a thing to be considered. If we can work the whole twelve thousand with him, the operation will be safe from beginning to end of the negotiation. But, if we go into market before seeing him, a false play may lose us the game. We cannot be too circumspect, Mr. Guy."

" But every hour is an hour of risk, Mr. Glastonbury," said the young man, not able to conceal his nervousness.

" The risks are less to-day, than they have been at any time since you obtained the notes," replied the lawyer. " Legally, they have been already negotiated, and no valid plea to their collection can be set up. A public notification cannot, now, render them worthless."

." But it can prevent my realizing the money on them," said Guy.

" True. Still, our case would not be desperate; and that is a great gain, you know."

" You will not, then, be able to see this person for two or three days? "

" He may get back to-morrow; and I will see that no time is wasted after his return, but gain the earliest possible interview. Don't grow impatient, my young friend, nor do any more desperate things. The well done is, in most cases, slowly done. Rome wasn't built in a day."

Guy had partly made up his mind, in case none of the notes were discounted, to get them back into his possession again. But, sitting face to face with the lawyer, and hearing what he had to say, left him in doubt as to the propriety of asking to have them returned. If Glastonbury meant in anything to play him false, he was now too much in his power to take the risk of making him an open enemy. To his hasty and obscure thought, it seemed wisest to let things rest as they were. So, he went away, but half satisfied.

In the mean-time a reconciliation had taken place between Mr. and Mrs. Larobe. The former had left his rooms at the City Hotel, and was now domiciled under the shadow of Washington Monument. A fact like this produced the usual gossip and remark, and a great many stories bearing on the causes that produced the reconciliation, circulated from lip to lip. Some of these were wild and improbable enough. Hints of unaccountable things, said to have occurred in the family, found their way to the public ear. Servants are keen eyed, and not always discreet. The visit of Edwin, and its effect upon Mrs. Larobe — the call of a mysterious stranger, the very sight of whom caused Mrs. Larobe to drop to the floor as one dead — the summoning of Mr. Larobe, and the establishment of a policeman in the house for a night and a day — all these things were, in some form, reported by the domestics, and variously exaggerated afterwards. Visitors spoke of a singular change in Mrs. Larobe. She was no longer the cold, self-poised woman, who, under all circumstances, had borne herself so evenly. In a great many cases she denied callers on the plea of indisposition, or gave the custom-sanctioned falsehood — "Not at home;" but, the few acquaintances who saw her, rendered sad accounts of her condition. "She looks ten years older," said one. "You'd think her just recovering from a long illness," remarked another. "She has a scared look," said a third, "and is so nervous, that she starts at the slightest sound."

"Doctor," said Doctor Hofland, speaking to his son-in-law, the husband of Lena — "there are some strange stories about in regard to Mrs. Larobe. Have you seen her lately?"

The two men were alone in Doctor Hofland's office, where the younger physician had called one night for consultation, touching a difficult case.

"I was there yesterday."

"Ah! Is the change in her appearance and state of mind so very remarkable?"

"It is; very remarkable. I nave been calling every week to see her oldest boy, for whom, I fear, medicine will not do much. I noticed some time ago, a change in Mrs. Larobe's appearance; but, she evaded with apparent displeasure, the few inquiries I ventured to make in regard to her health. Yesterday, however, she consulted me about some of her symptoms. She said, that she had spells of dizziness, followed by fainting — that she was not able to sleep at night — had no appetite, and felt herself growing weaker every day. She thought there must be heart disease — enlargement, probably."

" Ossification, if anything," remarked Doctor Hofland, in so cold and ironical a tone, that his son-in-law looked at him in surprise.

" No symptom of either," was returned. " Every valve and muscle is doing its work well. The disease has another origin."

" What ? "

" It is mental."

" You think so ? "

" Yes."

" Have you obtained the clue ? "

" No. The cause is hidden. But, there is no mistaking the signs. Something has occurred to shock severely her nervous system."

" She has been reconciled to her husband," remarked Doctor Hofland.

" Yes. Mr. Larobe is with her again, and, when I have seen them together, he has been kind and attentive. But I notice in her one peculiarity. She never looks at him ; but, always aside or beyond him. This reconciliation, depend on it, is only on the outside, and for mutual safety, or mutual gain. There is no heart in it."

"How could there be; when both are selfish and cruel? You are, doubtless, correct in saying, that this apparent reconciliation is for mutual safety, or mutual gain. For mutual safety, I opine. They have been, I fear, partners in some great wrong that is now struggling towards the light."

"Do you really think, Doctor, that Mr. Guy had foul play?"

"I have always thought so," replied Doctor Hofland. "The circumstances attending his removal from home, and subsequent death, were, to my eyes, veiled in mystery. Depend on it, Adam Guy's passage from this world to the next, was not in the orderly processes of nature."

"Some people say that he is not dead," remarked Doctor Holbrook.

"What!" There was unfeigned astonishment in the countenance of Doctor Hofland.

"When some people get to surmising, they will surmise anything. I thought you had heard this wild conjecture among the rest."

"No. Not dead! What basis is there for such a story?"

"I am unable to say. The gossip runs, that it was

not Mr. Guy who fell from the mad-house window, but another lunatic ; and that Mr. Guy is still living."

" A wild conjecture enough," remarked Doctor Hofland.

" And it is further said, that he has recently escaped from confinement, and is now, or was within a few weeks, in Baltimore."

" Why Edward ! You confound me ! "

" And furthermore," continued the young physician, it is said, and believed by many, that he actually called, not long since, at the house of Mrs. Larobe, and that at the sight of him she fell insensible to the floor. When the servants, alarmed by the fall, ran to her, she was lying as one dead. A strange, wild looking man had been admitted, who would not give his name ; and in meeting him in the parlor, this result followed. The stranger went out hurriedly, and the servants found their mistress alone."

" Is all this talked of seriously ? " asked Doctor Hofland.

" O yes ; and credited into the bargain. There are people who stand ready to believe any improbable thing. It is said, moreover, to make the story good, that her husband, from whom she had been living separate, was summoned immediately on her restoration to life, and that he procured a policeman, who remained in the house all night and through the next day. The presumption is, that the escaped lunatic was captured, and restored to his prison."

Doctor Hofland drew a long breath. His brows fell — his lips were shut tightly — a dark shadow fell over his countenance.

" Strange ! Very strange ! " he said, speaking in an undertone.

" But improbable," rejoined the young physician.

Doctor Hofland did not respond.

" You don't think there can be anything in all this ? " Doctor Holbrook spoke in some surprise.

" It has a strange look, Edward. Let us go over it again. A man of singular appearance called on Mrs. Larobe, and at the first sight of him, she fell to the floor insensible ? So the story runs ? "

" Yes."

" Do you credit this on any sufficient evidence ? "

" Something of the kind actually occurred. This, I believe, is a well established fact."

" What about the story of a policeman being estab-lished in the house, by direction of Mr. Larobe, for a night and a day ! "

" On occasion of one of my visits, I saw a man sit-ting at the lower end of the hall. He was standing near the same place when I came down stairs."

" Had he the air of a policeman ? "

"He was a stout, firmly set man, of rather coarse texture."

"Did you see Mrs. Larobe at this time?"

"Yes."

"What was her appearance?"

"She was so altered that I scarcely knew her. The change since my previous visit, a week before, was most extraordinary. There was not a particle of color in her face; and it bore the impression of a painful shock of some kind, the remembrance of which had not yet faded from nerves and muscles. 'Are you ill?' I asked, showing the surprise I felt. She turned her face partly away from my earnest eyes, answering faintly — 'Not now. I had a terrible sick headache all night.'"

"Were you satisfied with her answer?"

"No. Sick headaches are bad enough, sometimes. But, no sick headache ever wrought, in a single night, the effects she displayed. "She did not recover from the shock, whatever it was?"

"No."

How long afterwards was it before she and her husband made up their difference?"

"I saw Mr. Larobe at my next visit, within three or four days."

Doctor Hofland became silent. After musing for a while, he resumed.

" What else is said ? "

Before the young physician had time to reply, the office door opened, and a woman came in. She was coarsely dressed, and untidy.

" Are yez Docthur Hofland ? " she asked, looking at the elder of the two men.

" I am Doctor Hofland," was answered.

" Can I spake wid yez a minit ? " The woman's air became slightly mysterious.

" Certainly." Doctor Holbrook arose, and retired to the inner offiice.

" Well, my good woman, what have you to say ? "

The visitor commenced fumbling in her bosom, from which she drew a crumpled piece of paper.

" Maybe it don't mane ony thing," she said, in a low, half confidential way, " but my mon jist thought he'd humor him ; and I've brought it till yez." And the Irish woman reached out the paper.

Doctor Hofland saw that it was folded and sealed, and bore his address. Opening it, he read, in an almost illegible hand, to his deep astonishment, the words —

" Save me.   ADAM GUY."

Repressing as far as he had power to do so, all visible emotion, Doctor Hofland requested the woman to be seated, and then asked —

" Who gave you this ? "

" My mon, Hugh."

" Hugh ? "—

" McBride, an it plaze ye."

"And who gave it to your husband ? "

" Ye'll not do ony thing to bring harm on him, sir ?
Ye'll not give information. My mon is tender-hearted,
he is, and couldn't deny him. It's all agin the rule.
But Hugh is tinder-hearted, you see ; and the poor mon
was so coaxin' and wheedlin'. An it's sich a pity on
him ! Hugh says, he's not so fur gone as thim that's put
him in wants to make believe."

" The man that gave Hugh this ? "

" Yis, y'r honor. An ye'll promise not till give information on Hugh. He's so tinder-hearted."

" Don't have any fear about that, my good woman.
Nobody shall touch a hair of Hugh's head. Where is
he now ? "   ·

" He's there, y'r honor."

" Where ? "

" Wid the lunatics. Och ! Sorra ! An it's a dreadful place to be in for my Hugh, he's so tinder-hearted,
ye know."

" In what street is the asylum ? " asked the Doctor.

" Asylum ? 'Taint the asylum, Docthur. There's
no childther there. Oh no, 'taint the asylum."

" A private institution ? "

The woman shook her head in a mystified way.

" The house where Hugh takes care of the lunatics,
I mean.

" Dade y'e honor, and thot's jist the perplexin' thing.
We darn't tell."

" Then why did you bring me this letter ? "

" Don't the letther tell ? "

Doctor Hofland thought it best not to give an answer
to this question.

" Then there must be something wrong; and it's my
advice that you get your husband out of this business
as quickly as possible," he said, with a soberness that
made a visible impression on the woman.   Then rising,.
he stepped to the door that opened into the office where
Doctor Holbrook was seated, and said, in a low, hurried
whisper —

" Go for a policeman, Edward !   And be as quick as
possible."   Shutting the door with a gentle hand, so that
his visitor might not, through betrayal of excitement on
his part, suspect anything wrong, he came back, and resuming his chair, went on —

" You were right in bringing me this letter, Mrs. Mc
Bride.   I know the poor man, and must see him at once."

" Och, indade, sir !   And thot'll niver do.   We'r
bound till sacracy."

" Are you bound, Mrs. McBride ? "

" Not meself, sir ; but Hugh's bound, and thot's all the same."

" I don't know about that," said the Doctor. If a man goes into unlawful business, and become a party to wrong and oppression, I am not able to see how his acts bind his wife to the same things. This, let me tell you, is a very serious matter ; more serious, a great deal, than you have imagined, and the quicker both you and your husband are out of it, the safer will you be. I must see this lunatic immediately."

" Och, Docthur, Docthur ! I'm all bewilderment. Let me go home till Hugh. I must talk wid him. You've set me to shiverin' all over. If ony harm should come till Hugh ! Oh, sorra ! sorra ! " And the frightened Irish woman commenced wringing her hands.

" No harm will come to him if he does right. But, right or wrong, he is safest with the law on his side."

" Wid the law ? How dy'e mane Docthur ? "

" Through this letter," answered the Doctor, holding up the crumpled note he had received, " I am advised that an old and wealthy citizen is unlawfully confined under pretence of his being a lunatic ; and it has, therefore, become my duty, to see that he is released, and harm be to all who stand in my way ! " The Doctor's voice grew stern and menacing ; and the woman's fright increased.

" There is no occasion for you to be alarmed, Mrs.

McBride," resumed Doctor Hofland. " Your way is plain. Take me to the house where this man is confined, and none shall be the wiser for your agency in the matter. I will see to that."

" Twon't do, Docthur! Dade un I can't. I must go home and talk wid Hugh."

" Better say nothing to Hugh. He may get bewildered, and betray himself. Just show me the house, and I'll take all the responsibility beyond that."

But the Irish woman insisted upon it, that sno must see her husband, and made a movement to go.

" Sit down, Mrs. McBride ; sit down ! " said Doctor Hofland, as the woman rose from her chair. " I want to ask you more questions. Do you know who the person is who gave your husband this letter ? "

" Indade not, sir."

" Does your husband know ? "

" He don't know ony on um. Only Mr. Black knows who they be."

" Mr. Black, who keeps the house ? "

" Dade, an' Docthur, I can't stay here another minit. Ye'r jist confoundin' me. I must see Hugh." And Mrs. McBride started up, and was at the door ere Doctor Hofland could make a movement to prevent her departure.

" Stop, stop, ma'am ! A word more — "

But the Irish woman gave no heed. She jerked open

the door ere Doctor Hofland was half across the office,
and gaining the street, disappeared from view in the
darkness of a murky night. He was on the pavement
in a moment afterwards, glancing eagerly up and down
the street, but she was nowhere to be seen. Any attempt to follow her, must, he saw, be vain work; so, after standing a little while, quite as much confounded as
the Irish woman had been, Doctor Hofland went back
into his office to await the arrival of his son-in-law, Doctor Holbrook, with a policeman.

CHAPTER XVI

N the same evening, sat Mr. and Mrs. Larobe, alone, in agitated conference. Mr. Larobe had said to his wife, in re-monstrance —

"Jane, you must rally! Your ap-pearance and conduct are attracting universal attention, and occasioning remarks and conjectures so nearly ap-proaching the truth, that I am in terror every moment."

"I try to rally," was answered, in a gloomy, depress-ed tone of voice; "but have lost command of myself. I seem to be like the Italian prisoner — in a cell, the walls of which contract around me every day. Imagi-nation goes constantly forward to the moment, when flesh and bones will be crushed into a lifeless mass."

"Madness, Jane! You are but holding out your hands to destruction. Be the calm, self-poised woman again. Throw off this nightmare. All eyes are upon you, and the word of wonder, touching the change in

9

your appearance, goes freely from lip to lip. People look at me in a strange, curious way, as I pass along the street; and I know it is because of you. Everything is safe now. Day after to-morrow, he will be removed from the city."

"Only from the city." Mrs. Larobe's voice had in it something so icy, in its low, even utterance of this sentence, that her husband felt a chill along his nerves. He looked into her face; but her leaden eyes did not return his gaze — did not hold outward things on the sensitive retina.

"If my advice had prevailed, this would not have been," she said, with a slight quickening of the voice.

Mr. Larobe understood his wife, and shuddered inwardly. The movement of his chair a few inches back, was involuntary.

"There is no safety in these timid measures, Mr. Larobe," she added, with stern emphasis, her voice rising to a fuller volume. "Unless strong enough to walk resolutely to the end, it is folly to enter a perilous way. I saw and urged this in the beginning; but you temporized and interposed, thus cursing our years with a perpetual menace. While he lives, we are in imminent danger. It is his life or our lives! Shall we hesitate in our election? Justin Larobe! — answer me! — would not the news of his death, so you were freed from any responsibility touching the act, be the sweetest that could this moment sound in your ears ? "

" I will not deny it."

" You would not care as to how he died ; whether by violence, or in the order of nature — so you were not involved ? "

" No ; I would not care."

" The passage can be made swift and easy."

Larobe shuddered again, as if a cold wind had struck him.

" And it must be made ! " Mrs. Larobe's pale face grew dark from sudden congestion of blood in the veins. She spoke like one fearfully in earnest.

" Murder will out, Jane ! " answered her husband, in a voice so altered, that his own ears scarcely recognized the sound. " Murder will out ! Blood stains are never washed away. Risk anything but that ! "

" I am not superstitious," replied Mrs. Larobe, with covert contempt for this weakness, in her tones. " If the door is left unguarded, murder will out ; if the washing be careless, blood will remain. But, there are locks and bolts a-plenty ; and whole rivers for cleansing. Let the work be well done, and all signs removed ; and it must be done ! Death itself were better than this horrible life. He must not be taken from the city. A feeble, exhausted old man, the prick even of a needle would let life and misery out together. Why torment him longer? It is cruel! Let him die; and in his rest and peace, we shall find rest and peace also."

"The murderer never has rest and peace," answered Mr. Larobe, solemnly. "The world's criminal record is full of admonition. Call it superstition, or what you will, Jane — earth refuses to hide the blood of murder. No — no. This, depend on it, is not the way of safety; but the way to sure destruction."

"I have made up my mind to walk in this way," said Mrs. Larobe, with a cruel resolution in her voice.

Her husband felt the shivering wind sweep over his spirit again; and, with an involuntary movement, receded to a greater distance. The dull, leaden hue had left her eyes which now had a steely glitter. Her body was more erect; her head drawn back; her lips shut firmly.

"This present life is intolerable, Justin!" she added. "I am not strong enough to bear the burden. You see that I am sinking under it, daily. I shall lose my senses in a month, and betray everything in unconscious ravings. Even now, I catch myself muttering aloud, in the presence of servants, all of whom seem to be watching me with sharp suspicion. So surely as you live and as I live, Justin, there is but one way of safety. If that be not taken, we are lost. My poor brain cannot hold out much longer. I feel that it is giving way. If this terror is left hanging over me, madness is in

evitable; and then, though I may be safe from punishment, you will be lost, for confession will drop from my
unsealed lips. I am sure that I shall be moved to confess everything."

A change in Mr. Larobe's face, showed that his wife's
last argument had reached him. He did not reply immediately, but took time to weigh the argument, and get
to its real value.

"I am disappointed in you, Jane," he said, at last, in
a voice that was hoarse and impeded. "I never expected to see you break down in this way. Self-reliant,
unimpassioned, cool and wary, I thought you able to
walk steadfastly to the end. What does it mean?"

"I cannot tell what it means," was answered, in a
depressed tone. "But the fact is upon us, and we must
deal with it as best we can. The nerves are not wrought
of insensate brass. At least, not mine; and under the
present strain, they must give way. When that calamity reaches me, I shall have stepped past all danger;
but you, Justin Larobe, will be in most imminent peril!
I warn you in time! Two ways are before you; both
difficult to walk in,— and it is for you to take that which
is safest."

There was dead silence for nearly ten minutes. Both
sat motionless.

"I must sleep on this," said Larobe, breaking, at
length, the stillness. "To-night, all my thoughts are

confused. In the morning, they will be calmer and clearer."

"Sleep!" Ejaculated his wife, with an emphasis that made him start. "Sleep, on the edge of a volcano! or over a mine with the train ablaze! There is no more sleep for me, until this terror is removed. Why hesitate, Justin? Why put off until to-morrow, what so needs to be done now. Let to-night's darkness hide from us, forever, this hideous skeleton, that is blasting our eyes at every turn."

"I cannot see the means," said Larobe. "Work like this may not be done with ordinary agencies. There is no living soul that I would trust with the power over me which an accomplice in such a crime would possess. If he is to be taken out of our way, by whose hand shall it be done?"

There followed a long pause.

"Is not Black to be trusted?"

"I would not trust him."

Another long pause.

"It might be done, and the mystery of the doing left impenetrable." Mrs. Larobe spoke slowly, but with confidence.

"How, and by whom?"

"First the will, and then the way. You had him taken to Black's, and can remove him at pleasure."

"Yes."

" Remove him to night."

" Whither ? "

" To some place where he will be wholly in our power."

" You talk without reason," said Larobe, with some impatience. " The very fact of removing him to-night, and without previous notice of intention, would of itself create suspicion. Depend upon it, Jane, this deed cannot be done with safety. Every step will be in difficul-. ty, and no matter how lightly and cautiously taken, foot-prints must remain behind ; foot-prints, along which the bloodhound of justice will follow as surely as fate."

The brief animation died out of Mrs. Larobe's countenance. It grew pale, contracted, and shadowed again.

" I must sleep on this," resumed Mr. Larobe, repeating what he had said a little while before. " To-morrow morning, I shall see clearer. To act now, would be to act blindly."

Mrs. Larobe made no response. Her husband did not look at her while he spoke. Indeed, he rarely looked into her face, for it had become a thing repulsive in his eyes ; a sight to be avoided. For nearly a minute, he sat waiting her answer — but, as she still kept silence, he glanced towards her without turning his head. In doing so, he met a glance stealthy as his own, watching him from the covert of half shut lids — snaky, cruel, and malign. In an instant it was withdrawn ; but, it left a strange shiver of fear in his heart.   In all his life, he had never seen so remarkable an expression in any eye.   It was as if a fiend had looked at him — a fiend thirsting with an insatiate desire to do him harm.

"Sleep if you can," said the woman, coldly, and rising, she left the room.

He did not sleep.   And the long delayed morning found his brain no clearer than on the night before.

CHAPTER XVII.

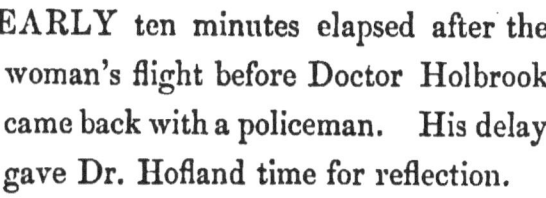 EARLY ten minutes elapsed after the woman's flight before Doctor Holbrook came back with a policeman. His delay gave Dr. Hofland time for reflection.

"The bird has flown," he said, as the two men entered. He spoke so quietly that both the policeman and his son-in-law wondered at his manner; for the latter, having been enjoined to go quickly on his errand, had, on finding the officer, hurried him with all possible speed to the Doctor's office.

"Who was she?" asked Doctor Holbrook.

"An Irish woman, who has a secret that I meant to penetrate; and I wanted your good offices in the matter," looking at the policeman. "But, as I said, the bird has flown. I pressed her so closely with questions that she got alarmed, and flitted away before I could arrest the movement."

"Do you know her?" asked the policeman.

9*

" Never saw her before in my life."

" Does her secret involve anything criminal ? "

" I fear that it does. Not, probably, on her part ;
but, she has knowledge of things that are wrong, and my
design was to secure her person, and so get, if possible,
to the bottom of certain transactions of which I gained
dark hints in my brief interview. Her escape leaves
me at fault. But the intimations she threw out are of
so serious a character, that I deem it best to confer
with the Mayor. Can I see him to-night ? "

" I think so."

" Will you ascertain the fact, and then bring me word
at what time he will give me an audience ? "

" How long will you remain in your office, Doctor ? "

" For an hour."

" Within that time you shall have the information
desired." And the officer withdrew.

" Common report was nearer the truth than you or I
imagined, Edward," said Doctor Hofland, as soon as
they were alone. " Old Adam Guy is not dead."

And he related the particulars of his interview with
the Irish woman.

" Whatever is done, must be done speedily," remarked Doctor Holbrook. " To-morrow he may be taken
from the city, and removed no one can tell whither."

" To be murdered," said Doctor Hofland. " That

will come next. I wonder, seeing how much his wife and her accomplice have at stake, that this last act in the tragedy has been so long delayed. The fact that he was believed to be dead, would have made the crime comparatively a safe one. Yes, Edward, whatever is done will have to be done speedily. To-night he must be released."

"If possible to discover where he is confined."

"There will be no trouble in that," said Doctor Hofland. "A place like the one in which he is held an unwilling prisoner, can hardly be unknown to the police. Mrs. McBride let drop the keeper's name. We shall find him, Edward, I am confident of this."

The two men sat silent for a short time, each busy with his own thoughts.

"So much for money!" spoke out Doctor Hofland, breaking in, after awhile, upon this silence. So much for money!" he repeated. "It was to fill his lap with blessing; yet has it proved only a curse. Wretched, wretched man! In all these dreary years of imprisonment as a lunatic — dead to the world — what fearful things must he not have suffered? When my thought touches this point in the case, I shudder as in the presence of vague shapes of horror. To a man like him there was no help. No materials were laid up in his mind out of which to build a house for his soul to dwell in, and find shelter from storms of passion. His head was naked and his body bare for sun and tempest to assail."

" The probabilities are all against him," said the younger physician. " His brief communication reads like the despairing cry of an insane man, uttered in a lucid moment. If we discover the place of his imprisonment, we shall find him, I fear, but a helpless wreck. A man such as you have described him, would hardly retain his reason through an ordeal like this."

" The worst, in that direction, is to be feared," answered Doctor Hofland. " But, no matter what his state of mind, he must be rescued from their hands, and placed under conditions the most favorable to mental and bodily health."

" The fact of his being alive — and with the knowledge of Larobe and his wife — will establish another crime."

" Bigamy," said Doctor Hofland.

" Yes."

" These accomplices are in a desperate strait, and to save themselves, will not shrink from desperate measures. The tempter who has lured them into this appalling danger, will not hesitate about the suggestion of murder as the only way of escape. He will magnify the safety and diminish the peril of this crime ; and they, bewildered and frightened, will go over to the fiend."

" If there was sufficient evidence to procure their

arrest," said the son-in-law, "so much would be done towards Mr. Guy's safety."

" That point I wish to talk over with the Mayor. It is barely possible, you know, that all may not be just as we infer. This letter, even, may not indicate the exact truth. The writer may only be a pretended Adam Guy."

The young physician shook his head doubtingly.

" All circumstances considered," resumed Doctor Hofland, " I think, with you, that the letter is genuine, and shall act on that assumption up to the limit of prudence. But, the gravest things are involved, and every step taken should be well considered. I may get myself into serious trouble without benefit to any one. Larobe is not the man on whom to make an assault, unless you are invulnerable at all points."

The policeman came back while they were yet talking, and said that the Mayor would see Doctor Hofland at nine o'clock. Precisely at the hour they met. The interview was a long one. At first the Mayor was wholly incredulous; but, after listening to Doctor Hofland's clearly given statement of all he knew about the insanity and confinement of Mr. Guy, and comparing the common rumor of the town with the recent singular change in Mrs. Guy, as noted by her friends, but particularly by Doctor Holbrook, he began to see the case differently. One duty, at least, was plain. The private mad-house — or prison — of Mr. Black, must must be discovered, and that without delay.

" I will place this matter in the hands of a discreet officer," said the Mayor, " who will get speedily to the bottom of it."

" To-night ? "

" Nothing can be done to-night, Doctor."

" A few hours, and all may be lost ! " replied the Doctor. " If Adam Guy be really alive, and held in constraint by Mr. Larobe, too much is periled by leaving him in the city — too much by suffering him to live, even. To-morrow may be too late, sir. Whatever is done, must be done speedily. Let me conjure you to act to-night, lest another crime be added to a dark catalogue. Nothing will be made public. No good name will suffer in this prompt movement, if discreetly made. Should no wrong be discovered, no guilt can be charged upon any one. But, if wrong be arrested, and further crime prevented, the gain will be incalculable."

The Mayor, as Doctor Hofland ceased speaking, lifted a small bell from the table, and rang it lightly. An attendant came in from the adjoining room, the door of which had been shut.

" Tell Mr. Joyce that I want him."

The attendant withdrew, and in a few moments a slender, keen-eyed man, entered. The first impression he made was that of a slightly built person; but a second glance, showed him to be compact and sinewy. His step had a spring that indicated both mental and physical confidence.

" Sit down, Mr. Joyce," said the Mayor, waving his hand towards a chair. The man sat down, yet holding his person erect, and with a prompt air, like one expectant and ready.

" Is there such a place in the city as a private hospital, or refuge for insane people, under the care of a man named Black ? " enquired the Mayor,

" I have not heard of it," was the unhesitating reply.

" Do you know an Irishman named Hugh Mc-Bride ? "

" A weaver by trade ? "

" I am not informed as to that."

" I know two or three McBrides. One, a weaver, is Hugh McBride."

" A married man ? "

" Yes."

" Where does he live ? "

" In Commerce street."

" Take an officer, Mr. Joyce, and bring McBride and his wife here with as little delay as possible. If he is not at home, bring his wife. If neither are at home, report immediately."

The man arose and went out.

" It will be desiriable for you to remain, Doctor, until

his return," said the Mayor. "Can you identify the
woman who called at your office to-night?"

"Yes."

"If we succeed in finding her, we shall obtain a clue
not likely to fail. Mr. Joyce will follow it up quickly."

In less than half an hour Mr. Joyce came back, and
reported the rooms of Mr. and Mrs. McBride closed
and locked. He had made no enquiries of the other
families in the house in regard to them, lest suspicion
touching the nature of his business should be awakened. So far, the movement was without result.

"Did you leave a policeman in the neighborhood to
watch for their return?" asked the Mayor.

"Yes, sir."

"You can depend on him?"

"O yes, sir."

"Sit down, Mr. Joyce."

The man sat down, holding himself erect, with the
prompt, expectant air before mentioned.

"We have intimations, Mr. Joyce," said the Mayor,
"of something wrong. We believe that a man is confined somewhere in the city under pretence of insanity.
Our information goes so far as to cover the name of the
individual who holds this man, with others, in confinement — it is Black. An Irishman named Hugh Mc-
Bride is one of his assistants. There are features about
the case that render prompt action necessary. We

must discover Black to-night, if possible, and remove the person of whom I spoke."

" Are you certain the name is Black?" asked the officer.

The Mayor looked towards Doctor Hofland.

" That is the name I received. But, it may not be the true one," answered the Doctor.

" There is a Doctor Black on East Baltimore street," said the officer. " He occupies a large house beyond Broadway, and has, I think, resident patients. This may be the man."

" Do you know anything of this individual, Doctor Hofland?" enquired the Mayor.

" Nothing," replied the Doctor. " In riding out East Baltimore street, occasionally, I have noticed the name. But, the person of Doctor Black is unknown to me. I infer, that he has no standing with the profession."

" You had best follow out this thread, Mr. Joyce, and see whither it leads," said the Mayor.

" May I suggest, the immediate despatch of one or two policemen to the vicinity of Doctor Black's house, with instructions not to let any one be removed there-from to-night. The fact that Mrs. McBride is away from home, gives me concern. She may have become alarmed for the consequences of her visit to my office," said Doctor Hofland.

" Did this woman call at your office?" asked Mr.

Joyce, with the smallest perceptible shade of surprise in his tone.

The Doctor glanced towards the Mayor, who answered the policeman's question.

" Mrs. McBride was at the Doctor's office this evening, and during her visit, let drop certain things, which, taken in connection with things already known, make it clear that a very serious wrong exists. The suggestion of Doctor Hofland is a good one. Set a watch in the neighborhood, and do not permit the removal of any person from the house of Doctor Black."

Mr. Joyce arose, promptly.

" A moment, if you please," said Doctor Hofland, as the man was about retiring from the room. " I feel deeply interested in this business. Every minute that passes will be one of painful suspense. How soon can we expect to hear from you ? "

" Within an hour," answered Mr. Joyce.

" It is now ten o'clock."

" By eleven I will report all that can be learned of Doctor Black. Will your Honor be here ? " looking at the Mayor.

" I shall remain, Mr. Joyce, until your return."

The officer bowed, and withdrew.

CHAPTER XVIII.

THE thoughtful silence which succeeded to the departure of Mr. Joyce, was not yet broken, when a policeman entered, having in custody an Irish woman.

"Mrs. McBride," said Doctor Hofland, in an undertone, to the Mayor.

The woman had a half frightened, half defiant look.

"You were at Doctor Black's, in East Baltimore street, to-night," said the Mayor, abruptly addressing her, as she was brought forward and placed before him.

"'Dade thin, un I'll not denoy thot same, y'r honor," replied the Irish woman, with an odd mixture of alarm and humor in her manner.

"Did you see your husband, Mrs. McBride?"

"Did I see Hugh, y'r honor?" She was trying to gain time for ready wit to serve her in this narrow strait.

" Yes, Hugh McBride, your husband ? "

" I saw him jist at dark, sir."

" At Doctor Black's ? "

" Yis, y'r honor."

" Have you seen him since you were at Doctor Hofland's office ?   Remember where you are, Mrs. McBride. There must be no evasion.   The truth, the whole truth, and nothing but the truth.   Have you seen Hugh since you saw the Doctor ? "

" I'll not denoy it, y'r honor."

" What did you say to him ? "

" Say 'till him ?   I sed jist these words, y'r Honor —un I'll make a clane breast ov it — I sed, Hugh, honey, the jig's up, and there'll be the divil to pay ; so come away home wid yez."

" And what did Hugh say to this ; Mrs. McBride ? "

" He didn't say nothin, but ' *whist!* ' y'r honor. For, you see, Musther Black came on us all ov a suddint.   Und he sed 'till Hugh, in angry, suspicious kind of way — looking at me, y'r honor —' Whot's thot woman doin' here agin ? '   So Hugh sed — makin' b'lieve mad, you know —' Go aff home wid ye, Biddy, and don't come a trapesin' here ony more.   I'll not have it.   It's agin the rule, as I've told yez more nor twenty times.   And so, y'r honor, I come away."

" And this is all that passed between you and your husband."

" Ivery blissed word."

" You'll have to stay here all night, Mrs. McBride,"
said the Mayor, in answer to which the Irish woman's
face was flooded over with ready tears, and she set up a
low howl of distress.

" Silence ! " cried the Mayor, sternly. " We must
have none of this. Take care of her for the night,
Wilkins," speaking to the policeman who had her in
charge, " and see that she is comfortable."

Mrs. McBride was removed, and Doctor Hofland was
again alone with the Mayor. A brief consultation followed, when it was determined to visit the house of
Doctor Black without delay, and remove Mr. Guy if
found there. A carriage was sent for, and in company
with a single policeman, they drove out East Baltimore street. The policeman sat with the driver, and
his orders were to keep a sharp look out for Mr. Joyce.
That person was espied, near the McKim school-house,
and taken into the carriage, when he was informed of
Mrs. McBride's arrest. A little beyond Broadway,
they left the carriage, and walked for a distance of two
or three squares, when they came to the building occupied by Doctor Black. It was a large, double house,
the lot fronting more than a hundred feet on each side,
and shut in from the street by a high board fence. The
entire area of the lot was more than half an acre, and
it was thickly covered with shade trees and shrubbery.

It was now nearly eleven o'clock. The house had a gloomy aspect. Through only one of its many windows looking down upon the street was light visible, and there it was feeble, as if from the low, burning lamp of a sick chamber. The bell was rung, and, almost immediately, the door swung open.

"We wish to see Doctor Black," said the Mayor, as he stepped in past a negro waiter who still held the door-knob in his hand. Doctor Hofland and Mr. Joyce followed. The door shut, and they found themselves in a large, square hall, from which the stairway ascended, and from which doors opened to the right and left. Before the waiter had time to reply, the left hand door opened, showing a small, well lighted office or reception room, and a man came out into the hall. There was nothing specially remarkable in his appearance, at the first glance, nor did he betray any surprise at this untimely visit of personages, at least two of whom, the Mayor and Doctor Hofland, were, in all probability, well known to him:

"Is this Doctor Black?" enquired the Mayor.

The man bowed assent, and then motioned his visitors to enter the room from which he had just emerged. They passed in, and he shut the door. The furniture of this room consisted of a table standing in the centre, on which were writing materials; a few chairs, and cases filled with books.

The face of Doctor Black was not one that impressed favorably. If it had any distinguishing peculiarity, it was immobility — a thoroughly hidden and inexpansive face. The eyes were blue and cold ; the mouth feeble ; the nose thin and long. He had small side whiskers, of a sandy hue, that were just a shade sandier than his hair.

The Mayor took a seat at the table, with the light full on his face, while Doctor Hofland and Mr. Joyce occupied chairs at the sides of the room. Doctor Black sat opposite the Mayor and in the light. Doctor Hofland, who could not remember ever having seen this man before, scanned his face closely, marking even the slightest change of expression, in order to form some definite opinion of his character. It was soon plainly apparent, that his calm exterior covered alert suspicion. His cold blue eyes, which dropped away from the Mayor's direct gaze, returned instantly to his face, the moment that gaze was withdrawn, with a keen, intelligent scrutiny. Doctor Hofland noted the constant repetition of this covert scrutiny. There were but few preliminary sentences. Then the Mayor said, coming directly to the matter in hand —

" Doctor Black, I am Mayor of the city. One of the gentlemen who accompany me, is Doctor Hofland, whom you probably know, an old resident physician ; the other is a policeman. Doctor Hofland has, this

evening, received a note from one Adam Guy, held by
you in this place as a lunatic, and we are here to take
him out of your custody."

Doctor Hofland was reading Black's face, while the
Mayor thus addressed him, with an almost breathless
scrutiny; but he could detect scarcely any change in its
expression.

" You may not be informed of all the circumstances
attendant on this case," continued the Mayor, " nor of
the peril in which you are involved as a suspected accomplice in one of the most shocking crimes, short of
murder, that our city has known."

There was a change now. Doctor Hofland read surprise, mingled with alarm, in the man's countenance.

" It will be safest for you, Doctor Black," continued
the Mayor, " to accept the necessities of this case, and
at once pass your patient into our hands.   For the present, considerations not necessary to mention, may lead
to the withholding of this affair from the public ; unless
you force us unto an arrest of yourself, which will be
done immediately.   A thorough search of your establishment will then be made.   If you are a prudent man,
you will interpose no obstacle."

Still, Black neither answered nor moved.

" You can have five minutes to decide on the course
you may deem best for your own safety and interests,"
added the Mayor.

" I have decided that already," answered the man, in a cold, even utterance of the words. " It is near mid-night, and I am in the hands of the first executive officer of this city. If I had any interest in resisting your demand — which I have not — resistance would be folly. The wretched old man after whom you have come, is at your disposal." And Doctor Black arose. " Shall I have him brought down ? "

" We would prefer being taken to the room where he is confined," said Doctor Hofland, speaking now for the first time. Black darted on him a sudden look, and the Doctor caught the glitter of his eyes ; but instantly the look was withdrawn.

" As you please, gentlemen." And Black moved towards the door. The four men passed into the hall, where a lamp was procured. From thence they ascended to the second story, preceded by Doctor Black, and through a passage to a wing built out from the eastern side of the house. At the extremity of this passage, a narrow stairway led to the third floor. Thither they proceeded.

" The presence of so many strangers will, I fear, greatly disturb him," said Doctor Black, pausing before a door, and taking a key from his pocket.

" It will only be necessary for Doctor Hofland to go in," replied the Mayor. " We can stay on the outside."

" He is probably sleeping, remarked Doctor Black,

in a repressed voice, as he turned the key. Doctor
Hofland entered with him. The apartment was narrow,
with a grated window at the lower end. An iron bedstead stood half way down the room. On this lay a
man, whose eyes sent back gleams from the light that
shone in suddenly upon him. He arose quickly, and
sat on the side of his bed. The rattling of a chain, in
the movement, showed that he was a closely guarded
patient.

"You, of course," said Doctor Black, in a low tone,
"take all the risks of a removal."

"All," was the simple, but emphatic response.

The two men went slowly towards the patient. His
figure was emaciated, one naked leg thrust out from the
bed showing little in its contour but sinew and bone.
A flannel shirt, open at the throat, exposed a lean and
knotted breast. His face was covered on the lower part
with a long white beard, that fell below the throat-pit.
His eyes shone away back from hollow orbits, with an
intense, almost fiery brightness.

"Thank God!" This man was first to speak, and
these were the unexpected words that dropped from his
lips, uttered in a low, fervent voice. "Thank God!"
he repeated, now with a tremor of eager life. He stood
up, reaching out his hands, all in a quiver of excitement.
"Doctor Hofland! Doctor Hofland! Oh, my friend!
my friend!"

Doctor Hofland went quickly forward, and the wretched old man fell into his arms, sobbing, moaning and
crying like a weak, long-suffering child, restored to its
mother's bosom. The recognition was not mutual.
Nothing in the appearance of this poor lunatic recalled,
with Doctor Hofland, a memory of his early friend.

"Why didn't you come before, Doctor? I've sent
for you, O, so many times!" The old man raised
himself as he spoke, yet still clinging to Doctor Hofland.

"No one brought me word till now," replied the
Doctor. "Did you ever write to me before?"

"Write! I've written a hundred times. And they
always said you got the letters. But, I couldn't believe
it."

"How did you sign them?"

"How?" The question was not understood.

"With what name, I mean?" said the Doctor.

"With my own name, Adam Guy." The answer
was prompt and outspoken.

"Unfasten this chain!" said Doctor Hofland, sternly,
looking towards Black. The rattle of its links had
wounded, that moment, his ears. The man drew some
keys from his pocket, and stooping, sprung the bolt of
a padlock that held the chain to the prisoner's ankle.

"You are free again, Mr. Guy." The Doctor spoke
softly, but with a meaning that no ear could doubt.

"Free! Free! Great God!" Then a strange cry

filled the room, as the man started up and tossed his arms wildly about his head. If reason had kept even partial supremacy until this time, now its dethronement was, alas! too sadly apparent.

"I feared this," said Doctor Black, moving quickly upon his patient, and endeavoring to seize him.

"Off, fiend!" shouted Guy, starting away with a look of fear and hate. "Off, I say!" Then crowding back on Doctor Hofland, he added, in a subdued and pleading voice —

"Don't let him touch me!"

"He shall not touch you," was the assuring answer.

"Wont you take me away from here?" Still in low, pleading tones.

"If you will compose yourself. Loud cries and tossings of the arms wont do among people, you know."

"I'll be all that you ask, Doctor. Only take me out of this horrible prison. They've nearly made an end of me. Flesh and blood can't stand it much longer. I forget myself sometimes. O, why didn't you come sooner?"

He was beginning to lose himself again, when Doctor Hofland said —

"Get on your clothes as quickly as possible: I have a carriage down stairs, and will take you right away."

Hurriedly the poor toilette was made — it was not very presentable — and then, clinging to the arm of

Doctor Hofland, eager, trembling with excitement, and like one fleeing in terror, Mr. Guy went down to the carriage, which he entered without an instant's hesitation, ejaculating —

"Thank God! Thank God!"

If, in all his life before, this unhappy man had not acknowledged a Divine agency in human affairs, that acknowledgment came now, and from the heart. Human prudence and human strength had been as nothing. They had not saved him from the worst of calamities ; and now, when succor came — in the conscious waning of reason — weak as a child amid giant enemies, he looked upward, and thanked God for deliverance.

"What next ?" asked the Mayor, drawing Doctor Hofland a little away from the carriage door, and speaking in an undertone. "Where shall we remove him ?"

"I will take charge of him for the present," answered the Doctor.

"You don't purpose taking him to your house?"

"Yes."

"An insane man! Think what consequences may follow."

"He will not give me any serious trouble. Still, as a matter of precaution, I would like a discreet officer to remain in the house during to-night and to-morrow. My profession takes me away from home at all hours, and while absent, he might get restless or alarmed, and attempt to get off."

"Mr. Joyce is at your service, Doctor," replied the Mayor.

"Thank you. With him at my right hand, all will be well. To-morrow morning I will see you at an early hour."

"If you please, Doctor. This is a strange affair, and must be well considered."

The two men, accompanied by Mr. Joyce, now entered the carriage, and drove away. During the ride to Doctor Hofland's, old Mr. Guy did not speak, nor show signs of uneasiness. When the carriage stopped, he aroused himself and asked —

"Where are we?"

"At my house," replied Doctor Hofland.

"Oh — Oh!" There was a prolonged tone of satisfaction in the almost murmured ejaculation of Mr. Guy.

"Good-night, Doctor," said the Mayor, as the four men stood on the pavement.

"Good-night, sir." The Mayor took Mr. Joyce, the policeman, aside, and after a whispered conference, re-entered the carriage, and was driven away.

"Who is that man?" asked Mr. Guy, almost sharply, and with an air of suspicion.

"The Mayor," answered Doctor Hofland.

" The Mayor ! "   Surprise took the place of suspicion.
" Then he's on my side ! "

" He's on your side, and against all your enemies,"
was the Doctor's assuring reply.

Again came the fervent " Thank God ! Thank God ! "
And with the words still murmuring on his lips, the pre-
maturely old man, a wreck in body and mind, crossed
the threshold of the earliest, best, and truest friend he
had ever known ; — the friend between whom and himself wealth had, years before, thrown up a wall of separation.

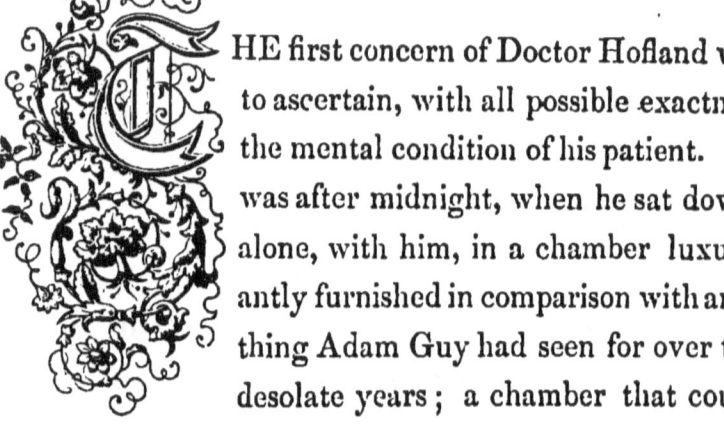

CHAPTER XIX

HE first concern of Doctor Hofland was to ascertain, with all possible exactness the mental condition of his patient. It was after midnight, when he sat down, alone, with him, in a chamber luxuriantly furnished in comparison with anything Adam Guy had seen for over ten desolate years; a chamber that could not fail to bring back a vivid remembrance of the past.

"You are safe here," said the Doctor, with a kind assurance. "Call this room your own, and occupy it as long as you please."

He gazed earnestly into the changed face of his old friend, trying to recall former looks and features; but the search baffled him. Adam Guy, if living, would not be over fifty-four years of age; this person seemed not less than threescore and ten. Doubts crept in, stealthily.

"Call this my room — my room?" With a dumb,

bewildered air, the man let his eyes wander around the apartment. "It's a long time since I called such a room mine. Ah, well!" He sighed deeply, dropped his eyes to the floor, and seemed to lose himself.

"You find me very much changed, Doctor," he said, looking up in a few moments, and speaking with the quiet composure of a self-possessed mind. "Would you have known me if you had met me on the street?"

"I think not."

He let his eyes fall again, shook his head, and seemed to have troubled thoughts.

"I'm very much hurt here, Doctor — very much," and he laid his hand on his forehead. "Very much," he repeated. Do you think I'll ever come right again?"

There was a mournfulness in Mr. Guy's voice, as he put the question, that touched Doctor Hofland.

"Why not?" was asked, in an assuring voice. "The past is past. You are free again."

"But, am I altogether safe, Doctor? Wont they find me out here?"

"You have all the power of the law on your side, and woe be to him who attempts anything against you. Yes, Mr. Guy, you are altogether safe; that is, if you will be discreet, and let the judgment of your friends . determine what is best for the present."

"Discreet? How? What?" The thin brows knitted themselves. He looked puzzled.

10*

"It is now late, Mr. Guy — past midnight," said Doctor Hofland. " Both of us need rest and sleep. In the morning we will have a long talk, and see what is best to be done. If, as you say, you are hurt here "— and the Doctor touched his forehead — "our first concern must be to cure that hurt. It can be done; but everything will depend on your giving yourself up to me, as your physician, and strictly following the rules I shall lay down. To-night there must be sleep. Compose your mind. Try to forget the past and its wrongs in a spirit of thankfulness to God who has wrought out for you a great deliverance ; and who will do for you still better things, if you will look to Him, and trust in Him."

" I prayed God to help me," said the poor old man. " I prayed all last night. I never prayed before. Do you think He heard me ? "

" His ears are always open to the cries of His children. Yes, He heard you."

" And sent me this deliverance ? "

" All good is from His hands. Keep that ever in your thought, and so always look to Him and trust in Him. He is the Great Physician, and will cure the hurt of which you complained just now. Good-night ! May His peace be with you."

The Doctor moved to retire.

" His peace — His peace." The thought seemed new

to Mr. Guy, as evidenced in his repetition of this part of Doctor Hofland's concluding sentence.

" Yes, His peace, which flows like a river," said the Doctor. Then added, as a suggestion came into his mind, taking up a book as he spoke, " Let me read you one of the Psalms of David. It will compose your mind." And he read aloud the fifty-sixth Psalm. Mr. Guy listened with an absorbed attention.

" If sleep does not come quickly, recall the words of this Psalm, and let them dwell in your thoughts." The Doctor closed the volume, and repeating his "good night," went out. In the passage, near the chamber door, he found Mr. Joyce, who had, by arrangement, remained within call. A room adjoining the one occupied by Mr. Guy, and communicating therewith, was assigned to the officer, and all needed precautions observed.

The night passed without further incident. Mr. Guy went to bed on the withdrawal of Doctor Hofland, and was soon fast asleep, not awaking till long after daylight. He was then supplied with suitable clothing, and at his own request, a barber was sent for to remove his long white beard. There was considerable change in him, as compared with his condition on the night before. His eyes had lost their glitter, and were dull. He showed no excitement of manner, and but little interest in things around him. The bow, tensely strung so long, was now for a time unbent.

For prudential reasons, Doctor Hófland thought it best to conceal from his own family, except his wife and son-in-law, the real name of the person he had received into his house. At an early hour, he called on the Mayor. Both men had thought, with much concern, over the difficult questions involved in the case of Mr. Guy. If he were really the man he represented himself to be — and they had few doubts on this head — crime had been committed, and justice must have way. When to act and how to act, were things not so easily determined. The decision was, to wait for a brief period — in the meantime, securing for Mr. Guy everything needed for his comfort and restoration to mental health. Mr. Larobe was to be closely observed, and his appearance and movements noted from day to day.

Returning home, after this conference, Doctor Hofland found his wife in much concern about their guest.

" He isn't at all in his right mind," she said ; " I can't make anything out of him."

. " Has there been any change since I left ? "

" Yes."

" Of what kind ? "

" He seems entirely lost. If you speak to him, he answers vaguely.

" Where is he ? "

" Sitting in the parlor, and as still as one asleep."

Doctor Hofland went into the parlor, and found Mr. Guy, as his wife had represented him, reclining in an easy chair. His eyes were open ; but there was no thought in them.

" How are you now ? " said the Doctor, in a cheerful voice, as he drew a chair and sat down beside him.

" Oh ! ah ! it's you, Doctor ? " A faint gleam of intelligence lit up Guy's dull face.

" Yes, it's me. How do you feel now ? "

" What did you say ? " Thought, startled from leaden sleep, was folding back its wings again.

" Yes, I'm Doctor Hofland."

" Oh ! ah ! Doctor——" The sentence died out in partial utterance.

No effort to arouse Mr. Guy brought him nearer to rational consciousness than this ; and Doctor Hofland, after spending an hour in observation and study of his condition, was forced to the conclusion that reason had, for the time, at least, passed under an almost total eclipse. Such being the case, it was necessary to have him in charge of a constant attendant. This duty was, for the day, and until better arrangements could be made, assigned to a colored waiter, whose instructions were on no account to leave him.

From this time until two o'clock, Doctor Hofland was absent among his patients. On returning home, he found no change in Mr. Guy. He was sitting where he left him, apparently unconscious of external things. Dinner being announced, he suffered himself to be taken to the table, where he eat sparingly, finishing his meal before the others were half done. This change partially aroused him, and several times the Doctor noticed a look of curious inquiry in his countenance, as he glanced, almost stealthily, from face to face, around the table. But, after dinner, the former stupor returned, and did not pass off during the day.

The position in which Doctor Hofland found himself was one of great delicacy. At first, on reflection, this course seemed plain :— To bring the facts in his possession to the knowledge of Adam Guy, jr., and place his father at his disposal, thusrelieving himself from all care or responsibility in the matter. But, the longer he pondered this course, the more did objections multiply themselves. He had no faith in the humanity of Adam Guy, jr. By inheritance, he had received from his father an absorbing love of money, which had become a god, on whose altars he was ever ready to lay the most precious things in sacrifice. No gain could arise to him from his father's reappearance on the stage of life. Loss, in all probability, would ensue ; for the will, by which a portion of the estate had been divided to him, must fall. In this view the Doctor did not wrong him, when he doubted and hesitated. It would be the interest of

Adam Guy, jr. to assume that the man claiming to be
his father was an imposter; and, therefore, instead of
searching for evidence in favor of the claim, he would
most likely collude with Mr. Larobe for the production
of proofs on the other side. Moreover, if his father
were given up to him in his present mental stupor, he
would be placed in an asylum, and might again come
under the power of Mr. Larobe and his wife, whose
stake in the case was highest of all, and who, if they
lost in the desperate game they were playing, lost everything.

The more Doctor Hofland dwelt on this latter view,
the less inclined was he to let the poor wreck in his
hands pass beyond all possible control.

"In providence," he said in his thought, "the guar-
dianship has been committed to me; and, as things are,
I cannot see that it would be right to pass it to another.
To give him over to them as he now is, would be, in
my opinion, little less than abandoning a lamb to the
wolves. He is in no condition to prove his identity, and
I have not the clue by which the mystery of this wrong
may be surely unravelled."

This opinion of the case strengthened the longer it
was dwelt upon, and the final determination of Doctor
Hofland, after further conference with the Mayor, was
to let everything rest, until some change in Mr. Guy's
mental condition, or some movement on the part of

Mr. and Mrs. Larobe, made action necessary. In the meantime, the restoration of Mr. Guy's darkened reason was to be the chief object in view, so far as he was concerned.

And now let us return to Mr. and Mrs. Larobe, whom we left shuddering in the face of a dreaded retribution.

CHAPTER XX

LL through the sleepless night that followed the last recorded interview between Justin Larobe and his wife, the former heard, at not remote intervals, movements in the room adjoining the one he occupied, which, to his excited imagination, had mysterious import. A door communicated with this room ; but before retiring he had turned the key, which happened to be on his side of the lock. Two or three times he fancied that a hand was laid on this door, and an attempt made to open it ; and on these occasions he would rise up in bed, and listen with that breathless concern which makes every heart-beat audible in the ears. It was a night full of strange terrors. Out of the darkness looked upon him a malign face. He saw it with shut or open eyes, just the same. Watching him from the covert of half closed lids, was a

spirit cruel as death — athirst with an insatiate desire to work him evil.   Well did he know the face!

Morning came at last, and with the first feeble intrusions of dull gray light, the haunting face withdrew. Rising, almost with the dawn, Mr. Larobe dressed himself, and went down stairs.   His movements had been quite noiseless.   No sound coming at this time from the adjoining chamber, occupied by his wife, he acted on the presumption that she was asleep, and moved silently in order not to disturb her.   Half way down he stopped to listen.   Had his ears deceived him? — or was that the rustle of a dress?   He stood still, hearkening.

"A mere fancy," he said to himself, and kept on. Only a dim light penetrated the hall.   One of the parlor doors stood half open.   Pressing it back with his hand, Mr. Larobe entered, and was near a window, which he designed opening, when a sound in the room arrested his steps.   Turning quickly, he tried to make out some object; but the light was insufficient.   A moment afterwards, and his hand had thrown a shutter open, letting in the day.   In the effort to conceal herself behind a column, stood Mrs. Larobe, with a face like marble — cold and changeless.   She did not move, as the light came in.

"Jane!"   The word dropped in sudden surprise from Mr. Larobe's lips.   No response was made.   Close against the column, which partly hid her person, the

woman continued to stand, with her eyes fixed on Mr.
Larobe — the same eyes that all night long had haunt-
ed him.

"Jane; why are you here at this time?" Mr.
Larobe came slowly down the room. He spoke with
assumed severity. She did not answer, nor for an instant withdraw her eyes. Something in their expression chilled him. On coming nearer, he saw that she
was dressed for going out; and that her bonnet and
cloak were lying on a sofa.

"Jane; there is one thing you had best understand,"
said Mr. Larobe, speaking with impressive earnestness,
not severely as just before — and in the tone of one who
appealed to reason. "Unless we act in concert, all is
lost. There must be no unconsidered step. A false
movement, and we are at the end. It is too late now
for retrograde action. Everything done, for good or
ill, will abide. I pray you, therefore, to be circumspect. Trust in me a little longer. My mind is calmer than yours. Imminent danger does not unnerve me,
as it unnerves you. The cool head, the alert will, the
self-reliance that cannot be overthrown — in these lie
our only hope."

"It is too late, sir!" she answered, in a dull, per-
verse way, as she moved from the column behind which
she had been standing. "Not the cool head, but the
fiery heart, now. This!"— half unsheathing a long

dirk — "Not that!"—touching significantly her forehead.   Mr. Larobe shuddered.

"Dead men," she added, "tell no tales. If you could have been made to understand the value of that saying years ago, our feet would have been on a rock."

Turning away, Mrs. Larobe went to the sofa on which her bonnet and shawl were lying, and catching them up in a resolute manner, commenced putting them on.

"Where are you going?" was demanded, in a tone of authority.

"To do my own will," replied Mrs. Larobe, with undisguised contempt, yet fiercely, as one who meant to have her way.

"I warned you last night, Jane!"

"You! Coward! A woman means to shame you!" The words were flung at him in bitter scorn.

She had fastened her cloak, and was now tying her bonnet strings. The stronger light that was coming in through the window, fell upon her face. Its cold impassiveness was gone. Flashes of insane fire shot from her eyes — cruel resolution dwelt on her firm lips. From an almost insensate image, she had become transformed to a fiend.

"There are some things more to be dreaded, Justin Larobe, than a conviction of murder," she said. "More fearful risks attend on his life than on his death. Place

the seal of eternal silence on his lips, and you remove a
witness whose testimony is destruction. The dead
body of a poor lunatic is voiceless. Let him die, and
his secret with him! As for after consequences, we can
meet them as they come; the worst having been escaped."

She was moving towards the hall while she spoke,
with a determined step, evidently intending to leave
the house; but Mr. Larobe started forward, and gaining the door, stood directly in front of her.

"It must not be, Jane!" He spoke with stern resolution in his manner. "You are beside yourself!"

"Hinder me at your peril!" cried Mrs. Larobe,
raising her hand quickly, and dashing it forward. The
gleam of a dirk knife caught Mr. Larobe's eyes, and he
leaped backward in time to avoid the blow which had
been aimed at him. In the fright and irresolution that
followed, Mrs. Larobe nearly succeeded in getting off;
but, he recovered himself in time to grapple with her
before she passed the vestibule door and wrest the instrument of murder from her hand. In the struggle,
she lost all self-control, and filled the house with wild
hysteric screams, arousing the servants and children,
who came running down with frightened faces, half
dressed, or in their night-clothes. Their presence had
the effect to allay, in a degree, the mad excitement of
Mrs. Larobe.

"Go for Doctor Holbrook," said Mr. Larobe, speaking to one of the servants, "and say that I wish to see him immediately."

Mrs. Larobe did not object. Even in her blind passion, she saw that it would be safest to let the mystery of this scene find explanation in supposed mental derangement, in order to draw conjecture as far from the truth as possible. So, she permitted herself to be taken to her chamber. Into this apartment, Mr. Larobe did not suffer either the servants or children to intrude; but, shutting them on the outside, attempted to deal with the case alone.

Pale, panting, quivering in every nerve, Mrs. Larobe sat down, and lifting her wild eyes to the face of the man she had no legal or moral right to call her husband, demanded of him his purpose in ordering the attendance of their physician.

"You can see him or not, according to your own good pleasure," was his coldly spoken answer.

"I shall not see him," she replied.

"As you will. But, if I were in your place, I would feign sickness. I covered your wicked attempt on my life, by ordering the physician. He will be here, I doubt not, in less than twenty minutes. Some good reason must appear for the hurried summons. Invent one to suit yourself—but see him; that is my advice."

"What will you say to him?" demanded Mrs. Larobe.

"I have not come to a decision yet," was evasively answered. She looked at him with sharp suspicion.

"One thing, madam, is clear," said Mr. Larobe, speaking now with a stern severity of tone, "from what has occurred this morning, it is clear that you are not a safe person to be at large."

He paused to observe the effect of this declaration, made almost without thought. There was little apparent change in Mrs. Larobe. Almost the only noticeable response was a repressed manner, as if she felt conscious of a superior force.

"Life is too precious a thing to be left unguarded." He paused again, but she did not answer.

"You have grown desperate, and would take the life that stands in your way Knowing this, my duty is plain."

"What!" She threw out the word with a quick, yet half repressed impulse.

"I would be guilty before the law, if I did not limit your power to do harm."

A long shivering sigh was the only response.

There came a knock at the chamber door. Mr. Larobe crossed the room, and partly opening the door, received a letter which the hand of a servant passed in. His name was on the envelope. Opening it he read —

"JUSTIN LAROBE, ESQ. —SIR: Last night after eleven o'clock, the Mayor of the city, accompanied by

Doctor Hofland and a police officer, came to my house, and removed the old man. I give you the earliest possible notice of the fact. I'm afraid there is trouble in the wind. I hope you have not deceived me as to this person's identity.

"Yours, &c., BLACK."

"What is it? Who is it from?" Mrs. Larobe was questioning eagerly before the contents of the letter were half comprehended. Mr. Larobe, after twice reading the communication, handed it to his companion, and sitting down, covered his face. The long dreaded catastrophe was knocking at his door.

"Fool! Fool! Fool!" Mr. Larobe started from his shrinking posture. The word was sent into his ears in a mad, despairing cry, the voice rising with each repetition.

"For heaven's sake, Jane, keep down this excitement! All is not yet lost; but, all will be, unless complete self-possession is restored. As things are, so must we take them and deal with them. Suddenly we come into new peril. Shall we sit down, like frightened children, or dumb animals, and let destruction overwhelm us; or shall we look right and left, upwards and downwards, for a way of escape?"

"There is no escape," Mrs. Larobe answered, her face a dead blank.

" When the ship is sinking, who escape ? " said the
other. " Those who fold their arms in despair, or
those who are on the look-out for means of safety ?
The courageous, the hopeful, the alert — they come
out of danger, while the doubting perish. Jane, if
there ever was a time when both you and I needed to
be cool, self-possessed, and united in action, it is now.
There is a magazine under us, and all the steps we take
are on grains of powder that friction may ignite.
Even caution may not save us ; but, blind dashing
about from side to side, and heedless stampings of the
feet, can only make destruction sure. Sit down, and
listen."

Mrs. Larobe sat down, and looked with a kind of
passive incredulity at her companion, who went on —

" Jane, there is one thing to be remembered. Proof
of identity in a case like this will be difficult. Almost
everything will rest with Du Pontz ; and his safety is
involved as well as our own. The death and burial of
Mr. Guy are things of record and public notoriety.
This man will have the disability of supposed imposture to contend with from the start. Adam will deny
and contest his claim from the very outset ; for, if
made good, it will dispossess him of twenty thousand
dollars, and the interest on that sum for ten years. My
standing in the community, and yours, also, will have
weight. The case will present unpleasant and humili-

11

ating features ; but, it cannot go against us, if we defend it bravely and with fair-fronted innocence."

Mrs. Larobe made no reply. In the pause that followed, came another rap on the door.

" What is wanted ? " called Mr. Larobe.

" The Doctor has come."

" Very well. Say that I will be down in a moment."

The servant retired. Mr. Larobe stood in thought for some time.

" How do you propose meeting the case, Jane ? "

" I do not intend seeing the Doctor," was replied. " Make what excuse you please. Anything to suit yourself. I am indifferent. You can have me put in the insane hospital, if that please your fancy. Perhaps, as things now stand, this course would be prudent."

Mrs. Larobe spoke in a dead level tone. The perplexed lawyer looked at her searchingly, but tried in vain to read her state. Was the last suggestion made in irony, or from a latent conviction that there might be safety in this direction? As Mr. Larobe went slowly down stairs, he pondered this view of the case.

" Good morning, Doctor," he said, in an assumed cheerful voice, as he met the young physician. " You were rather hastily sent for, in a moment of needless fright. Mrs. Larobe was up rather earlier than usual — having had a sleepless night from neuralgia — and in going down stairs, slipped and fell. In her fright.

she screamed out, and alarmed the family ; and you were sent for in the confusion that ensued. Fortunately, no hurt was sustained. She is now sleeping, and it will be best not to disturb her."

" You think there was no injury ? " The Doctor's suspicious eyes gave Mr. Larobe an uneasy sensation.

" None whatever," he returned, " beyond a slight bruise on the arm."

" Did the neuralgic pain continue ? "

" No. The shock received in falling, dispersed the pain entirely. Sleep naturally followed relief. This is a new remedy, Doctor, not down in the books." And Mr. Larobe affected a humorous state of mind.

" But one hardly safe in application."

" Hardly," answered the Doctor, but without responding to the smile Larobe had forced into his troubled countenance. " I will leave a prescription, the medicine to be taken when she awakes. There may have been an internal shock, the effect of which has not yet become apparent."

" Do so, if you please, Doctor. I will send for the medicine immediately, and see that she has it as soon as this sleep passes."

Doctor Holbrook wrote a prescription, and then went away. Something in his manner left an uneasy feeling with Mr. Larobe. He did not remember, until after the physician's departure, that he was son-in-law to

Doctor Hofland. When this recollection came, it was as if water had fallen on his head and trickled coldly to his feet.

" How the path narrows ! " he said, with a shiver and sat down alone to think. But, he did not long remain alone. There was a foot-sound on the floor, and looking up, he met the cold, hard face of Mrs. Larobe — hard with the congelation of bad passions.

" Where is the Doctor ? " She glanced around the room.

" Gone."

" Gone ! What did you say to him ? "

" That you were asleep."

" Ah ! asleep ? God knows if I shall ever sleep again ! It were better to be dead, than to live in this terror. Asleep ! Ha ! ha ! You are quick witted, Mr. Larobe, quick witted ! Game to the last — ha ! ha ! That was handsomely done ! Asleep, but somnambulic ! Don't look at me with such a scowl. I must laugh a little. And so we are rid of the Doctor. But, do you know who he is, Justin ? "

" Yes."

" Doctor Hofland's son-in-law ? "

" Yes."

" The Devil's net has many meshes. I doubt if we get free, Justin. Reynard, with all his turnings and doublings is generally caught at last. This is a hard way to

walk in — sore-footed and weary-limbed, I can go no
farther. Long and long ago our feet departed from
smooth and level roads, and ever since sharp stones
have cut, steep hills wearied, and miry sloughs exhausted
the strength. And now, as I look onward, I see stonier
ways and steeper hills, and blacker pools, down into
which we must sink and be lost. Let us end all this,
Justin." .

Her voice sunk into a calm, persuasive tone.

"Let us put the baying hounds forever off of our
track. What if, in the fierce struggle for all we hold
dear in life, that is now coming upon us, we are victors?
Will not even victory be defeat? What will be left
worth living for? I can see nothing — nothing. Tar-
nished honor — shattered fortune, most likely — social
ostracism. No — no — no! I am not now strong
enough to meet all this. I want rest and peace — rest
and peace, and where shall I find them but in —" She
paused, looking earnestly at Mr. Larobe, reading the
expression of his face. "The grave?" she added,
speaking the words in a rising instead of a falling in-
flection.

Mrs. Larobe shut her lips tightly, and with an erect
position of her body, awaited an answer. It came in
these words —

"While there is life there is hope, Jane. I have
still manhood enough left for a strife with fate; and I

will battle, bold-fronted, to the last. If you can stand up by my side, well; if not —"

The sentence was left unfinished, but his meaning was clear. A little while they stood opposite to each other, in a mutual effort to penetrate the veil that hid interior thoughts and purpose. Mrs. Larobe moved first. Slowly turning, but without remark, she went into the hall, and ascended to her room. Mr. Larobe did not follow her. It was impressed on his mind, that she would act in the line of her intimation; and he was not wrong. At the breakfast table they met again. She had the cold, stony look he had noticed earlier in the morning. The children observed her with strange, questioning eyes; and Blanche, the simple-minded girl, left her place two or three times during the meal, and putting an arm around her mother's neck, said plaintively —

" Don't look so, ma. It hurts me."

At dinner time they met again. The face of Mrs. Larobe was colder, stonier, and more unreadable. Neither was disposed to be communicative.

At early twilight they met again; but now it was as the dead and living meet. Another act in this life-tragedy is over, and as the curtain falls, you see the pulse-less body of Mrs. Larobe, lying upon a sofa, in her own chamber, where it had been lying for an hour. As to the cause and manner of this death, we will not curiously inquire. Enough, that life's fitful fever was over, and that she slept her mortal sleep. · Of the dreams that came in this sleep, we have no revelation; and so, the curtain that fell, as the act closed, must rise on other scenes.

CHAPTER XXI

T.WO months have passed. Mr. Guy is still at the house of Doctor Hofland, but the secret of his presence there has not transpired. The sudden death of Mrs. Larobe gave rise to many stories, some of them so near the truth, with all its strange and improbable features, that sensible people rejected them as the baldest kind of inventions.

Contrary to expectation, Mr. Guy did not rally from the mental torpor into which he fell after his prison door was opened and his fetters stricken off. The relaxed fibres of the overbent bow, did not contract and toughen again. A harmless, quiet, dreaming old man, he would sit for hours in his room, or with the family, not a thought seeming to stir the external surface of his mind. The book of his past life was shut, or the writing therein effaced. Memory was a blank. Sometimes, as the inner man looked out into the world of external things, and curiosity stirred as in a child, he would ask the name of some common thing, as a knife, a spoon or a chair, and repeat it over, trying to fix the answer in his thought. Observing him closely from day to day, Doctor Hofland saw that he was beginning to gather up a few shreds of knowledge, and that the possession of these was interesting him, and creating a hunger for further acquirements. Very, very slow was the progress ; but still there was progress. This fact, when clearly seen by Doctor Hofland, determined his future course. He recognized a Providence in the series of events which had placed Mr. Guy in his hands, and so far as his agency for good towards the now helpless imbecile would go, it must be freely given. The secret of his identity rested with himself and the Mayor, and, for the present, would rest there.

Very closely had Doctor Hofland studied the character of Mr. Ewbank, and that of his wife. Soon after Mr. Guy came into his house, he had conceived the plan of giving him into the charge of his daughter and her husband ; and with this in view, he had gone nearer to them, and made observation at all points. The more he saw, and the deeper he reflected, the stronger was his conviction that, with them, Mr. Guy would be in the best attainable condition. The question as to whether it were advisable or not, to let them into the grave secret of his personality, or leave it for time and

11*

circumstances to discover, was for a long time debated.
He had them frequently at his house, where they saw
Mr. Guy, and became much interested in him. The case
presented many novel features to Mr. Ewbank, and he
thought of, and talked of it with Doctor Hofland, a
great deal. When, at last, the Doctor suggested his
taking charge of the case, with a view to drawing forth
the slumbering faculties and educating them anew, the
proposition was not unfavorably received. Mrs. Ewbank
had been interested in him from the first, and he had
responded in a pleased way to her attentions. The
pecuniary consideration, which Doctor Hofland felt
justified in offering, was in itself so liberal, that taking
the limited means of Mr. and Mrs. Ewbank into consideration, it offered a motive not to be disregarded.

"I have heard, or read, of cases resembling this,"
said Mr. Ewbank, in talking over the subject with Doctor Hofland, "but always thought them exaggerated.
Standing face to face with a mental phenomenon so very
remarkable, I confess to being deeply interested. Memory is completely veiled. He is like one newly born,
with the pages of his spirit yet unwritten upon, and like
a child in the simple innocence of ignorance. He is not
insane — nor idiotic — but with the undeveloped mind
of a child. He must be taught and led. Have you
found him always docile?"

"Always," replied the Doctor.

"And gradually gaining interest in things around him?"

"Gradually, but very slowly."

"What do medical books say in regard to these cases. Memory is suddenly restored, I think?"

"That is the usual result. Suddenly the veil is rent, and the past revived."

"Do you know the particulars of Mr. Elliot's former life?" (Elliot was the name by which Mr. Guy was called in Doctor Hofland's family, and he accepted it as a true name, just as he did that of a chair or a door.)

"Something of them. But, as I have intimated before, there are circumstances which make it necessary to let former things, so far as he is concerned, lie buried for the present. I can only say, that the righting of great wrongs depends on his being once more clothed and in his true mind; and that if you can aid in the work, you will have done what must prove to you a life-long satisfaction."

"I try to hold myself ready for all good work, Doctor; and, somehow, my heart goes forth towards this, with a living desire. When I spoke of his former life, it had more reference to his interior than to his exterior state. Was he a selfish, sordid, worldly man; or, generous and humane? Did he live only for himself; or, was others' good kept in his regard?"

"He was selfish, sordid, worldly — seeking no good but his own."

Mr. Ewbank looked disappointed.

"I had hoped that it was different," he said.

"He lived only for himself. Even natural feeling seemed dead in his heart," said the Doctor. "I could almost wish the past never restored, if with the restoration his former life returned. Ah! if he could, as an innocent child, under better auspices, grow up to reasoning manhood. If tender and holy affections could be so ,stored up in his forming mental states, that in a second manhood he might be saved by their influence. My fear, Mr. Ewbank, is, that when memory comes back, and old habits of feeling and thought revive, he will be the hard, selfish man of old. But He, without whom a sparrow falls not, holds him in the hollow of His hand; and I have faith in the good to come from the great suffering through which he has been led, and now given, as a passive child, into our care."

"Was he religious in early life?" asked Mr. Ewbank.

"No."

"Have you any knowledge of his childhood?"

"Very little. It was not a pleasant childhood, however. A few times I heard him make reference thereto, and it was, generally, coupled with a sneer at bigots and hypocrites. With these he classed the majority of religious people."

"One thing is plain," said Mr. Ewbank. "The first and greatest work is, to teach him that there is a God, who loves him and cares for him — a God who is ever present, though unseen, and watching over him for good. If this idea can be fixed among the first things that find entrance into his mind, so as to be woven in with all that follows, we may sow precious seed in the ground of this new childhood; seed that may bear fruit even in the old manhood, if it returns."

"Ah, sir! There is a great work here. If you are equal to the task, a human soul in imminent peril may be saved." Doctor Hofland spoke with much feeling. "It looks as if in you, God has provided for the case of this man."

"I cannot say how that may be," answered Mr. Ewbank. "What seems right to be done, in the present, I hold it my duty to do — and it seems right that I should take charge of Mr. Elliot."

"You have talked it over with your wife?"

"Yes."

"How does she feel about it?"

"As I do. Something in Mr. Elliot has interested her from the beginning; and you have seen how like a pleased child he acts whenever she comes here. If she

were to ask him to go home with her, I am sure he
would answer yes."

" The way seems plain, Mr. Ewbank."

" It does."

" And you will walk therein ? "

" Yes."

As Mr. Ewbank had supposed, the invitation extend
ed to Mr. Elliot (as we will now call him) by his wife,
was accepted with manifestations of delight. He was
all eager for the visit, and entered the carriage that was
to convey him to the house of his daughter without a
shade of suspicion crossing his mind. Once there, under all the tender care and watchful solicitude with
which he was regarded — springing in the case of Mrs.
Ewbank from an impulse that she could not explain, and
in the case of her husband, from high moral and religious principle — Mr. Elliot seemed to have no thought
of going away. He remembered Doctor Hofland and
his family ; but more as one remembers a vivid dream
— to be dwelt upon, but not restored in actual experience.

Mr. and Mrs. Ewbank were not now in that poor
dwelling where Doctor Hofland found them on that
cold winter evening when the child Esther called for
him to go and visit little dying Theo. They had removed to a larger and pleasanter house, farther in the
western portion of the city ; the income of Mr. Ewbank

from pupils, justifying the increased expense. Mr
Ewbank's health was steadily improving. From the
time that Doctor Hofland arrested the progress of a
disease that seemed rapidly bearing him away, there
had been a steady accumulation of vital power, and
now he was strong for his work as well in body as in
mind.

It was on the afternoon of a pleasant June day that
Mr. Elliot found himself in the home of his new friends.
For a little while, Esther and Jasper, the children of
Mrs. Ewbank, were shy of the strange old man, who
looked at them in such a curious way — "Just as a
baby looks," Esther said. But they were soon drawn
towards him, and mutual good feeling established.
Before the afternoon had gone, they were so much interested in their visitor, and he in them, that, on a suggestion being made to Mr. Elliot about his returning
home to Doctor Hofland's, a joint demurrer was promptly entered.

" Why can't he stay here all night ? " asked little
Jasper.

" That might not be agreeable to Mr. Elliot," replied
Mrs. Ewbank.

" Yes, it will be agreeable.   Wont it, Mr. Elliot ? "
said the child.

" I like it best here," he answered.

"Oh, well, if that is so, we shall be happy to have you remain," said Mr. Ewbank, in a pleasant voice.

And so it was settled that he should stay all night.

During the two months in which he remained with Doctor Hofland, much time and care had been given by each member of the family to his peculiar mental needs, and pains had been taken to lead his mind as much as possible into that knowledge of things which had been so strangely lost. The names and use of most common articles by which he was surrounded, had been acquired, and he had not only learned his alphabet anew, but was beginning to unite letters into words. Thus, a fair commencement had been made. The children of Mr. and Mrs. Ewbank were not very liberally supplied with books and playthings; but, they had enough to afford interest and amusement to Mr. Elliot during the whole afternoon. He was attracted by pictures, and listened with all the pleased attention of a child to the explanations that were given by Esther. A box of building blocks afforded him an hour's employment; and when he had constructed, by their aid, some architectural form, he would gaze upon it with an expression of childish satisfaction not unmixed with wonder. Many times, during this first afternoon of his presence in the family of Mrs. Ewbank, did she pause in her work to look at him, and always with an irrepressible yearning in her heart. Something beyond his

mere helplessness touched her. What it was she did
not know, or even try to discover. It was, with her,
one of those intruding mysteries of the soul, that lie out
of the reach of thought or experience.

In the evening, when Jasper's bed-time came — he
was five years old — he retired with his mother, and
after being undressed, came back and knelt down by
his father, to say his nightly prayer. With small
hands laid together, face uplifted, and eyes shut softly,
the child repeated, " Our Father." The look of surprise, shaded with reverence, that fell on the countenance of Mr. Elliot, did not escape Mr. Ewbank. As
Jasper arose from his knees and went out with his
mother, after giving to all around his good night kiss,
the old man drooped his eyes to the floor and sat like
one lost in a dreaming reverie.

" What is it ? " he asked, speaking in a hushed
voice, and with an impression of mystery in his face, as
he looked up at Mr. Ewbank.

" Jasper was saying his prayers."

But Mr. Elliot was not enlightened.

" He was praying to God," said Mr. Ewbank, pointing upwards. " To God who made us all, and who
loves us and takes care of us."

" Did he make me ? "

" O yes. He made you and me, and every living

soul. And he loves you and cares for you, just as he loves and cares for all his children."

"Is he my father? Jasper said, Our Father in Heaven. Where is Heaven?"

"Heaven is where God is, and where good angels dwell with him; and God is your father and my father, and the father of us all."

Mr. Elliot looked down at the floor again. These things were almost too much for him. They crowded his feebly acting thoughts. He did not speak for several minutes, and Mr. Ewbank waited for his mind to fix itself on some definite idea. At last he said, with a sigh that expressed a state of relief, after effort —

"My father, and he loves me?"

The voice trembled just a little — trembled with feeling. The heart of Mr. Ewbank felt a thrill of pleasure. Just what he desired had taken place.

"Yes, your father, and he loves you," — giving back the thought in slowly spoken, emphatic words, that it might become fixed and remain among the first and most distinct things of his newly forming life. "And to be loved by One who is as good as he is powerful, is to be in safety. Only we must be obedient children. He says that we must be kind and good to one another, as he is kind and good to us."

"Does Esther pray, when she goes to bed?"

Thought was still searching about among the new things which had come into his mind.

" O yes."

" Do you pray ? "

" Yes."

A shadow came over the pale, exhausted countenance.

" I never pray." There was a touching sadness in Mr. Elliot's voice, mingled with self-condemnation.

" Never ? " As if in surprise.

" No; I have never prayed. I didn't know about God. How do you know about him ? Who told you ? " There was a rising eagerness in Mr. Elliot's tones.

" We have God's book, the Bible. In that he tells us all about what we are to do in order to please Him."

" The Bible ! " It seemed, from his manner, as if an old memory had awakened into life ; but, if it had stirred, its sleep was not broken.

" Yes, the Bible." And Mr. Ewbank lifted a copy of Sacred Scripture from the table near which he was sitting, and opening it, read aloud a portion of one of the chapters in Matthew — not selected with a view to Mr. Elliot's state, but simply as a portion of God's Word, trusting to Divine influence for the effect. It was a part of his faith, that, interior to the sense of the letter of Holy Writ, which comes to the natural understanding of man, was a divinely spiritual sense, by means of which God, who is the Word, is actually present to all who read or hear in states of innocence and true worship. And so, while not looking for this portion of Scripture to give distinct religious ideas to the mind of Mr. Elliot, he trusted to its interior influence — and not in vain. The disturbed condition in which he had been a little while before, subsided into a peaceful state ; and he said, after Mr. Ewbank had finished reading —

"I'll pray, if you'll teach me."

When bedtime came, Mr. Ewbank went with the passive old man to his chamber, and there heard him repeat, as he gave him the sentences, that all-embracing prayer, which has gone up from millions of Christian lips since Christ said to his disciples —

"After this manner pray ye."

Earnestly, innocently, as one of God's little ones, did he offer this prayer, kneeling as he had seen Jasper kneel, with hands uplifted and shut eyes. And then, lying down in peace, he was asleep ere a minute had passed from the time his head was on the pillow. For a good while Mr. Ewbank remained looking on his wan and wasted face, now so tranquil. His wife came in, and stood by his side, her hands drawn through one of his arms and clasped together.

"I don't know what it means," said Mrs. Ewbank,

in a whisper, " but, whenever I look at him, I feel tears coming into my eyes. It is the strangest case I've heard tell of. Everything lost ! His name even; for I don't believe that Elliot is his true name."

" Perhaps not. All that concerns him is shrouded in mystery." . Mr. Ewbank moved back from the bed, as he spoke, and they retired from the chamber. " But one thing is clear to my mind, Lydia," he added, as they sat down in the adjoining room, " in God's providence, he is in our hands, and we must do all for him that lies in our power. It is not probable that he will continue, for a very long time, in his present isolation from the past. As thought awakens, through the agency of instruction, it will break through the veil that has dropped between his inner and outer life. This may be gradual, or it may be sudden. Whenever it takes place, our work is ended. Now, we have him as an ignorant and innocent child; and we must do for him what is best for a child. It seems to me, that God has, in us, provided for the storing up in his mind of the elements of a new and truer life, by which, when reason is restored, he may have power to rise out of the old selfishness and sordidness that I learn shadowed his manhood. This work is more entirely in your hands than it is in mine, for it is a mother's work — dealing with affection more than with thought. Dear wife ! "— feeling trembled in his voice —" you are chosen of Him whose love reaches

down to the condition of every human being, to care for
this weak old man; to awaken kind, tender, loving, rev-
erent impulses in his soul.   To give him a new and
better childhood.   The seed now planted by your hands
may grow and bring fruit in his restored manhood.   The
new knowledge of things which we may impart, will be
of use only in the degree that they help in the formation
of tender, unselfish, and pious states.   If memory re-
vives, he will come back into all the former things of
his life.   My hope is, that something of what we give
him now, may so dwell with these things, as to form the
base of a new column in the structure of his mind, the
top of which shall reach far above the old building, and
stand where the pure sunlight of heaven may rest upon
it as a crown."

" I do not see in all things as you see," Mrs. Ewbank
answered, leaning towards her husband, and looking up
to him with loving confidence.   "My eyes are not so
clear.   But, as you lead, dear husband, I will walk.
The path of duty I have learned, after long discipline,
to be the path in which peace is to be found.   It is the
safest way, I am sure."

" Rightly said," answered Mr. Ewbank, "for they
who walk in it walk with God—and when he is near
us evil is far distant."

" How shall I plant this seed of which you speak?

How shall I awaken pure and good affections in his mind ? "

" Love kindles love," replied Mr. Ewbank. " Show him, in all your conduct, that you love and care for him — that you desire to make him happy ; this will draw his heart towards you, and give impressiveness to all you say and do. Then, into the love he will bear for you, cast seeds of reverence and love for God, as they are cast into the minds of children. These cannot perish. God will give increase, dear wife! A strange work has been committed to our hands. Let us, in all faithfulness and humility, looking to God for help, see that nothing suffers through our lack of diligence. If we can save a soul, we shall do the work of angels."

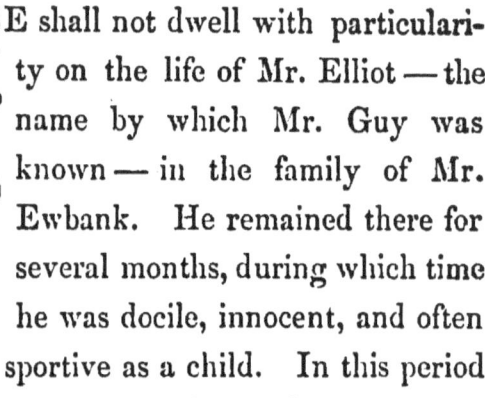

CHAPTER XXII

E shall not dwell with particularity on the life of Mr. Elliot — the name by which Mr. Guy was known — in the family of Mr. Ewbank. He remained there for several months, during which time he was docile, innocent, and often sportive as a child. In this period he had learned to read a little, and would often take a book and sit alone, trying to gather meaning from the sentences. For Mrs. Ewbank, he manifested the purest love; and was always happiest when by her side. Her word was his law; not her word spoken in authority, but the simple expression of her will. When she read to him, as her husband desired her to do frequently, those Bible stories which all young children delight to hear, — about Joseph and his brethren — the Hebrew children — of Abraham, David and Daniel — and of the nativity of our Lord; he would listen to her with that absorbed attention which appropriates every sentence. Thus, his newly forming memory became peopled with the men and women of olden times, whose words and deeds, representative of divine things, God has established as holy Scripture.

In all these months, Mr. Elliot had expressed no desire to pass beyond the threshold of his new home. He would sit or stand by the window, and look on the living panorama with a vague, childish wonder ; but the hard, strong, involved things on the outside, instead of attracting, made him shrink back with an emotion of dread.

But at last, signs of a new state were visible ; and the friends who had cared for him until care wrought itself into love, began to fear and tremble. Mrs. Ewbank, noticing one day that he was unusually quiet, asked, as we sometimes ask a child —

" What are you thinking about ? "

He raised his eyes, and looked at her for some moments ; then dropped them without answering. The expression of his face was so completely changed, that he did not appear like the same person.

" What are you thinking about, Mr. Elliot ? " Mrs. Ewbank repeated the question, after a little while.

" I must have been dreaming," he answered, looking up again, half perplexed, and with a faint smile breaking around his lips.

"Of what were you dreaming?" Mrs. Ewbank half held her breath for the reply.

"I don't know. It's all gone now," he answered, with a sigh of relief.

On the evening of the same day, Mr. Ewbank, in addressing his wife, called her Lydia.

"That's a sweet name," said Mr. Elliot, in a tone of voice that caused both Mr. and Mrs. Ewbank to look at him curiously.

"Do you think so?" remarked the latter.

"Yes. And I've heard it before. I used to know a Lydia. I wonder where she is?" And his face grew shaded and intent.

Mr. and Mrs. Ewbank turned to each other in silence. It was plain to them that a few pencils of light had penetrated the veil which hung between the past and the present.

"Oh, I remember now. She went away." There was a quiet sadness in his voice. "She went away somewhere and left me."

"And never came back?" Mrs. Ewbank ventured to enquire.

"Never!" He sighed again, but more deeply. "Never came back again."

With a quick motion, Mr. Elliot now lifted his hand and pressed it hard against his forehead, as if in pain.

"Does your head ache, Mr. Elliot?"

He did not answer, but turned partly away, so as to hide his face; and sat perfectly motionless. Presently, as they looked at him intently, they saw a slight movement of his head, and caught a stealthy look, that was instantly withdrawn. He was still again for some time. Mr. Ewbank now spoke to him, calling his name. Slowly turning, and withdrawing his hand from his forehead, Mr. Elliot asked, with a degree of intelligence in his voice that startled Mr. and Mrs. Ewbank —

" How long have I been here ? "

" Don't you know ? " said Mr. Ewbank.

Mr. Elliot shook his head.

" Five months."

A hand was pressed tightly to his forehead again. " Five months ! " He repeated the answer in a perplexed tone. Then withdrew his hand, stood up, gazed at Mr. and Mrs. Ewbank searchingly, then all around the room.

" Am I sleeping or waking? What does it all mean ? " There was something mournful in his voice.

" Awake, Mr. Elliot, and with true friends," replied Mr. Ewbank, not rising, nor seeming to be disturbed or surprised.

" Mr. Elliot ! Why do you call me Mr. Elliot ?" he demanded, with apparent irritation.

" It is the name your friend, Doctor Hofland, gave us," was replied.

" Doctor Hofland ! " He startled Mr. and Mrs. Ewbank with his emphatic repetition. Clasping his forehead again, now with both hands, he sat down and remained entirely motionless as before.

" Will you send for him ? " he asked, at length, with repressed feeling.

" To-night ? "

" Yes. I would like to see him to-night."

" He lives at a considerable distance from here, and it is growing late," said Mrs. Ewbank, in a gentle, persuasive way, going up to Mr. Elliot, and laying her hand on him. The touch was like a charm ; for, when she added —" Wont it do as well for you to see him in the morning ?" he answered submissively —

" Yes, it will do as well in the morning ; but I must see him then."

" You wont go away and leave us, I hope." . Mrs. Ewbank said this with real emotion, for her heart, so long interested in the docile old man, had learned to love him, and the thought of parting was painful.

" I will come back again, or you shall come to me," he answered, almost fondly.

His mind seemed to wander a little after this — to play between the past and the present, and to mingle remote with recent things.

" I wonder where she is ! Do you know ? " He lifted his eyes to the face of Mrs. Ewbank, after a period of silence, in which it was plain that he was endeavoring to untangle the confused things in his mind, and gazed at her with a look of troubled inquiry.

" Who ? " asked Mrs. Ewbank.

" My Lydia." And the perplexed look deepened. " My Lydia," he repeated. " Didn't you know her ? I'm sure you must have known her."

A sudden flush came — his eyes enlarged — his lips fell apart— a tremor seized him. For a short period, he was like one startled by an apparition. This passed, and he was in repose again.

" Your name is Lydia." He looked at Mrs. Ewbank with returning fondness.

" Yes, that is my name."

" And her name was Lydia."

" Who ? "

A shadow crept over his face — he sighed, and turned away.

" I'm trying to think," he said, speaking soon afterwards, but a little mournfully. " I don't know where she went. Oh-h ! " The ejaculation was sudden, prolonged, and uttered as a cry of pain. Some bitter memory had flashed into light.

" What is it, Mr. Elliot ? What hurt you ? " Mrs. Ewbank drew closer, and spoke with fond familiarity.

" Dead ! Dead ! " His voice was full of grief.

" Who is dead ? "

"Lydia — my poor Lydia! I remember it now. She grew sick and died. Poor Lydia! I'm afraid —" He checked himself; shrunk down a little, as if under the weight of some unhappy thought, and became once more silent.

"Was it a long time ago?" asked Mrs. Ewbank.

He started, with face flushing anew, and turned full around upon Mrs. Ewbank, rising at the same time to his feet. Eagerly, almost wildly did he search her countenance.

"There was another Lydia," he said, his voice shaking. "A dead Lydia and a living one. They had the same voice, and I heard it just now — the same eyes and hair. O, my God!" The trembling old man shut his hands over his face and stood for a few moments. Then withdrawing them, he said with constrained calmness —

"My name is Adam Guy!"

"And I am Lydia! Oh, my father! My father!" Mrs. Ewbank sprang forward, throwing her arms around his neck, and laying her head on his breast.

Past the form clinging to him, the old man looked to Mr. Ewbank, who had started up, and now stood near them — looked to him with an almost helpless, but imploring expression, as one in a swiftly running stream, ready to be swept away. Mr. Ewbank understood the appeal, and, astonished as he was by so unlooked for a

denouement, said, as he made an effort to lift his wife
away —

"If you are indeed Adam Guy, who was thought to
be dead, this is your daughter Lydia."

"I am Adam Guy," was almost solemnly answered.

"Father! Father! Father!" Mrs. Ewbank lifted
her face from his breast, and with eyes full of light and
tears, looked at him lovingly, yet wonderingly. "And
you have been with me so many months, and I did not
know it! O father! Do you love me? Do you love
your Lydia?"

He did not answer in words —only with kisses and
embraces. Love had begotten love. The old, sordid,
selfish father had not really loved his child; but love was
the chief element in that new state, which, through a
forming period of nearly half a year, had gained sufficient power to dwell in safety, even amid the hard,
cold, repellent things of his former life.

Mr. Ewbank, fearing the consequence of excitement
on the mental condition of Mr. Guy — as we must now
call him — drew his wife gently away, and in calm
words to both, suggesting gratitude to God for this
wonderful restoration, led their thoughts into smoother
channels. Still, in her eagerness to know something of
the great mystery enshrouding the past ten years of her
father's life, Lydia kept asking questions, that disturbed
instead of tranquillizing. Memory was still confused —

all its pages were not open. There was obscurity and incoherence in the old man's answers ; and a troubled effort to untangle many things. With a wise solicitude, that comprehended his state, Mr. Ewbank drew his thoughts as much as possible away from the unhappy past, that it might dwell with present good, and have, now that he was coming into his right mind, a distinct perception of that Christian love and charity, in the sphere of which he had been dwelling. Everything, he felt, depended on the crisis which had come. If the good affections and true thoughts that dwelt with him in the late childhood condition of his mind, could be linked, as a golden chain, whose staple was in heaven, to the thoughts and affections, which, on the return of reason and memory, would move his heart and brain, then he might become a true man, and his last days be better than his first. It was for this he had been working, and now must come a fruitful field, or rust and stubble. If the record of all that had passed in these months of planting and culture, was to be sealed up, alas for the restored! Old passions, intensified by wrong, would sweep him away, and he would be in the hands of enemies tenfold more cruel than those from whom he had escaped. No wonder that Mr. Ewbank, conscious of his ignorance and weakness in a case like this, looked up and prayed — " Lord, give wisdom and strength."

Right thoughts came at the right time. Into his unselfish desire to do good, flowed true perceptions. As the states of Mr. Guy varied, he was able to see what was best to be said or done, in order to keep those golden links fast to the newly forming life. And so, as the old past came slowly back, getting more and more distinct, with all its horrible wrongs, the present was clung to as an ark of safety, and the love that was to save him kept warm — love for his daughter, which so flooded his heart that coldness was impossible.

After that sudden awakening to a consciousness of who he was, Mr. Guy did not recover reason and memory in full strength for a long time.

In this slow restoration was his true safety. It gave opportunity for Doctor Hofland, who saw him frequently, and for Mr. Ewbank, who watched over him with a manly solicitude, to take counsel as to all that was best to be done. With a passiveness that was remarkable, he generally submitted to their judgment of his case, letting his indeterminate thought dwell with their calmer reason.

"If you think best." How often he so replied to their arguments against his expressed wish to summon Mr. Larobe to the defensive, and drive him to punishment and restitution. They understood better than he, the difficulties that were in the way. The proof of identity must be complete, and many links in the chain of evidence were lacking. Sometimes, in his varying states, Mr. Guy would grow restive, or impatient. Then it was that his daughter's power over him became manifest. A word of gentle remonstrance — the pressure of her hand on his hand or arm — a soft, persuasive smile — there was a magic in these that softened him into confidence and submission. The love she had awakened did not die, but seemed to gain strength daily, twining itself as a golden thread amid all his awakening thoughts, passions, desires and purposes. In the new future that opened to his onward-reaching eyes, he saw her always ; saw her, and the great reward of love and benefit that it was in his heart to bestow.

It is a fact to be noticed, that no suspicion of a selfish end in Mr. Ewbank, crept into Mr. Guy's heart. As one of the guards against this, Doctor Hofland had taken occasion, at the earliest moment in which he would be comprehended, to assure Mr. Guy, that neither his daughter or her husband had entertained a suspicion of who he was until he discovered himself. There was another reason. A man of pure motives bears with him a sphere of his quality, which those who come into intimate association perceive. Mr. Guy felt this sphere, and it had power not only to keep all suspicion back, but to win his perfect confidence. He felt safe with Mr. Ewbank — felt that he was a friend, in a higher and truer sense than he had before understood that term ;

and not only this, but of such judgment and discretion, that he might trust him as the wisest of counsellors.

Thus it stood with Mr. Guy, two months from the period when light broke into his mind. Without consulting him in regard to what they were doing, Mr. Ewbank and Doctor Hofland, through the agency of one of the soundest and most discreet lawyers in the city, were diligently, but secretly, at work, searching for evidence that, when brought together, would prove the identity of Mr. Guy beyond the reach of cavil, and so establish him in all his legal rights. The movements of Mr. Larobe were observed closely. The property which his late wife held in her own right, by reservation at marriage, and which, by will, she had left to her children, did not come under his control, as she named executors. But, a considerable portion of it was involved in mixed transactions under his old executorship of Mr. Guy's estate. The executors under Mrs. Larobe's will, early became satisfied that all was not right, and gave the lawyer peremptory warning of their purpose to press matters to a legal inquiry, unless the property claimed by the instrument under which they were acting, was placed, free from all entanglement with any other interests, into their hands. There was demur, and affected defiance on his part; but, standing as he knew himself to be, on the brink of a precipice, he took counsel of prudence, and yielded everything — so that the entire property claimed by the testator, amounting in value to over sixty thousand dollars, was safe for her heirs. Thus, only about twenty thousand dollars of all the large estate which Larobe had ventured upon the crime of bigamy to secure, actually remained with him. He had accepted the terms of settlement required before marriage, trusting to his future power over his wife, and ability to *mis*manage her affairs in a way to secure all the benefits contemplated in this criminal alliance. But, the events he would have shaped, were under that higher control which always limits the power of evil, and surely, sooner or later, casts down the wicked.

CHAPTER XXIII.

THE movements of Larobe, as we have said, were closely observed. It was plain to those who had him under surveillance, that he had lost much of the old self-reliant manner; was alert — suspicious — uneasy. Even in court, a change was apparent. He did not come up to the defence or prosecution of his cases, with that absorption of himself into the causes under trial, that distinguished him of old, and so often wrought the success which would not otherwise have been achieved. In a comparatively short time age had marked him, as though touched by years. His hair was losing its darker shades rapidly, and his flesh shrinking. Care-worn — that word gives the expression of his face, when in repose. He was beginning to stoop a little, as if yielding to the weight of a perpetual burden.

As far as could be ascertained, no changes in the condition of his real property were made, beyond what was necessary in his settlements with the executors of his late wife's estate. He seemed to be like one hiding and waiting for a danger to pass — a danger so threatening, that the very effort to escape might ensure destruction.

Mrs. Larobe's death took place before Edwin Guy had succeeded in negotiating the notes extorted from his unhappy mother-in law. Mr. Glastonbury's conduct in this matter did not seem open and fair to Edwin, and more than once he suspected him to be playing false. There was always some plausible reason why the notes were not sold, and always some new opening, with flattering chances. At last, losing all patience, Edwin demanded of his lawyer a return of the notes. A little to his surprise, Glastonbury took a pocket-book from his fire-proof, and produced the paper.

" Take them," he said, quietly, " but let me suggest caution. There is something in the wind that I cannot make out. You may stumble on a wasp's nest, and get stung."

" What do you mean? From whence is danger threatened?" asked the young man.

" I am not at liberty to speak of what is in my thoughts. Some under-current of things is moving adversely to our friend Mr. Larobe — I can see that — but of its character I am not advised. Since the death of his wife, he has changed rapidly. It is scarcely a

month since her sudden decease, and her loss, or something else — "

" Something else you may be sure," said Edwin, with
sarcasm in his voice.

" Has profoundly disturbed his peace," added the
lawyer.

" He may have murdered her, as he murdered my
father. It is the guilty conscience, you may depend on't.
No, not conscience either; that was seared long ago.
It's fear of retribution — a haunting terror, that is eat-
ing into his life."

" I know not how that may be. Such grave charges,
however, my young friend, should not be made, except
on very clear evidence, and I must caution you against
toofree speaking in this direction. Trouble, not anticipated, may be the consequence."

" What would you suggest in regard to these notes ? "
asked Edwin, not responding to Mr. Glastonbury's last
remark.

" Keep them in your own possession."

" They will not be paid at maturity, by the executors
of my mother-in-law's estate."

" I think not."

" Would you advise a suit, or an offer to abandon the
notes for a consideration ? "

" I am not, as things stand, prepared to suggest any
thing in the way of action. For the present, keep just

where you are. If there is no gain, there is no loss.
Before the maturity of these notes, events may happen
that will not only make them as worthless as waste
paper, but — "

Mr. Glastonbury checked himself so suddenly, that
Edwin looked at him in surprise.

" But what ? "

" You are not a very discreet young man, Mr. Guy,"
said the lawyer, speaking with entire self-possession.
" So far, in this business, you have acquired an advantage by some four thousand dollars, but in a way I could
not have advised.   On the principle, that a bird in the
hand is worth two in the bush, you have considered
yourself the gainer, and maybe you are ; but, we never
can tell what a day may bring forth.   I am of the
opinion, that events will prove you to have lost, instead
of gained in this transaction."

" Why do you say this?   What do you know ? " demanded Edwin.

" I know, from long observation, that operations of
this kind rarely pay ; and, without being much of a
prophet, I may venture the prediction, that it will not
pay in your case.   If we could determine the action of
events, all would be well ; but this is beyond our ability.
Man proposes, as it is said, but God disposes.   Unac-
ceptable as the truth may be, my young friend, it is a

fact in all experience, that we cannot make things come out in the line of our purpose."

> The best laid plans of mice and men
> Gang all aglee,'

as the bard has it."

"Mr. Glastonbury, there is something back of all this!" said Edwin, showing considerable disturbance. "You are in possession of facts that I should know!"

The lawyer's manner did not change.

"What are they?"

Glastonbury shook his head. His eyes and face were a sealed book. Edwin continued —

"Again, Mr. Glastonbury, I must put the question — what had I best do? You have said wait; but I am not of the waiting temperament."

"If my advice pleases, you will take it," answered the lawyer.

"I will be governed by what you say," replied the young man. "But we all like reasons for the course we are counselled to pursue. Blind action is of all things most distasteful."

"My young friend," said the lawyer, speaking with unusual seriousness, "it is always safest to undo what is wrong, than to let the wrong abide; for, somehow or other, there is in all wrong a hidden impulse towards retribution, that never dies. You were wrong in extorting money and notes from your mother-in-law ; and I believe, as I told you a little while ago, that you lost heavily in the transaction. As you seem to be in doubt as to what is best, I will say, in plain words, what I think."

" Say on."

" Go to the executors of your mother-in-law's estate, and offer to destroy the notes in their presence, if they will return your receipts."

" You seriously advise this ? "

" Seriously."

" Suppose you were in my place ? "

" Knowing what I do," said the lawyer, " I would not hold them a day."

" Knowing what you do ! " The young man s color came and went. " You confound me with mysteries. Why cannot you speak out plainly of what concerns my interests ? "

" I have spoken plainly enough, Mr. Guy, for all practical purposes. It is for you to act now in the way your reason may determine. But I warn you of danger, if you take any other path than the one I have suggested."

" Danger ! What kind of danger ? "

" Impatient — self-willed — unwise ! I have given you my best counsel, and can do no more. Follow it, or keep on in your own blind way. But, remember, that of all bitter experiences, that is among the bitterest in which is wrung from us the unavailing words : ' It is too late ! ' I said danger ; perhaps loss may better express what I meant. Let me repeat a declaration made just now. If I were in your place, knowing what *I* do, I would not keep those notes a single day in my possession."

Edwin lingered for a short time.

" What afterwards ? " he asked.

" After you have given up this paper ? "

" Yes."

" Wait."

" For what ? "

" Time will best answer that question. I only say, wait."

Beyond this, Edwin Guy was not able to get anything from the lawyer. He did not act immediately on his advice ; but, after a week's perplexed debate, concluded to abandon the notes, which was done.

CHAPTER XXIV.

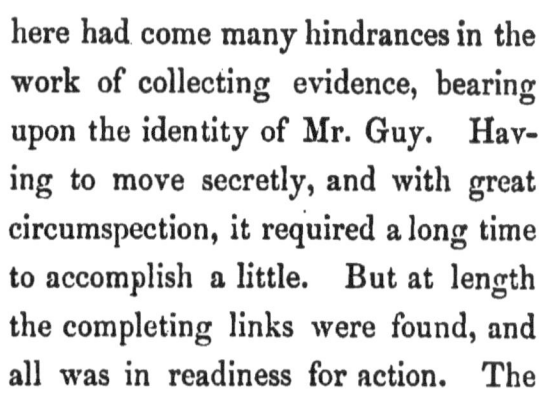

There had come many hindrances in the work of collecting evidence, bearing upon the identity of Mr. Guy. Having to move secretly, and with great circumspection, it required a long time to accomplish a little. But at length the completing links were found, and all was in readiness for action. The only thing to determine was the initial step. There had been fear that Larobe, forewarned, might escape, and put himself beyond the reach of justice, ere it would be safe to order his arrest. Doctor Hofland almost hoped for this, as such a flight would be regarded as conclusive of his guilt; but Mr. Guy was of another mind. The double wrong he had sustained at his hands, fired his soul with a thirst for retribution; and this became more intense, as mind and body grew stronger.

"He must not, shall not escape!" was his oft repeated declaration.

Mr. Ewbank was at the office of Doctor Hofland, and the two men were in final conference touching the case of Mr. Guy. The yet undetermined question regarded Adam Guy, Jr. Up to this point, no communication had been held with him, and every precaution had been taken to keep him in ignorance of his father's presence in the city. Still, he had been carefully observed, in order to know if anything passed between him and La-robe. The conclusion reached, at the present interview. was in favor of seeing him, and making a full statement of facts. While yet considering the subject, a student came in and said that a gentleman had called and wish-ed to see the Doctor. On going into the front office, he found, much to his surprise, the very person of whom they were talking. The countenance of Mr. Guy was very serious.

"Doctor," he said, with a natural contraction of the brows as he spoke, and a half mysterious, half troubled tone of voice, "I have called to ask the privilege of a private interview."

"I am at your service, Mr. Guy," answered the Doctor.

The student retired, and they sat down. There followed considerable embarrassment and hesitation on the part of Mr. Guy. He then remarked —

"There have been a number of strange things said recently, about my late father. I don't make any account of them, and yet such gossip is not pleasant. you have heard something of them no doubt.   In fact, your name is mixed up with the tattle."

Mr. Guy paused.   As the Doctor did not answer he resumed :

"It is even said, absurdly enough, that my father is not dead" — and he laughed faintly.

Something in the expression of Doctor Hofland's face, caused an instant change in the visitor's manner.

"What does it all mean, Doctor?"   Mr. Guy was sober enough now.   "Your look confounds me!"

"It means," replied Doctor Hofland, speaking slowly and emphatically, "that your father is not dead."

A sudden paleness swept over Guy's face, and he almost gasped for breath, as he stammered out —

"Not dead!   Not dead!   Impossible, sir!"

"What I have said, Mr. Guy, is the truth — nothing less, nothing more.   Your father, imprisoned for over ten years as a lunatic, has finally made his escape, and is now in this city."

"No sir! — No sir! — No sir!"   Guy shook his head slowly, as he repeated his emphatic rejection.

"No sir!   That story is too absurd.   But, have you seen this man who claims to be my father."

"Yes."

"And you credit his imposture?"

"I credit the man," replied the Doctor.   "As sure

as you live and I live, Mr. Guy, your father is now in the city! I say this knowing all that it involves."

" A bold attempt at imposture, Doctor. It can be nothing less. That my father was actually deranged, I know ; for I visited him at the institution on Staten Island, where he was removed from the Maryland Hospital. I went into the room where he was confined, and shall never forget the unhappy interview. He was a raving madman."

" Did it never occur to you, Mr. Guy, that the man you then visited in his gloomy cell was not your father ? "

" I know he was my father," answered Mr. Guy, most positively. " Do you imagine, for a moment, that I could have been deceived ? "

" You were deceived," said Doctor Hofland, speaking as one who had full knowledge of what he declared. " Du Pontz, the largely paid accomplice of Mr. Larobe and your mother-in-law, was notified of your coming, and prepared to receive you. Instead of taking you to your father, who was simply a prisoner, yet of sound mind, he introduced you into the cell of a confirmed lunatic, shocking you with the terrible sight of a madman, whom you thought to be your wretched parent. The same deception was practised in regard to his death. The insane man who fell from a window, in trying to make his escape, was not your father, although he now lies in your family vault at Green Mount."

" Ingenious, but it wont pass current with me," answered Mr. Guy, with cold incredulity. He was regaining the self-possession lost, when the Doctor so positively asserted the presence of his father in the city. " Such things happen in books, but scarcely in real life. That wrong was done to my father, I have always believed, but not a wrong like this. In my opinion, he should never have been removed from our own hospital to another."

" That removal was only one step in a contemplated series. Your father's mind was only partially affected when taken there ; and I had it from the resident physician, at the time he was removed, that he was fast recovering his mental equipoise, and in a fair way to an early and entire restoration. The physician was told by your mother-in-law, that she was going to take him home. Why this deception? Instead of taking him home, she had him sent away to a private madhouse, two hundred miles distant, and that is the last that was known of him, until the announcement of his death, not long after which she was married to her accomplice. She has gone to her reward in the other life ; but her partner in crime is yet within the reach of justice, and must not escape. With all solemnity, Adam Guy, I summon you to the vindication of your father's rights, and to the punishment of those who have done him such cruel wrong. All the evidence bearing upon his identity is secured, and you were about being placed in full possession of every particular."

"And pray sir," demanded Mr. Guy, his color rising, " under whose direction has all this been progressing, and why have I been kept in ignorance of what was going on until this time ? I don't like the look of it, Doctor. It smacks of imposture. If my father had, really, come back from the dead, as it were, to whom but to his own son would he have made himself known ? "

" His own son," replied the Doctor, with some severity of tone, " might have rejected him as an impostor, and refused to look at any evidence."

" And so, he came first to you ? " said Guy, with manifest ill-feeling, and some scorn.

" He managed to communicate with me, and I rescued him from his jailer," replied the Doctor.

" When ? "

" Months ago."

" Where ? "

" In this city. He had escaped from Staten Island, a weak, half-crazed old man — body and mind broken down by his long and cruel imprisonment. Here he was taken, and again placed in confinement But, be-

13

fore he was murdered, or removed to a distance, he managed to get word to me, and I saved him."

" You have been deceived, Doctor. The man is not my father ! " said Guy, with almost angry positiveness.

" And yet, sir, within twenty-four hours after the chain was struck from his ankle — I speak literally, for I found him chained to an iron bedstead — your stepmother committed suicide."

" Suicide ! I never heard that cause for her death affirmed," said Guy, with a confounded look.

" Yet, I know it to be true ; for my son-in-law was her physician."

" Where has this person been ever since ? " asked Mr. Guy.

" With your sister Lydia."

" And I kept in ignorance of the whole proceeding up to this time ! Doctor Hofland, this does not look well ! There is about it a savor of fraud and imposture. As the oldest son of my father, there lay with me the right to be consulted. With my sister Lydia, indeed ا " He said this with bitter contempt.

" Throughout this whole affair, Mr. Guy," returned Doctor Hofland, without manifesting any resentment, " I have acted from reason and conscience. After your father's rescue, the long agony of hope deferred being over, he sunk into a state of total oblivion as to the past. He was as a child, with memory like an unwritten page. In this state he had to be placed in the care of persons who would not only treat him kindly, but do all in their power to strengthen his feeble mind. Careful observation of your sister and her husband, satisfied me that they were, of all whom I knew, best fitted for the work, and at my solicitation, they received him into their family, both entirely ignorant as to who he was, and as unsuspicious of the truth then as you were. Nor did Lydia know him, until in the sudden rush of returning memories, he rejected the name by which she had been used to address him, and said that he was Adam Guy."

" Where is he now ? " demanded the son, without showing a sign of natural feeling. The lines on his forehead were stern — his lips hard and cold.

" With your sister still."

" Ah — yes ! And, of course, she is ready to swear to his identity. A nice little arrangement, truly ! But, it wont go down, Doctor, mark my word for it." The voice of Mr, Guy was pitching itself to a higher key. " I begin to see a little deeper into the affair," he added, still in a loud voice. " You are a dupe of that wench and her husband ! They have got up the whole thing. Her husband is, I'll warrant you, a scheming villian, who —"

The door leading into the Doctor's private office, or consultation room, which had been ajar, opened suddenly, and a man entered. He was tall, and of erect bearing. His countenance was refined and intelligent — his look dignified, yet a little stern. He had large, strong eyes, and a broad forehead, away from which the fine black hair curled short and clean.

" Mr. Ewbank — Mr. Adam Guy, Jr." Doctor Hofland introduced the two men. There was keen penetration on the one hand, and disconcerted surprise on the other; but, it was plain that Guy did not know Mr. Ewbank as the husband of his sister, a fact at once perceived by Doctor Hofland. The large, dark, powerful eyes of Mr. Ewbank, rested in those of Mr. Guy, until the latter wavered and fell away with a sign of weakness. Man to man, the stronger was felt, and, by force acknowledged.

" You spoke, sir, louder than you thought, just now," said Mr. Ewbank, in a deep, manly voice, that had in it a throb of indignation, " and I could not help but hear. I am your sister's husband ! "

" You ! " Guy stepped back, in manifest astonishment. Mr. Ewbank looked at him steadily, until he fairly shrunk in the presence of superior manhood; then said —

" Knowing your sister as I her husband, know her — pure, true, womanly and good — I cannot hear, with silent indifference, the coarse language you so wantonly applied to her just now. It does not hurt her; but it wounds me, and disgraces you."

"Sir!" Guy endeavored to rally under cover of indignation. But, he was in the face of one so far above him in moral power, that he felt himself almost as weak as a child.

"I regret," said Mr. Ewbank, "that our first meeting should be in this spirit. But I would be less than a man, if I did not rebuke your assault upon a sister, who, in the chiefest things that give beauty and worth to human character, is rivalled by few of her sex. For having ministered, in all tenderness and self-devotion, to your father, through months of watching and care, she merits something different from you. 'Wench' was not the word that should have fallen from your lips, Adam Guy!"

So stern and strong was the voice — so intense the eyes of Mr. Ewbank — as he stood drawn to his full height in front of the mean-souled man he was rebuking, that Guy shrunk, and cowered in silent confusion. There followed a brief pause. Guy rallied himself enough to affect a dignified air, with which, bowing low, he retired from the office, paying no heed to Doctor Hofland, who called after him to remain.

CHAPTER XXV

LITTLE after ten o'clock, on the next day, Adam Guy, Jr., entered the office of Justin Larobe. The lawyer was engaged, and he had to wait nearly half an hour before he could obtain an interview. He was sitting in an anteroom, where a student was writing, when a person came through, whom he recognized as Glastonbury, a well known counsellor at law. He had been all this time in conference with Mr. Larobe. It was now his turn. A look, searching and suspicious, met him as he went in.

"Ah, Mr. Guy." The lawyer arose and received him formally, and with an air of deference. What struck him was the great change in Mr. Larobe, who did not look, to him, like the same man he had known ten years ago, and, occasionally, met during the lapse of that period. Particularly did he note the absence of a certain steadiness of the eyes, which had once given him an advantage over timid people, and those not entirely self-confident. Now they fell away from his gaze, if he looked at him intently, but came back again, the moment his eyes were withdrawn, in a suspicious, searching scrutiny, that was detected over and over again. There was in his face a worn and exhausted air, and a pinching of the features, as if he had suffered from bodily pain. The long nose and wide nostrils were sharp and thin — his hair turning gray rapidly — his form beginning to stoop.

The men touched, rather than clasped, hands. Mr. Guy took the chair that was offered. Both were ill at ease. Guy was half doubting the policy of this interview which he had sought ; and Larobe was trembling in suspense for the words that should reveal what was in the mind of his visitor.

" Mr. Larobe," said Guy, forcing himself to speak — " I have called for the purpose of talking with you on the subject of certain extraordinary rumors that are afloat in regard to my father. You have heard them, no doubt."

A deadly paleness, in spite of his effort to be composed, overspread the lawyer's face.

" What is the purport of these rumors ? "

Mr. Larobe managed to keep the tremor that ran through his spirit, out of his voice.

" It is said that he is alive and now in this city."

" Do you believe it ? " asked the lawyer.

" Of course not."

The face of Mr. Larobe was no longer of a deadly
paleness. He leaned in a more confidential way, towards
Guy.

" What else is said ? "

" More than I can repeat. Chiefly, and of first concern to us, that a person, said to be my father, is in the
hands of designing and interested individuals — one of
them my sister's husband — who asserts that they are in
possession of all that is required to prove the claimed
identity. Of course, you are to be convicted of crime
and punished, and I am to be robbed of so much of my
father's estate as came fairly into my hands by his will.
A precious plot, truly ! "

" In the hands of your sister's husband ! And pray
who is he ? "

" A fellow named Ewbank. I never saw him until
last night. If I had heard the name, it was forgotten."

" Ewbank ! " Larobe looked confounded. " Not Ewbank the teacher ? "

" Teacher or preacher, it is more than I can say."

" And is he your sister's husband ? " Larobe's look
of surprise remained.

" Yes. But, what do you know of him ? "

To this interrogation, the lawyer made no reply, but
sat with looks cast down.

"Who is in league with Mr. Ewbank?" he asked, at length.

"Doctor Hofland."

"Who else?"

"I am not informed."

There was silence again.

"This Ewbank, then, is your sister's husband," said Larobe, after musing for some time.

"Yes. So I learn."

"Which sister?"

"Lydia."

"Lydia. I thought she married a low, worthless fellow."

"So she did. But he died, I believe; and this shrewd rascal picked her up, in order, no doubt, to make her a stepping-stone to fortune through the imposture now attempted."

Larobe did not answer. He looked stunned. Guy was troubled at his manner.

"Were you advised of this plot before?" he asked.

"In part."

"Did you know that Doctor Hofland had mixed himself up with it?"

"I have inferred as much. But, have you information, Mr. Guy, as to where the man now is who claims to be your father?"

"He is living with my sister."

13*

" In the family of Mr. Ewbank ! "

" Yes. So I understood Doctor Hofland."

" How long has he been there ? "

" For several months."

" It can't be possible ! " There was more than surprise in the countenance of Mr. Larobe. Even Guy
was startled by its expression. The gleam of his eyes
— the curve of his lips — the quiver that ran through
all the facial muscles — gave signs of evil passion ; of
malice, hate, and cruelty. For an instant, he looked
the wolf at bay.

" Where does your sister live ? " asked Larobe, as he
dropped a veil of apparent indifference over his face.

" I am not informed."

" Have you seen the man ? "

" No."

" It is a most extraordinary case ! " said the lawyer.
" And this long waiting, and working in secret, shows
that we have skilled plotters against us."

" The chain of evidence is complete, according to
Doctor Hofland."

" He said that to you ? "

" Yes. That all the testimony was ready, and that
I was about being informed of every thing."

" When did he say this ? "

" Last night."

" To you ? "

" Yes. I called to ask the meaning of some things that came to my ears yesterday, and he then made the astounding communication about my father '

" Who were implicated ? "

" You, and my step-mother. He says, that neither the man I saw at the Institution on Staten Island, nor the lunatic who was killed in falling from the window, and whose body now lies in our family vault, was my father. He was very positive, and talked like one who believed all he said."

" You don't know where your sister lives ? " Larobe had not replied to the last sentences of Guy. From a state of abstraction into which he fell, he looked up, asking this question in a tone of interest, that a little puzzled his companion.

" No," was answered.

They sat silent again.

" What can be done? " asked Guy, breaking the pause.

" Nothing, until a move is made."

The office door opened quietly, and a sheriff's deputy came in. Larobe looked up with a slightly annoyed expression —

" I'll be at leisure in a few moments, Garland. Wait in the front office."

But the deputy sheriff, instead of retiring on this invitation, said — ·

" Let me speak with you, Mr. Larobe."

There was something in the officer's tone, that caused
Guy to look at him curiously, and made Larobe's face a
little paler. Rising, the lawyer crossed the room and
stood near the officer, who said a few words in his ear.

" For me ! " exclaimed Larobe, his face becoming
white.

The officer handed him a paper. He did not read
the legal form, for he understood too well its import.
He was under arrest. For years, a haunting terror had
dogged his steps. For years, he had lived in dread of
this hour. For years, his steps had been close upon the
edge of a dark abyss, and in all that time had dwelt with
him a painful sense of danger. Now, his feet had slipped, and there was no arm to save him ! He must go
down to swift destruction. No wonder that his face
grew white as ashes ; nor that his knees trembled and
gave way.

" What is it ? " said Guy, advancing. He had observed the blank fear in Larobe's countenance. The
lawyer, aware of the presence in which he stood — of
the keen eyes that would read every look, and movement, made a feeble effort at self-composure. But, the
old strength of will was gone. He was unable to com
mand the hitherto obedient muscles — to look indifference while terror palsied his heart. There was an almost helpless waving of the hand towards Mr. Guy, as

if to keep him off. But, Guy pressed close upon him, grasping his arm, and crying out, sternly —

" Is it all, then, true ! Villain ! speak ! " He shook Larobe with violence, in his excitement.

All this was too much for the guilty man. He staggered back, and would have fallen, had not the sheriff's officer supported him to a chair.

" Leave me for a few moments, Garland. I wish to have a word or two alone with this gentleman," said Larobe, in a weak, exhausted way.

But the officer did not move.

" Don't be afraid. I shall make no effort to escape. Just a minute or two, Garland. I have something very particular that I must say to him alone." The pale, shivering prisoner plead with the officer.

" I'll be surety for him," said Guy. " Give us a few minutes alone."

A little while the officer hesitated, and then went slowly into the next room, leaving the door partly open. As soon as they were alone, Mr. Larobe, striving anew to compose himself, said to Guy —

" What if this man should be your father ? "

Guy did not answer. The question was unexpected.

" I do not say that he *is* your father. I only ask, *what* if he is ? This arrest is for the purpose of giving importance to the claim about to be set up for unknown person, who assumes to be Adam Guy, Sr. Now, suppose the claim, right or wrong, affirmed by legal decision ; how will you stand ?   I merely put the question."

" That is my affair, not yours," answered Guy, with considerable impatience.

" Very well.   I have no more to say."   The lawyer's voice was choked and husky.   Rising, he called to the officer, who immediately came in.

" I am ready, Garland.   Thank you for waiting." And the prisoner went out with the deputy sheriff. He was scarcely past the threshold, ere Guy repented of his stupidity in not accepting from Larobe the communication he had, evidently, intended to make.   He even called after him.   But the opportunity was gone.

CHAPTER XXVI

NOT in vain had Mr. Ewbank, through all the months of Mr. Guy's childish state, wrought with him for good — not in vain had Mrs. Ewbank ministered to him in patience, in gentleness, and in love. Too deeply had the impressions they sought to make, imbedded themselves in his consciousness. A sudden and entire restoration of the past, might have obliterated much ; but, old things came back so gradually, that opportunity was given to blend with them new and better states of life.

The old hardness — the old love of money — the old intense selfishness, manifested themselves at times — but, love for his daughter, born of her love and care for him, and a regard for, and confidence in Mr. Ewbank, upon which no suspicion could intrude, were softening and countervailing elements with Mr. Guy. Light had come into his mind, showing him a different relation of things. He saw higher truths than had ever before presented themselves; saw beauty in goodness, and a charm in self-denial. Limited, for a period of time, to the society of his daughter, her husband, and Doctor and Mrs. Hofland, he became familiar with traits in human character never seen before. In the old life, he did not believe that such a thing as unselfishness existed. It was a dream of the preacher and the enthusiast. But, in the new life, it was a conviction that no reasoning could disturb.

Everything in regard to his family that could be learned, from the period of his removal to the hospital until the present time, was communicated to Mr. Guy. By many things that were related, he was touched deeply; and many things aroused his fiery indignation. Always, Mr. Ewbank endeavored to draw from his anger the spirit of retaliation; to lift him above revenge into a regard for what was just and humane. Towards his son Adam, on learning how heartlessly he had separated himself from his brothers and sisters, and how basely and unnaturally he had acted towards Lydia, when informed of her presence in the city under circumstances of extreme destitution, his feelings were very bitter. No argument, ho excuse, no representation, could soften him towards Adam.

"He is unworthy the name of son or brother! Don't speak of him!"

In sentences like these, varied with harsher words, he answered all the attempts made by Lydia and her husband to draw, in his mind, a veil over Adam's heartless conduct; and they finally ceased all reference to a subject, that only made him sterner and less forgiving.

Late in the afternoon of the day on which Larobe had been arrested, Doctor Hofland received a note from him, asking an interview on matters of importance, at eight o'clock in the evening. The place named was the lawyer's office. He had given bond for his appearance at court, and was at liberty. At the hour mentioned, Doctor Hofland called, as desired. He found Mr. Larobe alone. His appearance shocked him. Never had he seen, in any face, a more exhausted, worn, and hopeless expression. But, his eyes were steady as he looked at him — steady, with some desperate purpose.

"Excuse me, Doctor, for having put to the trouble of coming to my office," he said, calmly. "I would have called on you, but here we shall be free from chance interruptions; and I have that to say which needs to be calmly considered. And, first of all, Doctor, will you receive from me any communication I may think best to make, and hold it sacred to the extent I desire. I can trust your honor. Your pledge given, I know it will bind."

The Doctor, after a few moments' reflection, answered —

" Is any good to arise from this communication ? "

" That will depend, mainly, on your judgment in regard to it.   If what I have to propose meets your approval, good will arise — if not to me, at least to others. If it does not meet your approval, I stipulate for an honorable silence touching all that I may communicate. On no other terms will I utter a sentence of what is in my mind.   You are, no doubt, aware that I was, to-day, placed under arrest."

" I am aware of it."

" And you know something of the cause ? "

" Yes."

" It is of this that I desire to talk with you.   Are you prepared to hear me, in the strictest confidence ? To hold my communication as sacred as if made at the confessional ?   I have no purpose of deception or hindrance.   What I shall say will not embarrass you in the smallest degree.   Your present relation to the case will remain undisturbed, if you decide not to act in the line of policy I wish to present for your consideration."

" I will hear you," said the Doctor, after a silence of over a minute.

" In honorable confidence ? "

" Certainly."

They were sitting at opposite sides of a table, and

Larobe was leaning, in nervous expectation, towards Doctor Hofland. At the answer he drew back, with stronger signs of relief than he meant to have betrayed.

"Of course," he said, after a pause for collected thought, "I have not been in ignorance of the movement for some time planned against me; nor of the nature of the evidence that will be adduced to convict me of crime. I know just how much it is all worth, and how to meet and dispose of it; and I feel sure of being able to thwart all the plans laid for my ruin. Still, I shrink from the infamous notoriety which must come when the case opens. Of late years, my health has not been good. I am losing in both nervous and mental stamina, and do not feel equal to the strain that must come. Therefore, I am looking for some door of escape; and will abandon much that I hold dear for the privilege of a quiet exit. You understand me?"

The Doctor bowed.

"Shall I go on?"

"Yes."

"Of course, I cannot obtain the privilege asked, except by yielding all this suit is designed to secure."

"Say, in the fewest and directest sentences, just what you wish to communicate, Mr. Larobe." Doctor Hofland drew himself up, and spoke with firmness. "I have passed my word of honor to betray your confidence in nothing."

"In a sentence, then, Mr. Guy is living." Larobe's face crimsoned slightly; and then became paler than before.

"I am aware of that," replied the Doctor, unmoved.

"But the evidence in possession of his friends is not, in all respects, complete, and may be so obscured by the testimony of witnesses on the other side, as to make the issue doubtful. I shall fight in this contest hard, and without scruple as to the means employed to gain success, for, with me everything is at stake. A desperate man, Doctor, will use desperate means. But, all doubt as to the issue may cease if you will. I am ready, if permitted, to retire from the field. It is to say this, that I have asked an interview."

"What are your stipulations?"

"The abandonment of this suit, on condition that I place in you hands such evidence as will, at once, restore Mr. Guy to his proper legal status."

"It is not with me, Mr. Larobe, to say yea or nay to such a proposal," replied Doctor Hofland.

"I am aware of that. But, being in possession of my offer, you may ascertain without committing me, the chances of its acceptance. It will be better, all round, I think. The issue of the suit will go no farther, at the worst, than the establishment of Mr. Guy's identity. I shall escape legal consequences. The loophole is open."

" What then ? " asked the Doctor.

" Within twenty-four hours after I am satisfied that the suit is to be abandoned, and my surety safe, I shall retire from this city."

" Whither ? "

A shadow of pain swept over his face.

" I shall drop down, like a wind-blown seed, in some unknown spot," he answered, in a sad voice. " But whether the soil be rich or barren, my roots will not strike deep ; for there is no vitality in me. I have played madly, in life, Doctor, risking honor, happiness, safety, everything — and I have lost ! O, fool ! fool." He shivered as he said this, like one a-cold.

" Something more than you have offered will be required," said the Doctor.

" What ? "

" You will have to restore some twenty-five or thirty thousand dollars appropriated from the estate of Mr. Guy."

There was a look of blank dismay in the face of Larobe.

" That demand will be cruel and oppressive," he answered. " I am not debtor in any such sum to Mr. Guy's estate. All that I am worth, would not cover it."

" The executors under the will of Mrs. Larobe, find evidence going to prove the claim ; and this evidence is in Mr. Guy's possession. Of one thing you may be sure, he will never abate one jot or tittle of the demand."

" Then, driven to the wall, there is nothing left for me but desperate battle." The eyes of Larobe were fierce with a sudden gleam. His lips drew back from his teeth. He looked savage and defiant.

" And certain defeat," was replied. " Ah, sir ! You may well affirm that you have played madly in life, as all play, who seek, through wrong, a coveted good ; for in all wrong lies hidden the seeds of a just retribution, which, sooner or later, surely comes. If you give desperate battle, according to your threat, the more disastrous will be your defeat. Take my advice, and let your offer include full restitution in every particular. As I have just said, there is evidence now in Mr. Guy's hands, going to show that you have between twenty-five and thirty thousand dollars of his estate in your possession. He is not the one to yield a farthing of his just rights ; and of all other living men, you have the least title to his consideration."

For the space of nearly five minutes, Larobe sat with his eyes on the floor. Heavy lines furrowed his row — his face was rigid.

" What is the extent of your influence with Mr. Guy ? " he asked, at length. His voice had regained . its calmness.

" He has yielded in many things to my judgment," replied the Doctor.

" Do you think he will act according to your judgment in the matter I have presented ? "

" It is impossible for me to say, Mr. Larobe."

" What do you think ? "

" He may be influenced."

" What will be your course ? "

" That is not decided."

Larobe had not expected this answer, as the half surprised, half alarmed expression of his face showed.

" What I have offered, will secure all that can be gained through the courts, after long delays — for, I will fight him to the last."

" Possibly you may be right in this — possibly wrong. I will give sober consideration to what you have said, and then, after sounding Mr. Guy and his friends, see you again."

"When will you see me ? I want no delays."

" Say to-morrow night."

" Very well. To-morrow night. Will you call upon me at my office ? "

" Yes."

The Doctor arose, and withdrew. Larobe did not accompany him to the door. He was too much oppressed for courtesy. When alone, he bent forward on the table at which he was sitting, with an abandoned air, letting his chest and face rest heavily down upon it. A groan parted his lips. He did not stir for a long time. Then he arose, heavily, like one who had been stunned, and moved about the office with an uncertain air. Finally, he took from an iron safe a bundle of papers — title deeds, certificates of stock, and various securities — and, spreading them out on the table, passed several hours in examining and arranging them. In this work he was active and in earnest. It was nearly twelve o'clock when he replaced them in his fire proof, and throwing himself on a lounge, passed the remaining part of the night in a heavy sleep.

CHAPTER XXVII

HE two interviews held by Adam Guy, Jr., with Doctor Hofland and Mr. Larobe, left his mind in a state of doubt, anxiety and alarm. To him, the re-appearance of his father would be regarded as a calamity. No natural affection, no love of justice, no righteous indignation towards the alleged perpetrators of a dreadful crime, had power over his basely sordid spirit. "How will it affect *me?*" Beyond that, he had no concern — asked no question. It was not his interest to have his father alive; and, therefore, he assumed the negative, instead of examining all affirmative evidence; and, because he wished his father dead, tried to accumulate arguments against the possibillity of his being alive.

He could not help being profoundly disturbed. The fact that his father — or, as he had it, the person claiming to be his father — was with his sister Lydia, towards whom he had acted with such cold hearted indiffer-

14

ence, was particularly distasteful to him. On the presumption that this claim was valid, the fact suggested many unpleasant consequences. The meeting with Mr. Ewbank had left impressions and reflections by no means agreeable. He saw in him a man of superior mind and quality — one, so far as his sister was concerned, fully competent to maintain her rights in the impending contest.

Two or three days were spent by Adam Guy, Jr., in perplexed debate touching his own action in this strange complication. Then, with something of blind desperation, he resolved to call at his sister's and see for himself the man who claimed to be his father. The time chosen was evening. In reply to a note written to Doctor Hofland, he got the location of his sister's house. It was late — past nine o'clock — when he stood at the door of a moderate sized dwelling in the western part of the city. In answer to his inquiry for Mrs. Ewbank, he was informed that she was not at home.

"Can I see Mr. Ewbank?" he then asked.

"He is out also," replied the servant.

Partly turning, he stood for a little while; then said, like one who had constrained himself to speak —

"Is Mr. Guy at home?"

"No, sir. They all went away together."

"Went where?"

" To Mr. Larobe's, I think I heard Mr. Ewbank say — down by the Monument."

" When did they go ? "

" This morning ; and the children went with them."

Adam Guy, Jr., turned away without a word more. He was confounded. What could this mean ? Affairs were rapidly assuming most unwelcome shapes. All the family gone to the residence of his late step-mother!

He had returned to the central portion of the city before reaching a decision on the course to be pursued. Still undetermined, he yet walked in the direction of the Monument, and at last found himself in front of the house where, for the time, all his thoughts centred. Acting more from impulse than from any clear judgment of the case in hand, he ascended to the door and rang the bell. He had not even decided the question as to who should be inquired for ; and this decision had to be made in the face of an expectant servant.

" Is Mr. Larobe at home ? " He knew that he was not there, when he asked the question. But this would give him time.

" No, sir. Mr. Larobe does not live here now."

The answer dashed him a little.

" Mr. Larobe's children are still here ? '

" Yes, sir."

Mr. Guy turned away partly, and stood with an irresolute air for some moments.

"Is Mr.— Mr.— Ewbank —" He hesitated and faltered in his speech, leaving the sentence imperfect.

"Yes, sir. Mr. Ewbank is here," promptly answered the servant.

"Can I see him?"

"Walk in, sir." And the servant moved back. Mr. Guy entered and stood in the hall. The parlor doors were open, and a strong light from the chandelier poured through them. The sound of voices was on the air.

"I would like to see Mr. Ewbank here. And the yet undecided visitor, shrank back from the glare of gaslight towards the dim vestibule. In the few moments that elapsed from the time the servant left him until Mr. Ewbank appeared, Mr. Guy sought in vain to bring his thoughts in order, and to determine some line of action. Mr. Ewbank did not recognize him.

"Mr. Guy," said Adam, introducing himself.

"Oh!" Mr. Ewbank's ejaculation was in a surprised tone. He made no other response, but stood in a waiting attitude, for Mr. Guy to speak his wishes. But, what had he to say? All his thoughts were still in confusion. Half stammering, he uttered the sentence —

"I called at your house this evening, and they told me you were here."

"Yes, sir."

" I would like to have a few words with you."

" On what subject ? "

" About this person who assumes to be my father."

" Ah! He is here, Mr. Guy. Perhaps you had better see him for yourself," said Mr. Ewbank."

" Just what I desire. It was with this end in view that I called at your house."

" Walk in." And Mr. Ewbank moved back, followed by Mr. Guy, who, never in all his life before, had experienced such strange, confused, and oppressed feelings. Ere he had recovered himself, he was ushered into the parlor, where he found nearly a dozen persons, old and young, assembled. On one of the sofas lay a pale-faced boy, whose large bright eyes turned wonderingly on him as he entered. Sitting in a large chair with purple linings and cushions, close by the sick boy, and with one hand on his forehead, was a man, against whom leaned a singular looking girl, whose half vacant, half intelligent face, expressed wonder and delight. The moment he entered, he was transfixed by the eyes of this man, who leaned slightly forward, with contracting brows. All doubt left the mind of Adam Guy, Jr. He knew this man. As if the dead had been raised up, his father was before him. He stood still, all power of speech and motion for an instant suspended.

"At last," said his father, speaking sternly. At last, Adam ! "

There followed a breathless silence. Adam then came forward slowly, pausing within a few feet of his father, and looking at him with straining eyes.

" My father ! " dropped from his lips — not coldly — not with constraint — but with a kind of wild, gushing surprise, mingled with so much feeling that every heart felt the throb in his voice. " My father ! " he repeated. Then covering his face he stood trembling.

" Adam ! " The old man's voice softened a little ; and he made an effort to rise from his chair. Lydia was by his side in a moment, and her lips were at his ear.

" Forgive him ! " she whispered — and Adam heard her words — " He is your son. Forgive the past, father — the dark and dreadful past — and bless God's love for the sunshine that lies about us now. Don't let anger shadow this happy hour, dear father ! "

" Adam ! " Mr. Guy reached forth his hand. It was grasped and held tightly for a little while. Both father and son were strongly moved. Adam was first to recover himself. With returning composure, came a measure of embarrassment. The position he had maintained towards all his family — his conduct and language with reference to his father since becoming aware of his presence in the city — his conscious selfishness and cupidity — all had their effect. He felt humbled, unworthy, if not debased in the presence of his father, and of the sister he had despised, cruelly neglected and basely insulted. The sister who now said to his father — "Forgive him! He is your son!" — and said it with a manifest power that showed her influence.

At the earliest opportunity, Adam Guy, Jr., took Doctor Hofland aside, and asked —

"What of Larobe?"

"He has confessed everything," replied the Doctor.

"I am amazed! Confessed that he kept my father imprisoned for ten years!"

"Yes. We have the painful narrative in his hand writing, and sworn to, thus every impediment to the restitution of your father's legal rights is removed."

"But, such a confession must consign him to a criminal's cell. I wonder that he made it."

"He has fled from the city."

"And betrayed his surety," said Guy. "So, dishonor is the twin of crime."

"Your father will abandon the prosecution."

"Was this agreed to?"

"It was, no doubt, understood. Barred away from the city of his nativity — stripped of fortune — broken in health and spirits — and bearing with him the undying memory of all he had madly risked and lost —

I think his bitterest enemy might willingly abate the prison cell. Let not man follow him with retribution. His punishment, like Cain's, will be greater than he can bear. He is in the hands of the Just and the Merciful, and we may safely leave him there."

" I am not of your spirit, Doctor. I would hunt him to the death," answered Guy. " No retribution is too severe for such an infamous crime. He should never have been permitted to escape."

" Your father thought differently," replied Doctor Hofland. " As you have evidence to-night, he is under the influence of those who draw him towards forgiveness. Your sister and her husband, Mr. Guy, are not of your hard, stern, unrelenting quality; else, had re-- conciliation been a more difficult thing than you found it. You owe them much, if you set any value upon this reconciliation. A word, a motion, from Lydia or her husband, would have thrown up a wall between you and your father that you might have striven in vain to pass. But, they are above such base and selfish action. Lydia has been learning in a new school, under a new teacher, lessons of humanity and forgiveness, that you and all the members of your family should learn also. Mr. Guy, pardon me ; but, it has so happened in the order of Providence, that my relation to your father and some members of his family, has assumed features that make it my duty to use plainness of speech — and

I now say to you : — Let there be laid as heavy a mantle as possible over the past; and let the present, as it unfolds itself, be accepted in a new and better spirit than you have ever shown. Against you, Mr. Guy, as the oldest son and brother, all have cause of complaint. You did not act well the part assigned you in the Providence of God ; but drew away from the weak and the helpless and left them to the world's tender mercies. If they are ready to forgive, accept the proffer. Of all your sisters and brothers, Lydia was most cruelly neglected ; yet, is she the first to speak for you — the first to step in and turn aside your father's anger."

Mr. Guy was visibly affected. He saw his own image as he had never seen it before — distorted and hideous, in contrast with the beautiful image of his sister. Not answering, Doctor Hofland resumed —

" As for her husband, I have, during several months, observed him closely, and my testimony to his worth is without abatement. A purer, truer man, I do not know. And he is, also, a man of education and enlarged views. One of superior quality in all respects. Of necessity, taking all the peculiar circumstances of your father's restoration to society, Mr. Ewbank will, hereafter, exercise much influence over him, and I need not add, after what has just been remarked, that this influence will be for good. In everything, it will, I know, for I have talked with him freely, lead towards family re-

14*

union on the right basis. Accept him, Mr. Guy, as a
true friend — a wise, unselfish friend. Don't assume a
hostile attitude ; this will hurt only yourself, for he is
a strong, clear-seeing man, and brave as strong. In the
line of duty, he can be as inflexible as iron. I say all
this freely, that you may know just where you stand."

Mr. Ewbank joined them at this moment, and Doctor
Hofland saw, by Guy's subdued and respectful manner,
that his counsel would be heeded. He left them together, and was pleased to see them in earnest conversation,
for a long time.

" My son," said the father, holding Adam's hand, as
the latter was about going away — Lydia stood with an
arm drawn in one of her father's, and leaning her face
against him tenderly — " My son, there is for us all a
better and a truer life, if we will lead it. Your sister
and her good husband have helped to open for me the
door of this better and truer life, and my feet, I trust,
are on the threshold, trying to enter. Will you not
enter with me ? Touching the past, my son, I have
much to complain of you "— Lydia moved uneasily,
and looked up into her father's face. He went on —
" But I will throw a mantle over the past ; and I pray
you, Adam, not to remove it. This is now my home,
and the home of Lydia and her husband. Let there be
no jealousies towards them, for they will provoke none.
Had my impulses ruled, you and I would not now be

standing face to face; for my anger was like fire when I learned all that you had been and all that you had done. But for them, I would not have forgiven. Under this roof, my son, a new home is to be constructed, in which love and peace are to dwell. We have heard from your sister Frances. She is in the west, and is now returning to make one with us. Edwin has not been here. May I trust you to see him, and take a message from his father?"

"I will do faithfully, all you may desire." Adam's voice trembled.

"Say to him, that I know all that he has recently done; and that I understand the motives from which he acted. Say also, that I have laid it away with the past which I have forgiven, and desire to forget. I wish to see him. You understand me, Adam?"

"I do.

"And the spirit in which I speak?"

"Yes."

Father and son held each other's hands with a tightening clasp for some moments. When Adam turned away and left the room, his eyes were dim with moisture; and wet eyes looked after him.

"May God's peace be on this dwelling," said Doctor Hofland, taking the hand of his old friend, as Adam retired.

Mr. Guy lost his self-control, and leaning down, laid

his face on the head of Lydia, who was still at his side, and sobbed aloud.

On this last scene in our drama of life, the curtain falls. Its foreshadowings of days to come are full of promise — so full, that their blessing will not be counted dear even at the great price through which the purchase came. The fire is never too hot that burns out the dross, leaving only precious gold.

THE END.

www.ingramcontent.com/pod-product-compliance
Lightning Source LLC
Chambersburg PA
CBHW060530030726
47498CB00004B/1146